Following the Lead

The Sixth Isabel Long Mystery

Joan Livingston

Read the complete series:

Chasing the Case
Redneck's Revenge
Checking the Traps
Killing the Story
Working the Beat
Following the Lead

www.darkstroke.com

Discover us online:
www.darkstroke.com

Find us on instagram:
www.instagram.com/darkstrokebooks

Include **#darkstroke** in a photo of yourself
holding this book on Instagram and
something nice will happen.

For my mother, Algerina Medeiros

About the Author

Joan Livingston is the author of novels for adult and young readers. Following the Lead, published by darkstroke books, is the sixth in her Isabel Long Mystery Series, featuring a longtime journalist who becomes an amateur P.I. solving cold cases in rural New England.

The other five books are: Chasing the Case, Redneck's Revenge, Checking the Traps, Killing the Story, and Working the Beat.

She draws upon her own experience as a longtime journalist in Massachusetts and New Mexico to create Isabel Long, a sassy, savvy widow who uses the skills she acquired in the business to solve what appears to be impossible cases. She also relies on her deep knowledge of rural Western Massachusetts, where she lives, to create realistic characters and settings — from a country bars where Isabel works part-time to a general store's backroom where gossipy old men meet.

She credits her mother, Algerina — the inspiration for Maria, Isabel Long's 'Watson' — for instilling in her a love of reading and the power of the written word.

For more, visit her website: **www.joanlivingston.net**. Follow her on Twitter **@joanlivingston** and Instagram **@JoanLivingston_Author**.

Her author page on Facebook is: **www.facebook.com/ JoanLivingstonAuthor/**

Acknowledgements

I continue to extend my appreciation to those who have encouraged me to write, as well as those who read my books. In many cases, they are the same. I would like to mention three teachers who inspired me: Irma Darwin, Donald Graves and Robert Alan Rose. I am grateful for the support of my husband, Hank and our family. And a special thanks to Laurence and Steph Patterson, of darkstroke books, and my editor, Miriam Drori, who help make this series possible.

Praise for *Following the Lead*

"Livingston does it again, delivers a compelling whodunit that grips you from the first line!"

JD Spero
Author of *Boy on Hold*

"For those who have not picked up a book by Joan Livingston, you are missing out. A terrific, engaging writer, who spins a great tale. Livingston has become one of my go-to authors. *Following the Lead* is another great mystery, and one that begs to be read. From the first page to the last, you will be engaged and engrossed. You find yourself in the hills of Western Massachusetts, among a cast of colorful and memorable characters. Isabel and Ma have become two of my favorite characters, and I'm certain they will be yours, too. Livingston doesn't overwhelm you with detail, but gives you just enough to let you use your imagination. Each chapter leads you to a satisfying and surprising ending. *Following the Lead* is a great book earning a 5 Star Review and Rating from me! Highly recommended!"

Joseph Lewis
Author of *Lives Trilogy, Caught in Web, Spiral into Darkness, Betrayed,* and *Blaze In, Blaze Out*

"A mystery lover's mystery. Isabel Long has a decades old kidnapping on her hands, but she's up for the challenge, just as Livingston is, in this the sixth and best of the series. Livingston's resourceful characters, led by Isabel Long, could solve the world's problems and be home in time for dinner. Highly readable and engaging. I'd follow this lead anywhere. Bravo.

Kevin Carey
Author of *Murder in the Marsh* and *Junior Miles and the Junkman*

Have you ever found a series of books that grips you so much that you constantly await the next in the series with pleasure? I first experienced this as a child with the Famous Five mysteries by Enid Blyton. As an adult, I am always happy to see a new John Rebus thriller by Ian Rankin. However, most recently, the Isabel Long books by Joan Livingston are my guilty pleasure.

Following the Lead is the sixth book in the series and, as I open the pages and join the cast of characters in this most recent mystery, it is like catching up with old friends and meeting new ones. I love Isabel's feisty nature, her old mother Maria's acerbic comments, and her love interest, Jack Smith's care for her. This is a cleverly crafted plot with finely developed characters and a gripping plot. I always enjoy Joan Livingston's novels and *Following the Lead* is no exception. I highly recommend it to those who enjoy a good story.

Val Penny
Author of *Hunter's Chase, Hunter's Revenge, Hunter's Rules, Hunter's Force, Hunter's Blood*, and *Hunter's Secret (Edinburgh Crime Series)*

Praise for *Working the Beat*

"Joan Livingston at her best. An ingenious plot featuring the unexplained death of a young man at a country fair. It's always a joy to follow this canny, quick-witted, and unconventional detective through her investigations but this case looked especially hard to crack — until it all fell into place. Masterful! Can't wait for the next one."

Katharine Johnson
Author of *The Suspects, The Secret*, and *The Silence*

"With a narrative written from Isabel's point of view, Joan Livingston puts the reader right at the heart of the action. The plot and the dialogue have an immediacy that reels you in from the outset. The twists and turns keep coming as the investigation progresses and the author keeps you waiting until the very last few pages for the final resolution. A great read, with characters that live on the page and a story that keeps you gripped until the last word. Ms. Livingston's books are cosy-crime writing at its best — don't miss out on this series."

Angela Wren
Author of the *Jacques Forêt Mysteries*

Praise for *Killing the Story*

"I love everything about this brilliant 5 star series — the humor, the superbly drawn characters, the small town setting, the well-woven plot. It's like catching up with old friends again."

Paula Williams
Author of *The Much Winchmoor Mysteries*

"Intriguing tale, strong on description, and hard to put down."

Paula R C Readman
Author of the *Funeral Bird*s, *Stone Angels*
and *Seeking the Dark*

Praise for *Checking the Traps*

"A twisty small town mystery that stays with you."

J. V. Baptie
Author of *The Forgotten* and *The Departed*

"Tough, tense, and compelling, Joan Livingston's *Checking the Traps,* grabs you by the collar and shoves you into the mysterious underbelly of Western Massachusetts. Her gritty heroine, Isabel Long, finds herself once again at the center of a raucous whodunnit. Be careful. Once this book gets a hold of you, you might not be able to pull yourself away."

Tom Halford
Author of *Deli Meat*

Praise for *Redneck's Revenge*

"The second book in the Isabel Long Mystery Series bounces along with humor, plot twists, colorful voices and rich character development. *Redneck's Revenge* is also a human story, a well-crafted tale of small town secrets, complicated relationships, life changes and lies. A romantic storyline adds spice and warmth to this cozy mystery."

Teresa Dovalpage
Author of the *Havana Mystery Series* and *A Girl Like Che Guevara*

"Set in the frozen Northeast, author Joan Livingston's spellbinding descriptions of small town America and classic Yankee characters weave humor and a love story with murder. The story sweeps us along and there are enough plot twists and turns in this deftly written work to satisfy the most hard-core mystery fan. A great choice."

Brinn Colenda
Author of *Homeland Burning* and *The Callahan Family Saga*

Praise for *Chasing the Case*

"Written with meticulous attention to the details mystery readers relish and a welcome playfulness, this novel zips along like a well-tuned snowmobile. I can't wait for the next installment in what promises to be a great series."

Anne Hillerman
Author of the New York Times bestselling *Chee-Leaphorn-Manuelito* Mysteries

"Joan Livingston has delivered a smart, fast-paced mystery, with a savvy and appealing protagonist who knows her way around the backwoods of the New England hilltowns. I can't wait to read more about journalist turned private investigator Isabel Long."

Frederick Reiken
Author of *Day for Night, The Lost Legends of New Jersey,* and *The Odd Sea*

"Lurking beneath the surface in small town, Back East life, there is always a mystery. In *Chasing the Case*, Joan Livingston, as only she can do, digs down into the underbelly of a small town to solve a crime. Take a trip to the land of pot roast and murder with Joan. I did, and I liked what I read."

Craig Dirgo

Author of *The Einstein Papers*, *The Tesla Documents*, and *Eli Cutter Series*

Following the Lead

The Sixth Isabel Long Mystery

Envelope Please

Lin Pierce said not to open the envelope he gave me until I get home, but since when do I listen to what my old bosses tell me? I bet he said it only as a test, a tease, or knowing Lin, a joke. The manila envelope's contents have been on my mind since he handed it to me in his office and said, "It's your next case." And there it sits on the back seat of my car, bugging the heck out of me to stop and rip it open. Thanks a lot, Lin.

"Do you think it's another unsolved murder?" my mother asks after she gives the fat envelope another glance.

My mother and I are on our way home after I stopped to see Lin at his office. I shipped her to my brother's home when things got a little bit scary with the last case, but now she's back, and it appears ready for the next one.

"No clue," I answer.

Ha, my mother, who you may know as my partner in crime, that is solving them, is as nosy as I am. When I was a kid, she kept a close eye and ear on the neighborhood where I grew up in the eastern part of this state. In those days, the town would broadcast the location of a fire by a series of loud horns, and my mother would look them up in a booklet she kept on a table beside her comfy chair. She would announce the street and number where the fire was happening, although one summer when the call was for a business several streets away from our home, we walked there in the middle of the night to watch. The only difference between my mother and me, regarding nosiness, is that I turned it into a profession, journalism. As a reporter, then editor, being nosy is a job requirement. Now, I use that trait as a private investigator solving cold cases in the hilltowns of Western Massachusetts where we live. So far, I've solved five, and now it appears I will be moving onto number six sooner than I expected.

"You looked really excited when you left Lin's office," my mother says.

"Uh-huh. Lin wouldn't give me a case that isn't worth pursuing. He knows better than that."

Ma checks over her shoulder again.

"I guess we'll find out soon enough."

Hmm, not soon enough in my mind.

My mother and I have been talking about what could be inside that envelope ever since we left Lin's empty office in Jefferson. He's officially out of the private investigation business now that he's sold it to Bob Montgomery, the retired state cop who's still interested in solving crimes. Once a cop, always a cop although as a private investigator, he can't arrest people or shoot them. Lin, who I would rightly describe as a bit of a fuddy-duddy, isn't what comes to mind when I think of a P.I., certainly not the ones I've seen in movies and TV shows or read about in novels. He didn't solve crimes but took insurance cases, usually on behalf of the company trying to disprove one. It wasn't until I came on board earlier this year that he ventured into crime. Actually, I did the criminal part. I earned a buck a day and he got a cut of what I made from my client, including the case where I was paid free mechanical service for my vehicles for life. Lin does, too. That was the deal I made with Annette Waters aka the Tough Cookie when I investigated her father's death in case number two.

From now on, I will get two bucks a day from Bob Montgomery. His stipulation for buying the business was that I come with it. No, I'm not an indentured servant, but Bob likes the zip I added to Lin's business. Certainly, my solving those mysteries gave Lin's business some badly needed publicity after my cases were written up in the local newspapers and even covered by a couple of TV stations. As for me, Bob's offer is likely the best and only one I could get to continue what I love doing. I didn't bother applying to other private investigation firms since I need an arrangement that doesn't take me away from my mother, who is ninety-three. Besides, I

4

want to investigate cases that interest me and I sure as heck don't want to work full time because I plan to keep my part-time gig tending bar at the Rooster on Friday nights.

I tip my head toward the back seat.

"He said it was an old case. Maybe it was before he started doing business with those insurance companies."

"Could be something personal, Isabel."

"Now, that would be interesting."

We are on our way back home after my mother spent some time away with my brother while I finished up my last case. It just got a little too scary for Ma when somebody showed up at our house one night while I was at the Rooster. We suspect it had to do with evidence I found during that case and my big mouth for telling somebody about it. If you recall, Shirley Dawes hired me to investigate her grandson's death. She didn't believe it was an accident that he died after he fell into a ravine at the Titus Country Fair while everybody was watching a demolition derby. As I found out, she was correct. It was too bad who turned out to be the real culprit, but at least she has the truth. Who was the person presumably trying to break into my house? Funny, at the time I thought it was one person, but it turned out to be another.

My mother ended up missing out on the action at the end of that case. I did call, as I promised, every night to give her the lowdown. Ma may be up there in years, but don't let that fool you. Everybody says my mother doesn't look her age, and she truly doesn't. Naturally, she has gray hair, but her face doesn't have the deep lines you'd expect with someone her age. It must be that clean living. She's still one sharp woman although I do see her slowing down. Lately, she's talked about giving up driving for good, which is fine with me. If she needs to go someplace, I usually do the driving anyway. She doesn't know the area well since she didn't live here until recently, after my husband Sam died and she got tired of being alone. It's taken some adjustment on both of our parts. After all, there were years when I wasn't the model child, especially during my early adult years when I went full-bore hippie. But taking on these cases has helped. I joke she's my Watson. She laughs when I say that. "All right, Sherlock," she jokes back.

I take a left onto the road that will bring us home to Conwell. We have roads and not streets here in the hilltowns of Western Massachusetts, which makes sense, especially since about half of them are dirt. We are a couple of miles up the road, past the spot where our ears pop as we reach a certain elevation, when I see the turnout along the side of the road at the Penfield/Jefferson town line that the plow drivers from Penfield use to get back up the hill during the winter and the ones from Jefferson use to go downhill.

Ma and I give each other a glance. We laugh as we read each other's minds.

"Oh, why not," I say, as I pull into the turnout.

"I was wondering how long you'd last," my mother says.

"Uh, maybe three miles. Not long at all. Just needed to find a safe place to park."

I reach for the envelope, undo its clasp and remove the thick pile of papers. I smile when I read what's written on the sheet attached to what appears to be a newspaper clipping yellowed by age.

Dear Isabel:

I knew you couldn't wait until you got home. There's a lot to read in this envelope, so start with the article attached to this paper. Come see me after you get a chance to read the rest. I really want you to take this case.

Best,

Lin

"What so funny?" my mother asks when she hears me laugh.

"Here." I hand her the note. "Read for yourself."

Ma nods.

"He sure knows you well."

"Yes, he does."

My mood shifts quickly when I read the headline: **Baby abducted from family's front yard.**

My mother's mouth drops open when she sees it, too. My educated guess is the story ran on the front page of the Daily Star, top of the fold and across six columns. I don't recognize

6

the byline since the story was written decades before I worked there. If I do the math in my head, the article was printed forty-nine years ago.

I hold the article so we can both read it at the same time.

JEFFERSON — Police have launched a massive search for a 4-month-old baby stolen from her carriage Tuesday morning while she slept in the front yard of her family's home.

State Police, who have taken over the case from the local police department, say they are working on leads. They request anyone who might have been on Carter Road that morning to notify police about any vehicles they might have seen.

The baby, Elizabeth Pierce, is blonde and has a distinctive feature, one blue eye and one brown.

"Help us find baby Elizabeth," State Police Lt. Stephen Jacobs said. "Any clue might help."

Jessica Pierce, mother of Elizabeth Pierce, told police she was giving piano lessons to a student inside her home when her daughter was taken. Her 11-year-old son was supposed to be watching his sister, but the boy left her when the family dog got loose and ran into the woods behind the house.

According to Jacobs, Jessica Pierce said when the boy returned and saw the empty carriage, he thought his mother had taken his sister inside. He then went to a neighbor's to play. It wasn't until after her student left that Pierce realized her daughter was missing.

Jacobs said Jessica Pierce called the police dispatch and her husband, Benjamin Pierce at work. The couple have two children, a boy and the baby who was taken.

Police went door to door in the rural neighborhood. They even conducted a search of the woods behind the Pierce family's home.

The story goes on to say how people with information can contact the police. It has a heart-breaker of a photo of the baby Elizabeth with her parents, plus one of the family's two-story Victorian home. Of course, the boy is Lin Pierce although the story doesn't name him. I check the date. Yes, that would be the right age. And I am guessing his sister was never found because otherwise why would he be asking me to solve this case. Apparently, the loss has stuck with him his entire life. What did he tell me in his office? "I've held onto these papers for a long time. I got nowhere with them, so I'm turning them over to you. I hope you have better success than I did. Actually, I'm sure you will."

I sigh.

"Are you thinking of your cousin?" my mother asks.

"Yeah, Patsy," I whisper.

When I was a girl, my cousin Patsy, a couple of years older than me, went missing while she was riding her bike. She and I were real close. We played together a lot, we went to the same elementary school, and then she was taken. At first, all the police had was her bike, but years later her remains were found in a wooded area cleared for a subdivision. The person who did it was never caught.

"It makes me mad, really mad that somebody got away with killing that sweet little girl," my mother says in a hard voice I rarely hear her use.

They say most of the time it's somebody the victim knew. I hate to think that whoever killed my cousin was close to our family or even a member.

"That's a case I would like to take on some day," I tell my mother. "I definitely would."

"I hope you do."

I check the car's clock. I need to get going since I'm tending bar at the Rooster tonight. I flip quickly through the rest of the papers, which include more clippings, documents, and notes, before I slip them back inside the envelope. I hand it to my mother.

"Why don't you read this tonight while I'm at work?"

She nods.

"I'll give you a full report in the morning."

"Please do."

Junkyard Dogs

As usual, I arrive when the Rooster officially opens for business, which at this point on a Friday night means the folks already here came for an early dinner or are warming up for a good time tonight. I'm behind the bar doing a bit of cleaning and checking on supplies. I glance at my reflection in the mirror behind the three tiers of the hard stuff. I'd say I am still a good-looking woman for my age, which I will keep to myself, thank you, with high cheekbones and smooth skin tanned from this summer's sun. I have longish silver hair after I decided last year to stop dyeing it. I definitely look more like my father's family, especially when I see old photos of his sisters.

Jack's already filled the coolers with beer, so they'll be cold enough when things get rolling. Right now, he has enticed one of the early bird True Blue Regulars to help clear the space where the band will set up and for the dance floor. All it took was an offer of a free beer, but it's an easy job for a young buck like him who works in construction. They slide the pool table against the wall and cover it with a sheet of plywood to protect the felt. Everything else, the tables and chairs, is either stacked on top of the plywood or stored outside beneath the building's overhang. When the night gets going, most people will stand around anyway unless they've scored a stool at the bar or one of the tables remaining along the wall. If the weather's nice enough, they collect outside with the smokers.

The jukebox is playing "Highwayman," that hit song by The Highwaymen, the country super group of Johnny Cash, Waylon Jennings, Willie Nelson, and Kris Kristofferson. I glance around the Rooster's customers and laugh. Yeah, I bet they all wish they were one of those wild guys living it up out West.

Jack's all smiles when he gets behind the bar. I snap the cap off the free cold beer for the True Blue Regular.

"Here you go. This Bud's for you," I joke. "Glad I got out of that chore this time. Thanks a bunch."

"Aw, Isabel, you gettin' soft on me?" Jack jokes.

I give his side a pinch.

"Talk about soft."

Jack chuckles. He doesn't mind my ribbing him about his size. He's a good-looking guy with a square jaw, brown eyes, and mostly dark hair even though he's in his sixties. If anyone had asked me when I was a young girl if I would ever hook up with a real country guy, I would have said they were nuts. The same goes for Jack falling in love with a former hippie. But it did happen when we were older and wiser.

"Yeah, I'm an ol' softy," he says. "Your mother glad to be back?"

"Yes, she is. She says she missed the dog, cat, and you, uh, in that order. I think she missed me, too." I laugh at my little joke. "Anyway, she's happy cause it looks like we might already have another case."

Oops, me and my big mouth. Jack's eyes are steady on me. He scratches the side of his neck as he mulls over that news. You all know by now how Jack feels about my being a private investigator. He understands how important it is for me to help desperate people, and so far, I have had success doing that. But as Jack has lectured me several times, he doesn't want me to get hurt, which has happened, or put myself in danger, ditto.

"Another one already? What's it this time? Another dead body?" His head pivots side to side. "I never realized I lived with a bunch of criminals until you started snoopin' around, Isabel."

I give the counter a swipe with a damp rag to stall my response.

"This one's different. Lin Pierce, my old boss, wants to hire me. It happened a long time ago when he was a boy." I stop and eye Jack. "I only know a little bit, but it appears his baby

10

sister was kidnapped. He was supposed to be minding her in the front yard but got distracted. He was only a kid. Just eleven. It happened in Jefferson forty-nine years ago. Do you remember hearing about it?"

Jack squints as he thinks.

"All I remember is my parents warnin' me to be careful, that I had to look out for my sister. I couldn't leave her out of my sight. They said strangers were stealin' little kids. Scared the shit outa me. Eleanor couldn't play by herself in the front yard. She had to stay close to the house and barn. It was a real big deal. Then it went away." He pauses. "I forgot all about that story. So you say they never found the girl or the person who took her?"

"I'm guessing no if Lin wants me to look into it. Ma is reading all of the materials Lin gave me. We should meet with him this weekend."

"Forty-nine years. That's gonna be a tough one to solve, don't you think?"

"Maybe," I say, but before I continue, we are interrupted by a commotion at the Rooster's side door as a guy carries a keyboard inside. He yells over his shoulder, presumably to his bandmates. They're here extra early. The band doesn't typically start until eight. Maybe they've come for dinner, or maybe they're brand new and eager.

"I better show 'em where to set up their stuff," Jack says.

"Who's playing tonight?"

"New band. Called the Junkyard Dogs," he says with a chuckle. "You might recognize a couple of those dogs."

But before I can quiz Jack further, he's striding across the room and shouting at the guy with the keyboard.

The Rooster has a band playing Friday nights, with the one exception being during the Titus Country Fair when Jack wisely figured nobody is going to pass that up to listen to music. The musicians are all local guys and gals with varying degrees of talent but an unbridled enthusiasm for playing that familiar mix of country, rock, and blues. I remember when the Plowboys attempted semi-successfully James Brown's "Papa's Gotta Brand New Bag." It took a while for the dancers to catch

11

on, but they finally did to my amusement. Anyway, Jack pays the bands what he can afford and throws in a couple of beers. One of my jobs is to keep tabs on how much more they drink, so he can deduct it from their pay. I believe one night a hard-drinking band barely got enough for gas money.

I'm on my toes and leaning forward to see what's what or rather who's who I will recognize coming inside. A couple of Rooster Regulars who just came through the front door are blocking my view. I raise my finger as I scoot around the bar's corner.

"Be right back, fellas," I say.

Jack leaves the building, and then a very recognizable person does come inside. A grinning Annette Waters carries a guitar case and gives me a wave with the hand that's free. Now I get it. Annette owns a junkyard. Her son Abe is behind her with a drum. He's got to be one of the Dogs, as are the two other guys who are hauling speakers. I wasn't aware the Tough Cookie, my secret nickname for her, plays music although earlier this summer when my mother and I were at Rough Waters Garage and Junkyard to have my car serviced, we heard Annette belt out that Tammy Wynette number "Stand by Your Man" inside her garage. She had a great voice although Ma and I joked whether the Tough Cookie had a new guy or she would actually do what the song's lyrics say.

Annette, who has dressed for the occasion with a sequined halter top, tight jeans, and a black Stetson walks toward me.

"You one of the band's groupies?" I joke.

Annette slaps my arm, a form of endearment from the Tough Cookie, and laughs.

"Nah, this is my band. I'm the lead singer." She tips her head toward the other side of the room. "Abe plays the drums. Those other guys work at that garage in Rossville. Rick and Rob. Brothers. Don't think you know 'em."

"No, I don't. What kind of music do you play?"

She rolls her eyes as if I really need to ask, but she plays along.

"What kind do you think?"

"Jazz?"

12

She sticks out her tongue and makes a gagging noise.

"Try again."

"The usual?"

She grins.

"You got that right."

I glance back at the bar. A line of thirsty customers has formed. Duty calls.

"Hey, I gotta go."

"Any requests?"

I smile.

"How about something from Patsy Cline."

Annette winks.

"You got it. I know just the song."

Then it gets busy, real busy pouring beer, making the occasional mixed drink, and chatting it up with the customers. Everyone is real curious about the Junkyard Dogs and that Annette, one of the True Blue Regulars, will be singing. During one quick break in the action, I use the bar's phone to call my mother. This is the first night Ma has been alone at home in a while. She assures me she's fine and is naturally amused when I tell her about Annette and the Junkyard Dogs.

"I might go to Jack's bar just to see her play," Ma says.

"Really? I'll remind you the next time," I say. "How far have you gotten with Lin's papers?"

"Isabel, there's an awful lot in there. I skimmed half of it, but I think the information will mean more to you than me since I don't know the towns around here or the people he makes notes about," she says. "This one's going to be tough. But it's clear Lin never forgot his sister. He even thinks he might have seen her once, which makes him wonder if she could still be living in this state."

"He saw her?"

"Yes, they were adults, about fifteen years ago."

Ma complains she can't hear me over the noise at the Rooster even with my back turned to the room, so I cut our conversation short. I don't want to yell into the phone and let everyone within earshot hear my business. Besides, I have a couple of drinkers who want to get served.

13

"What'll it be, fellas?" I ask as if I don't know.

Yes, I serve them the King of Beers, and about twenty minutes later during a lull in the action at the bar, I call Lin Pierce.

"That was clever of you to write that note," I tell him.

"So, did you open the envelope before you got home?"

"Of course I did, on the side of the road. It was too long of a drive home."

He chuckles.

"I knew you would."

We decide to meet at his house Sunday. I will take Ma first to Mass at the Catholic church in Jefferson, which will make her happy.

Jack's cousin, Fred Lewis, who I still call el Creepo because I haven't come up with a better name, has taken the choice stool at the bar, the one that gives the sitter a back against the wall shared by the men's room and within hearing distance of whatever is going on in there, which can be annoying or amusing depending on who's using the toilet, I've found.

In between serving beers, I check on Fred, who appears to be moping big time. No jokes or quips about the customers or me. Not even a grin when I try to be humorous. And no, I didn't dare ask Fred so why the long face. I'm smarter than that. The latest in the Rooster grapevine is that Fred and the woman he's been seeing, Amy Prentice, called it quits. Maybe it just wasn't going anywhere since they hadn't been together very long or she wants something different from him. I'm talking about two months and that's a long time for Fred. He's even brought her to the Rooster, which, of course, set the tongues of the True Blue Regulars wagging. I wonder what the future holds for him, like how long he will rent the other side of Jack's house, which the family divided into two a long time ago. You might recall Jack's late sister used to live where Fred does.

I haven't had a chance to ask Jack about it, especially since it appears I will be stuck with Fred tonight. He's drinking steadily although not heavily, but I will keep an eye on him. He's guaranteed a safe ride home with Jack anyway.

I take Fred's empty and replace it with a full bottle.

"What do you think about Annette having a band?" I ask.

Fred stares at me as if I should know better, and he's right although give me credit at least for trying to break his bad mood.

"Isabel, do you think I give a shit about what she does?" he says dead-panned.

"Cause you used to be married to her?"

"Give the little lady a prize," he says before he takes a swig of beer.

For those who just joined, Annette and Fred were once married but not for long. Both would like to forget all about it, but that ain't gonna ever happen. Given Annette is a True Blue Rooster Regular and also a frequent flier at Dave Baxter's place in Caulfield, it would be pretty hard for them not to bump into each other. About the only good thing I've heard Fred say about Annette is that when they were married his truck never ran better. The Tough Cookie never talks about him, but then she has had a steady line of guy friends since that marriage. And, no, Fred isn't Abe's father. Young Abe was the result of a hook-up with another regular here, Gary Beaumont, one that was so brief, he doesn't even know he's a father, and that is just fine with Annette. It happened when they were kids in high school. I sincerely hope that's enough gossip for you tonight.

Jack returns with a tray of empties.

"Annette's chompin' at the bit to start," he says. "I told her to let it rip."

As if on cue, Annette goes to the mic and tosses the Stetson onto the silent jukebox. She gives the boys in the band a nod, and then her attention is on the crowd.

"Here's somethin' by Gretchen Wilson that should put the fear into you boys here tonight." She gestures toward the bar. "And thanks, Jack, for havin' us play."

Annette flicks her head to get the music started and, after the opening chords from the lead guitarist, she begins singing "Redneck Woman" in that full-throttle voice I heard inside her garage. Everybody in the room who hasn't been privy to that

15

experience stops and stares at Annette, startled I presume that she has the voice to carry off that song about one tough woman. There's no doubt in my mind that this could be Annette's theme song. Rick and Rob grin as they play guitar. Her son, Abe, is behind the drums, with one eye to his mother. Their performance draws rebel yells from a few of the guys before the dancers scurry onto the floor.

Jack is back with a stash of empties.

"I didn't know Annette had it in her," he tells Fred.

"Me neither," he says with a glance in my direction. "By the way, that's all I'm gonna say on the subject, Isabel."

"Sure, Fred," I say.

At Home

My mother is in her nightgown, washing her face in the downstairs bathroom when I finally get home, later than usual because Annette wanted to hang around to celebrate the debut of the Junkyard Dogs. Despite bombing on a couple of songs, Dolly Parton's "Jolene" comes to mind, the band was definitely a hit, and Jack agreed to give them another gig in a few weeks. Abe split soon with his friends who showed up at the Rooster but only after his mother made him load the equipment into the van. The other guys in the band, Rick and Rob, we didn't bother with last names, stuck around, swapping stories about the local bands they played for until they decided to go on their own. They picked up Abe when their drummer left. As the story went, one day, Rick, or was it Rob, heard Annette singing when he stopped at her garage to pick up some parts. It didn't take much to convince her to join but only if they let her choose the name, Junkyard Dogs. By the way, Annette did play a Patsy Cline for me, "Crazy," a nice slow song that inspired Jack to hold me close and end the song with a good spin. Of course, he let the whole bar know it was closed while we danced. He doesn't want any of the customers helping themselves to beer.

Ma is amused when I describe how the Beaumont brothers acted when they saw Annette performing. I gauged their reaction as a mix of disbelief and amusement when they stood there staring. The last time Annette and the Beaumonts were together was when they posed with the trophy they shared at the Titus County Fair's demolition derby. Annette and Gary were driving the last cars in the final heat, and in a surprising move, they ended it with a crash that put both vehicles out of commission. I heard the trophy now has a place of honor at Baxter's. They probably could have asked Jack about keeping it at the Rooster, but there's really no place to put it. Besides, we all know how Jack feels about Gary and Larry, who now can drink at his bar only because I interceded on their behalf. They will forever be on probation as far as he is concerned.

Anyway, a small group stuck around after the place cleared, even Fred, I was surprised to see. He sat on the edge of the group, nursing a beer and not saying a word. Yeah, I found out later, his bad mood does involve a woman. He wants to spend time with her, but she's made it clear she's looking for something more meaningful than what he's suggesting. Fred's bummed. What did Jack tell him? "Hey, cousin, how long do you want to keep livin' on the other side of my house and spendin' all your free time here? Don't get the wrong idea. I don't mind. But do you wanna be one of those guys who's still doin' that when you get old?" I waited for some wise ass remark from Fred, and he didn't disappoint me. "You mean like you did?" Ouch.

With a "good-night, sleep tight" from Ma, she is in her bedroom and shutting the door behind her. I make my way through the kitchen, where I eye the fat envelope on the table, and then the headlights from Jack's truck shining through the living room windows as he parks. I sigh. It's not the right moment to be picking through those papers. I'll have plenty of time tomorrow. I shut the kitchen light and go to the front door instead. Jack sits in his truck like he's deciding whether to come inside. He flashes the pickup's headlights. Nosy me has to find out what's going on.

"Hey, what's up?" I say when I open the passenger side door.

He grins.

"It's too nice a night to go inside just yet. How about you join me?"

I can't stop smiling as I climb onto the front seat and shut the door. Jack cranks down the windows, then shuts the engine. Now, the only sounds come from the tree frogs living in the woods surrounding my home. Jack stretches his right arm behind me and pulls me closer as he leans back.

I laugh. I can't help that either. I know full well what's going to happen next, and thank goodness my mother's asleep and so are the neighbors. Here we are like two teenagers with no place to have sex, except inside the cab of a pickup. I don't want to even guess how many times Jack has done it in a truck or the back seat of a car. Me? I never had to, but then we hippie types were more liberated about those things. But as they say, there's a first for everything. I move closer to Jack and slide my hand along his thigh.

"Hmm, yes, it's a nice night all right."

Paperwork

That fat manila envelope from Lin sits on the table taunting me as Jack and I eat breakfast, and then when my mother joins us at the kitchen table. Jack doesn't seem to be in any rush to tend to his Saturday chores. He jokes and tells stories. At one point my mother says, "My, Jack, you're sure in a good mood. Did you win the lottery?" Jack gives me a wink. "Something like that." I return the wink and don't say a word. Of course, Ma wants to hear Jack's version of what happened last night at the Rooster, in particular Annette and the Junkyard Dogs' first appearance. I wait patiently while he gives her the blow-by-blow. In the meantime, I map out my day in my brain. Besides diving into those papers, Ma and I will do the Conwell Triangle, hitting the dump first, then the general store, and the library to replenish her supply of mysteries and smutty romances. Tonight, we'll have dinner at the Rooster.

Jack taps the envelope.

"So, is this for your new case? Looks like a lot of papers in there. Maybe I should hit the road so you can get to them, Isabel."

I smile and thank him.

"Let me walk you to the truck."

As soon as Jack leaves the driveway, I run up to my office for a notebook and pen, and then I am back in the kitchen, pouring myself what's left of the coffee. Ma watches from across the table as I remove the papers from the envelope. I glance at the stack and then her.

"How did you do it?" I ask.

"I went through the newspaper clippings first, then the police records, and notes in two different types of handwriting. To me, it looks like one of them was written by a woman. I'm

20

going to assume the second was done by Lin. But I will let you see for yourself. There's a map in there you'll probably find useful. And that white envelope has two photos."

I will do as Ma did and separate the yellowed clippings from the Daily Star and a few other in-state papers. It's curious Lin's family would have so many of them. Some are copies, presumably from when, I am assuming, Lin went to the library in Hampton to search through the Star's microfiche archives.

I glance up as Ma slides back her chair.

"I'll leave you to it," she says.

For the next hour, I read the news stories about the disappearance of Baby Elizabeth as she came to be known. Here are some headlines: **Police hunt woods for baby** with the drophead **House to house search for baby begins**; and **Where is Baby Elizabeth**. Then there is this one: **Town reacts to missing baby**. I pity the reporter who was sent to corner people outside the local store and Town Hall to get their reaction. The people he interviewed all said the same thing: How could this have happened here or I hope they find her soon. I can only imagine the people who told the reporter to get the hell out of their way.

This one interests me: **Police question parents of missing baby**.

Here's how it starts:

JEFFERSON — State Police met with the parents of Elizabeth Pierce, the 4-month-old baby that was reported taken from their front yard two days earlier, on Monday.

State Police Commander Barry Walton declined to say whether the parents are suspects in the girl's disappearance.

"We have to consider all possibilities," Walton told reporters. "At this point, we are hoping for any information that will help us find that little girl."

Jessica and Benjamin Pierce were seen being driven from their home in a cruiser Wednesday. Neither spoke to any of the reporters gathered outside their home.

The story goes on to give the back story and how frustrated the police were about this case. But I can only imagine how traumatic it must have been for the parents, who had just lost their child, to be questioned as suspects.

As time passes, the articles are farther apart until finally, **Police call off search for missing baby**. Articles are written on the first anniversary and tenth. The parents aren't interviewed in either of those, but Lin is for a story that was reported twenty-five years after his sister was taken. Actually, he talks about being able one day to reunite with her, that he remained hopeful she is alive and the people who had Elizabeth took good care of her. **"I even wonder if she will ever know she was taken," he said. "She was just a baby when it happened."**

I am going through the police records when Ma comes into the kitchen to make lunch. I concentrate on my reading while she feeds the animals, lets them out, gets dressed, lets them back in, and then she's in the living room going through the stack of books she will return to the library. She has them bagged and ready to go.

"Do you want me to stop, so we can run errands?" I ask her.

She opens the refrigerator door.

"No, you finish up there. I'll make lunch. I can see you are really into it. I felt the same way last night."

"I'm glad we won't be meeting Lin until tomorrow. There's a lot to absorb."

The police records tell the official story, the who, what, when, where of this case but the why part is unknown and certainly who took Baby Elizabeth, which will be my name for her from now on.

What else is in the packet? There's a handwritten map of the neighborhood and notations with the last name of who was living where around the time of Baby Elizabeth's disappearance. Asterisks mark who still remains there, just a few. Lin's family lived on Carter Road in Jefferson's main village and not in the sticks, where people farmed and where Lin now lives. I am guessing Lin created the map as well as the family tree of his kin living at the time of his sister's disappearance. There's a typed list of people's names, addresses, and phone numbers although with the loss of landlines in favor of cell phones I don't know how useful they will be.

I find pages of notes, lots of notes. One group is written by a woman, a perfectly graceful style I once had until journalism ruined my handwriting. I am guessing Lin's mother wrote them because the dates she gives are a few years after her baby was taken. It appears Jessica Pierce was attempting to do her own investigation, and perhaps that inspired her son to go into the P.I. business. The notes contain her observations, what she remembers from that day, what her neighbors and the police told her, her distraught feelings, and her suspicions. One sheet has a list of her students, with one name underlined. Beside the name Tim Todd, she wrote: **He was there that day**.

The rest of the notes, including a timeline, are written by Lin. I recognize his handwriting. The most interesting was the time he allegedly saw his sister fifteen years ago.

I swear I saw Elizabeth. The woman was the right age and she looked a lot like my mother did then. Plus, like my mother, she had one blue eye and one brown. She wore a classy dress and a black pearl dangling from a silver chain was around her neck. I saw her walking toward me on a sidewalk in Mayfield. I tried not to stare, but I followed her into Luella's restaurant, where she met a man. I sat at a table near her, ordered something, and watched her while she ate. That's all I could do. What could I ask her? Were you stolen? How would she know? Instead I stayed until she and the man were nearly done. I went to the cashier to pay and waited in the lobby. I told her, "Excuse me, but you look a lot like somebody I know. Is your name Elizabeth?" "No, it's not," she told me, but she didn't say hers. It's what I expected. I just wanted to hear her speak. I was sure about the voice. My mother's voice. I went outside and stepped into a store's doorway to watch her walk away. She and the man got into a car across the street. A Mercedes. He took off before I could see the license plate number.

I get to that white envelope last. One is a darling photo of Elizabeth smiling and gazing at whoever took the photo as she lies on a quilt. Her eyes are open enough that I see they are not the same color. The second is of a woman who appears to be sitting at a table in a restaurant. This must be the woman Lin suspects could be his sister. He took it with his phone, keeping his distance across the other end of the room. The woman sits with a man at the table. Her straight, dark hair falls to her shoulders and she wears a red blouse. But the photo was taken too far away and under poor conditions for me to see if her eyes indeed had different colors. I will have to take Lin's word for it. But with this blurry image I would have a tough time trying to pick her out of a crowd never mind a lineup. Lin probably didn't want to be caught taking her photo. Plus, fifteen years ago, the crappy phones back then didn't take quality images. I replace the photos in the envelope for safe keeping.

Ma is back in the kitchen with her purse. She is raring to go. I've reached the end anyway.

"So, what do you think, Isabel?" my mother asks me.

"There's some helpful stuff in here, but like you said, this one's going to be tough. It was forty-nine years ago. Who's alive now that remembers what happened then?"

"I guess we'll start with Lin."

"Actually, I need to call Bob Montgomery first. He is my boss after all."

"Do you think he will turn you down?"

I laugh.

"That would be a first if he did."

Chance Meeting

My mother and I are at the library on our final leg of the Conwell Triangle. The substantial amount of trash and recyclables I accumulated while Ma was staying with my brother are gone, a bag of dog food is stashed in the back of my Subaru, and my mother is perusing the latest releases on the bookcase near the library's checkout desk. At some point, Mira Clark, the town's librarian forever it seems, will go over to make her recommendations. She might even have some books set aside since she is well aware of my mother's taste and the amount of sex she will tolerate in a book. How much? My guess is she prefers to use her imagination when it comes to what a couple does alone.

Meanwhile, I am stationed in front of the mystery section, looking for something good to read although I have less time these days. What do I like in a good mystery? A smart detective or P.I. with serious flaws but a genuine desire to right wrongs. But my search is interrupted when my mother appears on the other end of the aisle.

"Isabel, you'll want to talk with somebody I just met," she says. "It might help your case."

Those are magic words, and I follow Ma to the large table near the circulation desk, where Mira Clark talks with Vivian Franklin, one of Conwell's old-timers. Vivian taught my kids when they went to the town's elementary school. They had her in fourth grade. She had a no-nonsense style of teaching, which meant my Matt got into trouble now and then, but my kids say she is one of their favorites. When I was a reporter ages ago, I recall she was a regular at Town Meeting, raising her hand to speak on the issues that mattered to her, especially funding for the schools. I'd catch a couple of the people on the

25

Finance Committee rolling their eyes when she spoke. The Franklins, the family she married into, are one of Conwell's founding families.

"So nice to see you, Vivian," I say. "It's been a while."

From the expressions on the women's faces, something is up. I decide to let my mother lead the conversation.

"Isabel, I was telling Mira about your new case and Vivian says she was living in that town when Baby Elizabeth was taken," Ma says.

Vivian nods.

"I actually lived on that street, two houses down. My maiden name is Allen. I was in high school when it happened. I used to be the Pierce family's babysitter. Lin was playing with my brother that afternoon." She shakes her head. "I've always wondered what really happened and where that girl could be ... or if she is even alive. Such a tragedy. Who would have thought something like that could happen in our small town."

Vivian was the family's babysitter? Her brother was playing with Lin? I nod at my mother for this bit of luck.

"I believe if anyone can find out, it will be my daughter," Ma says.

Vivian gives me a steady look as if she's sizing me up.

"So I've heard."

I have yet to do an interview for a case in the town library, but I don't want to lose this opportunity.

"Do you have any time to talk? We're meeting Lin Pierce tomorrow, so it might be nice to have more information before we go. Of course, we could meet another time if this isn't convenient."

"This works."

It appears this is indeed a convenient time. Besides, the library is empty except for the four of us.

Vivian takes a seat at the table. She's a large woman with thick white hair cut conveniently short. Ma and I sit across from her. Mira returns to her desk, but she won't have any trouble hearing anything we say. I pull out my phone, and Vivian says okay when I ask if I can record our interview. She makes a pleasant grunt.

"What can you tell me about the Pierce family?" I ask.

"Nice people. Mrs. Pierce was my piano teacher although she stopped after the baby was taken. She still played. I could hear her during the summer when the windows were open. Mostly sad songs."

"Were you home the day Baby Elizabeth was taken?" I ask.

Another grunt.

"Baby Elizabeth. That's what everybody started calling her." She pauses. "It was the summer before I went away to college. I had a waitress job, the breakfast shift at Cappie's Kitchen, a breakfast and lunch place that used to be in town. It's where they put in that fancy gas station. Nice place for the locals although I bet you can guess the nickname." She shakes her head. "But I'm getting off track here. As I was walking home from my shift, I noticed Lin pushing his sister's carriage along the sidewalk. When he stopped, I saw she was asleep. I remember the clothes she wore were a pretty pink, including her bonnet. She had kicked off her flannel blanket that was printed with teddy bears and bunnies. I covered her back up." She pauses. "It's funny what I can remember after all these years. Anyway, Lin went on his way and I went home. It was the last I saw of her." A sigh. "She was such a good baby. And he was a kind boy. Later, he was playing with my little brother, Stuart. He said his mom had taken his sister out of the carriage. But, of course, we found out that wasn't true. I know Lin took it hard."

Vivian rubs her fingers beneath her eyes to smear the tears that have formed. I wait so she can compose herself.

"Is it okay to continue?" I ask in a soft voice, and Vivian nods. "Do you recall what happened later, after she was found missing?"

"I was reading on our back porch when I heard the yelling. Then these cars started arriving. Then State Police cruisers. The town didn't have a police car in those days, so I knew whatever was going on had to be serious. When I left to take a look, people were gathered on the sidewalk near the Pierce family's house. An officer was keeping everyone off the grass.

I remember one of the neighbors, George Harvey, saying somebody took the baby. Lin was supposed to be watching her, but it might have happened when he chased the dog after it got loose. I started crying."

"Where was the Pierce family?"

"They had to be inside the house. I didn't see them or Lin. The baby's carriage was still parked in the front yard. They had a close-up photo of it on the Star's front page, which many people complained about, that it was, what do you say, oh, over the top. I guess they wanted to sell a lot of papers that day. You once worked for that newspaper. Would you have allowed something like that?"

"I understand why they did it. But frankly, I would have said no."

She nods.

"Eventually, I went home. I was too sad to stay." She thinks for a moment. "I remember people searching our backyards. A police officer talked with me because he heard I saw Lin and his sister that morning. I told them I heard Lin calling for his dog, Patches, when I was on our back porch reading. He sounded like he was in the woods behind our house. And then he played with my brother, Stuart."

"What about after that day?"

"The commotion didn't stop for a while. Reporters. TV crews. Police. As each day went by, I felt they weren't going to find her. She was a sweet little baby. Easy to take care of. I didn't believe for a second her parents could have hurt her. But then I went away to college a few weeks later. My mother would talk about it when I called home. And then it all stopped." She takes a breath. "I don't know if any of that is helpful."

"It's going to be hard going back that far, but you gave me a good picture of what it was like then," I say. "What do you think happened to the baby?"

"It had to be planned. Someone must have known the family or of it. Isn't that usually the case?"

I glance at my mother. We share the same idea.

The library's front door opens for a woman and a noisy

28

group of kids. I fish into my bag and remove one of my cards. I place it on the table.

"You have been most helpful, but if you can think of anything else that might be useful, don't hesitate to call."

Vivian studies the card.

"I certainly will," she says.

Talking with Bob

I call Bob Montgomery when we get home. He answers right away.

"You ready to sign that paperwork?" he asks.

Bob is being a stickler that I sign a contract laying out our agreement so, as he puts it, there are no misunderstandings. Like I can't take on a case with another P.I. firm, which has never been my intention, how much work I will do for him, and our financial arrangement. Plus, just like I did with his predecessor, he has to give the okay for any case I want to take.

"Sure, we can meet to do that. But that's not why I'm calling. I have a potential new case."

"Already? Another unsolved murder? Or is it that treasure buried in that old man's backyard?"

"No, not that one. Actually, it involves a kidnapping. Forty-nine years ago, a baby was taken from the front yard of a home in Jefferson. Are you familiar with that case? Lin Pierce wants me to investigate it."

"No, I'm not. I didn't move to this part of the state until after the academy. What can you tell me about it?"

So, for the next several minutes, I go over what I learned from the documents I read earlier today. He interrupts me at certain points to ask questions. His biggest concern is the amount of time that has passed. It's mine as well.

"Look, Isabel, I trust your judgement. If you want to pursue this case, then I'm game. Just keep me up to date. That work?"

"Yes, it does."

What Lin Has to Say

As planned, Ma and I go to the eight o'clock Mass at the Catholic church in Jefferson before heading to Lin's. That's early for my mother, but she joked that she'd make the sacrifice for this case. I could say she could skip Mass, but I am aware of the reaction I would get. I'm just grateful to have her along. And as she reminded me, it would do me good to continue going to church with her. I might even want to go to confession. Right, Ma.

Not surprisingly, given his obsession with the West, Lin lives on a farm on one of the backroads of Jefferson. It has a modest farmhouse with a large front porch. There are mowed hayfields, barns, and appropriate fencing to keep the livestock he raises from getting loose. The largest barn has a painted sign that says: **Go West Farm**. Okay, Lin.

As my mother and I get out of the car, farm boy or rather cowboy Lin comes down the front steps of his house to greet us. Retirement has taken years off Lin's face. He's still on the pudgy side, with glasses and a double chin that hangs like a turkey's wattle. He's a short guy, maybe five-foot-two. The first time I saw Lin, when I interviewed for the job, he was wearing a cowboy hat and a long canvas coat as if he were a cattleman out West. But when he opened his mouth, it was obvious he wasn't with those added Rs and missing Rs, which are typical of the way we New Englanders speak. Let's just say Lin is one of those wannabe cowboys.

"Nice spread," I say.

He grins.

"Bought this years ago from one of the town's old farming families, the Monroes. You hear of them? I see you nodding, Isabel. Anyway, the last generation wasn't interested in farming, and lucky for me, they were willing to sell it to me. Here, let me show you around." He turns to my mother. "That all right with you, Maria?"

My mother smiles.

"Lead the way," she says.

And so he does, taking us inside the barn, well-maintained, I would say, and to the corrals out back for his animals. Horses, cows, pigs, goats, you name it, he's raising them. He's kept up the fields for hay, and now that he's retired, he says he wants to try his hand at maple sugaring. He gestures toward an old sugarhouse to the right of the barn.

"It wouldn't take much to get that in shape," he says.

Okay, Lin, enough of the farm tour. We're here for a reason, to hear about this case and why after forty-nine years he wants me to pursue it. The man made a living as a private investigator and has the know-how to do it on his own. But maybe, as my mother said during the car ride here, he's too emotionally involved in this one. Or maybe he's changed his mind.

My mother stops and tells Lin, "Thanks for the tour. This would be a good time to talk about your case." She smiles. "Besides my legs are killing me. I need to sit down for a while. I'm no spring chicken, Lin."

"Of course, Maria. This way."

Good one, Ma, using that old lady trick again. We follow Lin to his home's side door, through the kitchen, and then to the dining room, where stacks of paper are on the table top. He pulls out a chair for my mother.

"Could I get you two something to drink?" he asks.

"Water is fine," I say, and my mother nods in agreement. "Make it two."

As we wait for Lin to fetch our water, I sit, amused that most of our interviews take place around a table, but it makes sense. It's where we can meet people face to face. I pull out my phone to record our conversation and my notebook with the list of questions I want to ask, just in case I forget. Lin is back with three glasses of water, and I wait until he sits before I pounce. He knows the drill.

"I should tell you, I've already spoken with Bob about this case. He has his concerns but will go along if I decide to take it," I say, and after he nods, I continue. "So why don't we begin. We both read the paperwork you gave me. By chance, we got to meet Vivian Franklin, who grew up on your street, at the town library yesterday."

He nods.

"Well, that was lucky. Her maiden name is Allen. You'll see that name on the map I gave you." His hand wraps around his glass of water. "I was only a boy when it happened, but it was one of those experiences that sticks with you. I remember every detail, what my sister wore, what song that damn student was playing over and over, the weather, everything."

I glance at my mother, who gives me the slightest of nods.

"What was the song?"

"Mozart's Piano Concerto No. 21. I never want to hear it again. If it comes on the radio, I shut it off."

"Your mother gave piano lessons in your home," I say. "How often did she do that?"

"She used to be a music teacher at a local school but left just before she had my sister. There weren't the possibilities for daycare like there are now. So she gave lessons in our home for extra income."

"Who were her students?"

"They varied. Mostly little kids and teenagers, a few older students who were musicians with serious aspirations. One of them was with her when my sister was kidnapped. A young man. I believe I wrote his name in those papers I gave you. Tim Todd. He came once a week. He was preparing to audition for an orchestra, at least that's what my mother said."

"I saw from the police records they questioned him but not much more than that."

"I read that, too. Frankly, I don't know what happened to him. I tried at one time to find him but couldn't. I see you writing down his name. Go for it, Isabel."

"Were you in the house when she gave her lessons?"

"If I was home, I stayed in my room. I could go into the kitchen to get something to eat. I wasn't supposed to watch her students or bother her at all. She timed it so when the older students came, it was during my sister's naptimes. If Elizabeth woke up and wasn't fussy, my mother brought her into the music room. If she was, she would have me entertain her in my room. But that wasn't often. She was a good baby. A very good baby." He pauses. "But none of that applied when Tim Todd came. I had to take Elizabeth outside for a ride in her carriage. Usually she fell asleep. The ride never lasted an hour, so I would bring a book and read while she slept until he left."

"You only took your sister out of the house when Tim Todd was there?"

"Yes, like I said, she was preparing him for an audition. It was supposed to be his big break. My mother did pay me for it."

"Did he come the same day and time every week?"

"Yes, he did, which made it easier for my mother to plan."

"I wonder if it made it easier also for somebody to keep track of your sister when she was with you." My mother nods at me after she says it. I give props to her for that observation. "Did you ever feel like you were being watched?"

"No, but that didn't mean I wasn't," Lin says. "You two make a great team by the way."

"Yes, we do," my mother says.

"Tim Todd didn't come again after my sister was taken. Actually, my mother stopped giving lessons altogether. She still played the piano. I could hear her when I was in my room at night."

"Do you play?" I ask.

"My mother taught me the basics, but she gave up when she saw I wasn't interested. She told me later she didn't want to force music on me like she saw other parents do. I thank her for that."

"She sounds like a good mother."

"Yes, she is."

"From that paperwork you gave me, I see she tried to do her own search. I'm curious why your mother wrote Tim Todd's name in her notes and not the ones for the others students."

"Curious," Lin repeats.

34

I pause, trying to claim the right words to frame my next question, but I better get something out of the way.

"Lin, like a lot of the other people I've interviewed for my cases, I might ask you some questions that will make you uncomfortable." I wait for his nod. "Looking back, did you think your mother and Tim Todd might have had a different relationship than teacher and student?"

There, I said it. Even my mother brought it up. Maybe Lin's mother was having an affair with her student. I study the man as a red blush creeps up his neck and face.

"Yes, I've thought of that. I always wanted to ask my mother but was too afraid to hear what she would say. Maybe you could ask her yourself. She still lives in the same house."

"I see. And your father?"

Lin shakes his head.

"He and my mother were divorced many years ago. The loss of my sister was really hard on them. She blaming herself was bad enough. His doing it was awful. " He pauses. "Actually, I believe you know him, Isabel. He lives in your town. Benjamin Pierce. He goes by the name Ben."

Ah-ha, Ben Pierce is the true name of the Bald Old Fart, yes, one of those guys who hang around the back room of the Conwell General Store to gossip and joke. I call them the Old Farts, but they haven't a clue I do. Besides the Bald Old Fart, there are the Fattest Old Fart, Serious Old Fart, Silent Old Fart, Skinniest Old Fart, and the Old Fart with Glasses. The gossip mongers have been helpful with my other cases because they are plugged into the hilltown pipeline of news. Plus, two of them had a personal connection to my previous cases. Now, it appears it is the Bald Old Fart's turn. I'm so used to calling him that, not to his face, I forgot that he and Lin have the same last name, one that is not uncommon in the hilltowns, so I semi-forgive myself for not making this connection.

And now that Lin has shared that information, I see the family resemblance in the facial features between the two men although Lin still has some hair and the Bald Old Fart, one of the older members of the group, is heavier. I wonder if he has an inkling his son wants me to pursue this case because he was oddly quiet during my last visit to the store's backroom. I don't go every week, just when I need their help with a case or for a little local levity.

"I do know your father. Is he aware you want to solve this case about your sister?"

"Let's say my father and I aren't very close, but I told him. I felt I had to. Besides, he may have useful info he hasn't shared with me. At first, Dad wasn't happy about it, but he changed his mind when I told him it would be you. He said he was impressed how you handled your other cases."

"That's nice of him."

"Oh, and just so you know, I paid for one of the services where they use your DNA to tell you about your ancestors." He frowns. "That didn't turn up any long lost family members or even the ones I have. But it was worth a shot."

"Glad you told us that," I say. "Ma?"

As planned, I let my mother ask a few questions. She reminds him we would need a list of other persons of interest. It gives me the opportunity to think about the Bald Old Fart and how I should handle him. Certainly, the other Old Farts must know his back story since they all grew up in the hilltowns. The Bald Old Fart is married to a local gal, his second wife it seems. He taught math at a local high school and is retired like his backroom pals. If my memory serves me better, I believe my son, Alex, the engineer had him in class. Maybe even my daughter, Ruth. Matt, the heavy equipment operator, didn't as he went to a vocational high school. I will have to quiz them the next time we are together although Ruth won't like it that I took another case. She worries about my safety too much. Alex and Matt? They actually think it's cool their mother is a P.I. Thank you, boys.

"That must have been hard on you as a young boy," I hear my mother say. "I take it your parents didn't have another child."

"No, they didn't. My father didn't when he got remarried. My mother never married again. Once was enough. And, yes, it was hard on me as a kid. Really hard." He clears his throat. "I heard it over and over from my father. Why did I have to leave my sister to go chase a stupid dog? Why didn't I check with my mother to make sure she had her? Why did I make a big fuss when she asked me to watch her? The list goes on. I tell myself I was only eleven. Just a boy. Dad has tried to make it up to me in his way. Sometimes it helps." He looks at me directly. "Here's why I am hiring you. I want to know for sure what happened to my sister. If she's alive, I want to meet her, to tell her about her real family. If she isn't, I want to grieve for her like a brother would."

"You mention in your notes about meeting a woman you thought could be your sister. I saw the photo you took of the woman at Luella's. But I couldn't make out her face very well."

"Unfortunately, that was the best I could do under the circumstances. Plus, it was a piece of crap phone."

My mother speaks, "What features did she share with your mother?"

"The eyes definitely. One was blue and the other brown, a trait on my mother's side that unfortunately I didn't inherit. And the long nose. She had what I would call an elegant face. When you meet my mother, you will understand."

As I jot down that detail, I have to ask the all-important question.

"Does your mother know that you want to hire me to investigate this case?"

"Yes, we've talked it over. She's fine with it." He pauses. "But she wants to meet you and your mother alone the first time without me. I understand. I believe she'll be more comfortable talking with you than me. Maybe there are things she doesn't want me to know. I've tried in the past but she pushed me aside. Too much pain, I believe. I was surprised she didn't resist when I brought it up recently. She, of course, knew of your success. That won her over."

"When can we meet her?"

"She mentioned Wednesday. I'll give you her number before you leave, so you can set up a time."

I glance at my mother, who gives me a nod. A day of surprises for certain.

"Yes, that would work for us."

"I will let her know." He finishes his glass of water. "So, how would you two like to go for a ride? I'd like to show you my old neighborhood."

"Please do," I say. "I did bring a copy of that map you gave me."

Lin nods.

"Too bad someone with your brains wasn't investigating this case when it happened."

My mother speaks up.

"Yes, it is."

Old Neighborhood

Lin is at the wheel of his extended cab pickup truck. My mother is in the front seat and I'm in the back, which works fine for our short trip to Jefferson's main village. Lin used a wooden box for a step and held Ma's hand, so she could climb easier, which upped her opinion and mine of the man. Country people, I've found many times, have excellent manners, well, except for the criminals I've come across. I've even heard the Beaumont brothers use "ma'am" and they were raised in a feral household. Now, Lin's chatting up a storm about the town of Jefferson mostly for my mother's benefit. But that changes when we get closer to the village, which is off the rural two-lane state highway that runs through many of the hilltowns. I retrieve the map from my bag.

Lin drives slowly as he tells us who used to live in each house as I follow along on the map and which ones are still around, unfortunately only a couple. I note their names: Frieda Payne who lives on 25 Carter Road and Lawrence McGowan, in 31, who very recently went into a nursing home but in Lin's opinion is still with it, so he plans to add him to his list. Lin explained that Lawrence spent a lot of time that summer on his front porch due to two broken legs. He was in a bad car accident and lucky he didn't get himself killed.

In all, there are about ten homes, none newer than early last century.

"The houses are pretty much the same on this street as they were when I was a boy, except for some improvements after new people bought them, and we did have one fire," he says loud enough for my benefit as he slows the truck. He steers with his left hand and points with his right. "A few like that one were converted into a two-family. The owners of that one closed in the front porch and put in vinyl siding. Too bad. It ruins the look of that bungalow. New paint job on that one."

"This is a really nice neighborhood," my mother says, and I mentally fill in the rest like how could a crime like kidnapping a baby happen here.

Lin pulls the truck to the curb in front of a two-story Victorian with a large porch in the front. He turns toward my mother.

"Maria, are you up for a little walk?"

"For your case, of course."

Lin retrieves the box from the pickup's cap for Ma's step and we are onto the tour. He points toward the Victorian.

"That's where I grew up. Mother's not home today." He glances as I take photos with my phone. "She didn't mind it when I told her I wanted to bring you here today."

The Victorian, painted a sage green with gold trim, is well-maintained with gardens now at the end of their growing season since we are heading deeper into fall. The garage, painted the same color as the house, is to the right. Woods are behind the house. He says the property has two acres of them, unbuildable because there is no access from the street and it contains wetlands. The woods border land now owned by a conservation trust. I recall from one of the photos printed in the newspaper, that controversial one, the baby carriage was left on the walkway leading to the front door.

"Where did your neighbor Vivian live?" I ask.

He points toward a house, another Victorian, two doors away from his mother's.

"Over there. It's been sold a few times since the Allens owned it."

"When we met Vivian at the town library, she said you were playing with her brother that day."

"That's right."

"Ma, what are you thinking?" I ask.

"When my kids were babies, I had the same kind of carriage we saw in the photo. The way they are designed, with that hood, it might be awkward for an eleven-year-old boy to

40

take a baby bundled in a blanket in and out of the carriage. There's a stone step and a walkway from the door, so I bet your mother wouldn't risk you dropping her." Lin's head bounces as she talks. "So that day, when did your mother put the baby in her carriage?"

"She did it before Tim Todd came," he answers. "He was pulling up in his car when I started pushing her carriage. He stopped and looked at her. I remember him saying, "That's a pretty baby," and then he was inside the house. My mother told me not to come back inside until after he left. I pushed the carriage around the neighborhood, but I got tired of doing that. Elizabeth had fallen asleep, so I figured I would wait in the front yard with her. I had a book, but I wasn't that interested in it. I started looking at the pack of baseball cards I had with me instead but stopped when I had to go after the dog. She had broken from her leash, barking her head off. Our neighbors didn't like her running around like that."

"Where was the dog tied up?"

He glances toward his mother's house.

"She won't mind if I show you."

Ma and I follow Lin to the shady side of the garage where he says the dog was typically chained.

"Patches had slipped from his collar."

"Or did somebody help him?" my mother says.

Lin stops.

"I've thought of that myself." He points toward the woods. "He ran off there."

"So if my mother is right, this must have been well-planned. Somebody knew your family's habits."

"Anyone in the neighborhood would know that, but nobody here took her."

My suspicious mind wonders but could they have helped.

"Was she a friendly dog?"

"Yes, but a barker. That's how I knew she got loose."

"If we want to follow this theory for a while, the person who released the dog, was using her as a distraction. Did you hear a vehicle?"

He shakes his head.

"I was only a kid. I wasn't paying attention to anything like that. I wanted to get Patches back. She'd gotten loose before and chased the ducks belonging to a man on the street. He wasn't happy about it. And I wanted to stop watching my sister, so I could play with my friend, Stuart."

I study the woods. The trees are large but not old growth. At one time, when this town was first settled, the original trees were cleared and these grew in their place. I don't see much in the way of undergrowth.

"If I were to walk through the woods, what would be on the other side?" I ask Lin.

"Now, houses. Then, a field off a road. Proctor Road."

"So somebody could have parked there and come through the woods. Is there anyone still living on that road who was alive then?"

He shakes his head.

"No. The Proctors passed it onto their kids. They live in Florida now."

"So after the dog broke loose, what happened next?"

"I tied him back up and made sure his collar was on right. That's when I checked on my sister. Her carriage was empty. I could hear music inside the house. I figured my mother took my sister and went inside with her."

It's a perfectly understandable situation. He was only eleven. He had instructions from his mother to stay out of the house, so he wasn't going to go inside and check. Off he went to play unaware of what had happened.

I glance at my mother.

"How are you doing?" I ask, and when she responds with a nod and a smile, I continue, "Could you show us where you went to play?"

"Of course," Lin says.

We walk slowly for my mother's benefit to Vivian Allen's childhood home. He stops and points toward the back yard.

"There used to be a treehouse with a ladder in that catalpa tree. That's where I was that day my sister was taken."

"What could you see from up there?"

"A lot I suppose. But Stuart and I were busy playing."

"Of course."

"So, Isabel, are you willing to take on my case?"

I had decided I would as soon as I opened that envelope. Lin wouldn't ask me unless he felt it was worth my while and that I would actually solve it. Thanks, old boss. My mother leaves the decision-making to me. While she is my worthy adviser and accomplice, I am the one who takes the risks.

"I've already spoken with Bob, and he's letting me decide," I say, building up a little suspense. "But, yes, I would like to give it a go."

Lin barks out a laugh.

"That's great, Isabel. Really, great. Now, let's talk business."

Stacking Wood

After I bring Ma home, I head to Jack's where I promised to help him stack wood for a couple of hours before he heads to the Rooster. Ma wants nothing to do with this chore. Besides, she's a bit tuckered out from going so early to church and visiting Lin. I don't mind. Stacking wood is one of my favorite country chores. I've been heating with a woodstove since Sam and I moved to Conwell. It was our only source of heat, which made for a warm spot near the stove but much cooler temps in the rest of the house, particularly the bedrooms, which suited us. That changed when my mother moved in with me. Now, I use the furnace to keep a certain base of warmth and only light the woodstove for nostalgia or those really cold days when I will be present to man it. I don't want to risk Ma trying to load a heavy log into the stove or forget about adjusting the flue or the air vent. It turns out I only had to buy two cords of green wood this fall to let sit a year since I have still plenty of dry wood to burn. I'll be bringing those logs into the cellar since I have lots of room without Sam's workshop. The green wood will be stacked outside to keep up my supply. But that's not the case for Jack, who depends on wood to heat both halves of his house instead of the furnace, which he keeps on low. When I pull into the driveway, he's sitting on the house's stoop.

"Well, it's about time you showed," Jack jokes as he tosses me a fresh pair of work gloves. "I was about to give up."

"You were going to start without me?"

"Nah, I'd just found somethin' else to do instead."

I smile. Our relationship has a certain quota of humor that makes it interesting for the both of us. I will tease him about his country boy ways. Yup, he gets back at me for being a hippie in my previous life and no matter how long I live here, likely until I drop dead someday, I will be a newcomer. I take a look at the work ahead. One of the True Blue Regulars, the same guy who sells me firewood, dropped off six cords, seasoned one year, he assured Jack. Of course, the man is aware of what would happen if he's lying. He'd become one of the Rooster's outcasts. As smart ass me reminded Jack, the smartest and cheapest trick would be for him to get ahead by buying an additional six cords of green firewood, let them sit this year and burn it next winter.

Jack told me, "Isabel, I thought you were a city girl."

"Not anymore," I answered.

Jack is usually on top of these country things, but he got distracted last winter with what happened with his sister. I surely don't have to remind you about that. But Eleanor was the one who took on a lot of the farm chores. Handy with the chainsaw, she'd fell dead trees in the woods behind their home, then drag the logs to the house with the tractor, cut them to size, and even man the splitter. They never had to buy firewood. Jack has told me the stories, including how Eleanor stacked their firewood all by herself. He got spoiled. Well, that's not happening today, so the plan is for me to help him stack this wood in nice straight rows near the house's doors with flat pieces stacked three over three at the ends to anchor the rows. This chore will take days. I don't mind. I like the solid sound a log makes when I drop it onto the others. No split log is exactly the same, but they fit together in a nice puzzle.

And so we work together, building the first row. At one point, Jack goes inside the house to place a radio in an open window to play, do I really have to say, the country station, and returns with glasses of water. Waylon Jennings and Jessi Colter are singing "Storms Never Last" when we resume.

"So it went okay with Lin?"

"It's a start." I drop a nice piece of maple in place. "I didn't know his father moved to Conwell."

"Yeah, a long time ago when he married a local woman. So, how are you going to handle that with your buddies in the backroom?"

"I guess I'll find out tomorrow morning. I might as well get it over with. What's your take on him?"

"He can be kind of a grouch sometimes, but we all felt sorry for him because of what happened in Jefferson."

I bend for a couple of logs. We have a lot more to go by my estimate, so we definitely will not get this chore done in one afternoon. Jack has to leave at three to open the Rooster. Carole, his cook, will join him. I heard chili, which she makes as spicy as the locals can handle it, is on the menu tonight.

Jack says if I come back tomorrow, he will make it worth my while.

"What does that mean?" I ask.

"Just don't bring your mother."

"Ooh, you bad boy," I say. "Hey, where's Fred? Doesn't he want to keep warm this winter? He should be helping."

"I'm not countin' on him. He had somethin' else to take care of." He chuckles. "And I bet you're dyin' to know what it is."

"Of course, I am."

"Did anyone ever say you are one nosy woman?"

"Yup, you all the time." I laugh with him. "So, let me guess. He's moving in with that woman, Amy."

Jack's mouth drops open.

"How'd you figure that out?"

"I didn't. I was just making a joke." I drop two logs onto the row. "Is that where he is now?"

"Well, he didn't come home last night. He told me after you and your mother left he's movin' out."

"Really? So what are you going to do?"

He grins.

"I have a couple of ideas. One of them includes you."

Jack has my full attention. I study his face. He's being serious, real serious. This isn't one of our playful jokes. This is about the next step in our relationship. If Jack knew about his cousin leaving last night, he must have been waiting for the right moment to bring it up. But then again, he didn't sleep over last night. He knew what Ma and I were up to today, and he had to meet the guy who was dropping off the firewood.

"So, Jack Smith, is this your way of asking me to live with you?"

"What do you think?"

Jack steps over a few logs and stands in front of me. This isn't the first time we've talked about living together. We both agree this would be a big step for us. I couldn't ask him to give up the house and land that's been in his family four generations although he might make a killing if he did. I would be giving up the house Sam built when we didn't have much, except three kids. Guys who had worked with him for years helped out for free on the weekends or gave us a great deal. Building that house was a labor of love for his family, that and some of the furniture I have. And there is my mother to consider. Live with Jack? Now, that would be a life changer. What are you waiting for, Isabel? You love the guy.

Jack's hands are on my arms.

"I've been thinkin' about this a lot. The best days of the week are the ones when I sleep, eat, and be with you. I see you smilin', honey. You feel the same way too." He pauses. "I was thinkin' your mother could live where Fred does. You move into my end. And maybe you could rent your house. I'd get the rooms in my place repainted and we'd move your things up here. There's even an extra bedroom on my side. It's full of junk, but I can get rid of it. And, cross my heart, I promise I won't stop you from working on your cases."

Shoot, I can't stop smiling.

"Seems like you've got this all figured out, Jack."

"Well, hon, it only works if you agree." He strokes my cheek. "Look, I don't want an answer right now. You need to talk with your mother about this. It'd be a big change for her." He moves in for a kiss and afterward says, "Think it over, but don't take too long. I hear my ex might be movin' back to town. That's a joke, Isabel."

I shake my head.

"Oh, you funny guy."

Bald Old Fart

Jack's still sleeping when I duck out for my visit with the Old Farts in the backroom of the general store. This is definitely going to be tricky considering the seriousness of my case and who is involved. From the vehicles parked near the store, I assume I will have one hundred percent attendance, and as I make my way through the stockroom, I hear a chorus of laughter. Naturally, the Fattest Old Fart, the group's lookout, announces my arrival.

"Where in the heck have you been, Isabel? We've been waiting to hear all about your last case." He pats the spot beside him on the school bus seat. "Sit yourself right down, kiddo. We had to read about it in the Daily Fart."

Laughing, I do as I'm told. I forgot that's what this group of old men called my old newspaper just to tease me when I still worked for it. Little do they know that it inspired their secret nicknames.

The Serious Old Fart is already up getting my coffee. As expected, he jokes, "How about a cappuccino, Isabel," which is a far cry from the crappy coffee he will serve me. But I graciously accept the cup before I proceed with a detailed narrative of my last case. Of course, they've read about it in the Daily Star. I imagine one of them brought in a copy and read the article aloud to the others. What they want to hear is what wasn't in the paper, and I gladly oblige their comments and questions, except for the really personal details. While we talk, I take in the Bald Old Fart, trying my darndest not to be obvious he's the primary reason I am here. And then I get hit with the question I've been expecting. It comes from the Silent Old Fart, who isn't living up to his name this morning.

"So, Isabel, when are you starting your next case?" he asks.

The Bald Old Fart and I exchange glances.

"I have one already," I say quietly.

"Speak up, Isabel," the Fattest Old Fart says. "We can't hear you."

I'm about to do just that when the Bald Old Fart clears his throat.

"It's about my family," he says. "My daughter ..."

For once there are no wisecracks as the Bald Old Fart's voice trails off. Just serious faces. The Old Farts already have the intel on his sad family history. Perhaps they've even discussed it as a group. I decide to let him off the hook.

"His son, Lin, has hired me. He wants closure after all these years."

The Bald Old Fart nods and wipes away a tear.

"Closure. That's a good way to put it," he says. "I believe we should meet in private, Isabel. Yes? Fine." He puts his attention on his buddies. "If you don't mind, fellas, I'd like to find something else to talk about. If I, er, we have news to report on this case, I will let you know."

This is an interesting turn of events. I've been here before when the Old Farts were gabbing about somebody's missteps or misfortune, and even being a little free with the facts. Certainly, they have been a source of info for my cases, but like the good reporter I once was, I backed up whatever they told me with more research. As I mentioned earlier, two other Old Farts had a connection to my cases but none were as close as this one.

"All right, fellas, let's move on," the Fattest Old Fart says. "Before you got here, Isabel, we were talking about the town's latest romance."

"Oh, you mean Jack's cousin, Fred?"

"Ha. Heard he was moving in with Amy Prentice."

"How'd you hear ... oh, was he just in here?"

"No, but thanks for confirming it."

I check the wall clock. I bet Jack should be up by now.

"And with that I will be leaving you, fellas," I say, drawing the typical chorus of protests, all part of the fun since they will be skedaddling it out of here soon to whatever they do back home.

I have my hand on my car's door when I hear my name being called. You guessed it, the Bald Old Fart has followed me outside.

"Thanks for your discretion back there," he says.

I throw my bag into the car and face him.

"Be honest. How do you feel about your son hiring me for this case?"

He shakes his head.

"I have mixed feelings. I'm the father, so I have a different take on what happened almost fifty years ago. He was just a boy." He raises his hand. "But I agreed to speak with you. When would you like to do that? How about tomorrow morning, say ten?"

I check the store's windows as we agree on a time. The rest of the Old Farts are staying put out of consideration for their friend, nice guys. I decide that I will go solo on this visit. I'm sensing there might be some sensitive adult issues involved that Lin isn't aware happened.

"See you soon."

What I Tell Jack

I find Jack in my bedroom, buttoning his plaid, flannel shirt and tucking it into his jeans. I am amused he has made the bed. He must be trying to butter me up as my mother would say. I stand there watching him as he fixes his hair in the mirror, smiling at me, I believe, before he drops the comb beside my brush. Jack keeps enough stuff at my house, so he doesn't have to bring a bag and I just wash his clothes with mine. I've only slept overnight at his place once, largely due to my mother, the dog when she's not here, and the fact I have a much better mattress than Jack's, as he has told me a number of times. "Make sure you bring that with you, if you decide to move in," he joked last night as we lay in bed.

I went to the Rooster last night after having dinner with my mother and a long conversation about the future. What was my mother's response when I told her about Jack's proposal to move in with him? She surprised the heck out of me when she laughed and said, "What are you waiting for, Isabel?" She went into a lecture about changing times, that she really didn't mind it when Sam and I lived together before we got married, that it was really my father who had old-fashioned ideas. She also reminded me I wasn't getting any younger, thanks, Ma. Then came the clincher: my mother would like her own space and kitchen, plus that side of the house has a glassed-in porch thanks to an addition Jack's sister had built. I did remind my mother that a body was once buried beneath it. I found that out during my first case. But she joked, "Well, a dead body wouldn't be a deal breaker for me. Good job by the way solving that one." Taking over Fred's place would suit her just fine.

"So you can cook whatever you want?" I joked.

51

"That's right, Isabel. I'm getting awfully tired of that brown rice you keep serving me," she joked back. "What are you going to tell Jack?"

Yes, what am I going to tell him.

Jack turns around with his hands out. He raises his eyebrows.

"So how do I look?"

"Pretty handsome for a guy who's going to be stacking wood most of the day."

"You're not plannin' to bring your mother, are you?"

He doesn't even have to wink. I know what he's implying, a romp in bed or maybe the barn, the recent tease about our lovemaking.

"No, but I will when I move in with you." Jack looks at me like he thinks I'm fooling him. "I'm being serious, Jack. I want to do it. But there are a few things I have to take care of first."

"Go ahead."

"I need to tell my kids myself. I already told my mother, and she's totally fine with it. But I don't want my kids learning about it from somebody else, and you are well aware as soon as somebody at the Rooster hears I'm moving in with you, there'll be no stopping the entire town from finding out. That includes those guys in the backroom of the store. I swear Conwell's biggest pastime isn't hunting or fishing but gossiping. Am I right?"

"Absolutely."

"That includes Fred, especially him. You'll just have to stall him if he asks. I promise to get it done by tomorrow. I will ask them all to dinner."

"I'd like to be there for that if you don't mind."

Now, I am sure I made the right decision.

"I'd like that, too. Who you tell after, well, that's up to you." I hold up my hand as Jack moves forward, I presume for a hug and a kiss, so I smile. "Sorry. I'm not done. I have to figure out what to do with this house. I'm not ready to sell it, that would be a big deal, and I don't want to rent it to just anybody. I also have to figure out what to do with my stuff because it won't all fit in your place. And you have to figure out what to do with yours. The pets come, but they can stay on my mother's side. They love her more than me anyway."

"You done yet?"

I keep that smile going.

"Almost. You don't have a mortgage, but my mother and I will pay our fair share of the utilities, maintenance, and taxes." I pause. "I believe I'm done."

Jack is all grins.

"You sure about that, Isabel?"

"Oh, yeah," I say. "Now give me a kiss so we can seal the deal."

A Serious Talk

The Bald Old Fart and his wife Linda live in the town's main village, close enough that he could walk to the Conwell General Store if he wanted. It's a rather large house for two people, but my understanding is that his wife, who is a Conwell native, inherited it. I am familiar with Linda as she is a poll worker at town elections and active with anything to do with the only church in town, Congregational, of course. I believe she used to run the school system's cafeteria program, and perhaps that's how she met Ben Pierce, the name I will use as I pursue this case. Given the case's seriousness, it'd be a bit disrespectful to use his secret nickname although the man's baldness is indeed his salient characteristic. But after it's done, and hopefully I find some closure, the catchword these days, Ben Pierce will again be called the Bald Old Fart.

Ma agreed to stay home for this interview. She agreed Ben, who she hasn't met, would be more comfortable talking with me alone since we have that backroom connection. She has been invited by a couple of its members to come along, but that's far too early for my night owl mother although I honestly think she would enjoy the group's lively exchange of facts, real and imagined. Besides, she's busy prepping for tonight's meal with the kids and Jack. My sons, Matt and Alex, who are always game for a free home-cooked meal didn't question my invitation. Ruth, my naturally suspicious daughter, asked why the sudden invite and on a Tuesday. My answer? It's the last barbecue of the year and Jack's day off. I believe I might have fooled her. We'll see.

Ben ushers me through the side door. Linda, he informs me right away, isn't here.

"I thought I would spare her the interrogation," he says with a sly grin. "She said you're welcome to meet with her another

54

time. But keep in mind she and I didn't get together until many years after that all happened."

I follow Ben to the kitchen, where he says we can meet. What did I say about my meeting people around tables? And this one, something from the fifties with Formica and steel legs just like the one my mother had in her kitchen, has a photo album, a short stack of papers, and a pitcher of what he says is lemonade. Homemade, Ben informs me, so I accept his offer for a glass. I set my phone to record as he takes the seat across from me.

Softball questions are the ones reporters use to make the person comfortable if it's going to be a lengthy interview. If that's not the situation, like trying to get a comment from a town official or a cop, especially when they probably aren't going to say much, then reporters get right to it. My line of questioning will not be a one and done. I will just do my best to be sensitive about this situation while trying to wrangle as much helpful information as I can from Ben.

So here goes. Softball question number one: "What was your life in Jefferson like before?"

"Before."

He takes a sip of lemonade before he launches into a narrative about growing up in Jefferson, when it was half the population it is now. It even had a high school then. Now, the kids are bussed to a regional school. Most people were born there and never left. Newcomers were those who married into the old families like his, although that changed when people wanted to try small town life, plus homes were cheaper than in the city.

Softball question number two: "How did you and your first wife meet?"

Ben and Jessica, who grew up in another town, were school teachers fresh out of college. He taught math and she, music, but in different high schools. They met on a blind date through friends and had a one-year courtship before marrying. Lin was born a couple of years later.

"Was it a happy marriage?" I ask, which I acknowledge is not a softball question.

He doesn't answer right away.

"Happy? The first few years, definitely. But that faded away. I suppose that happens with lots of couples. You get involved with raising a kid. You buy a house and fix it up. You have family gatherings. There are vacations and holidays. You kinda forget about each other. At least we didn't stick it out until we were old and waiting for the other one to die."

Ouch, at that last sentence. Ben was reverting to his backroom persona.

"There's an eleven-year gap between Lin and his sister. Was that intentional?" I tip my head. "Sorry, but some of these questions might get personal."

"Elizabeth was definitely a surprise. My wife loved her job teaching music. She was in charge of the high school's band and chorus. She didn't want to give that up. She was definitely not happy about it." He hits the pause button. "Options for child care were minimal then, and her parents made it clear they weren't going to be full-time babysitters. We certainly couldn't afford a nanny."

"The only photos I've seen of your daughter were two in the newspaper clippings and a snapshot your son supplied."

He reaches for the album, spins the book so it's facing me, and flips the cover. The first page says: Elizabeth Pierce. As he turns the pages, he gives me a narrative, of the baby coming home from the hospital, her Christening, and lots of photos with her brother, parents, and other family members, who's who and where they were taken. There are no newspaper clippings or anything tied to her taking. He pats the last page of photos.

"This was the last one of her. It was taken a few days before …" His voice fades. "She was such a pretty baby. That blonde hair. Those eyes like her mother's."

A young Lin sits on a couch, smiling down at the baby sister he holds in his lap. She is bundled in receiving blankets. I recognize the one with the teddy bears and bunnies.

Ben leaves the book open.

"Your son says his mother gave music lessons in your home," I say.

Ben nods.

"Jessica started doing that in the middle of her pregnancy and planned to continue until she could go back into the classroom. She mostly played the piano but also the violin, guitar, even the flute. She was quite good. I believe at one time she aspired to be a professional musician. There was a piano in a room downstairs with a door that closed for privacy, so the sound of bad piano playing didn't fill the house. Have you been inside yet? No? I haven't since I moved out my things and that was a long time ago." He pauses. "Actually, that's not true. When her mother and then her father died, a few years apart from each other, Linda and I went to the receptions she held at her home after their funerals. It was cordial."

"Does the name Tim Todd mean anything to you?"

He presses his lips.

"He was with my ex-wife when our baby was taken."

"Who was he?"

"I never met him. I didn't meet most of her students. I was usually at school when she was teaching. During the summer, I got a full-time job. I had to. In those days teachers weren't paid what they get now. And Jessica wasn't working. That summer, I worked on my uncle's painting crew."

"Lin told me how he was supposed to watch his sister only when she was teaching Tim Todd, because he was preparing for an audition."

His eyes are focused on mine.

"You'll have to ask Jessica about him."

"I'll be meeting with her next. Tomorrow."

Ben shakes his head.

"I'm afraid I was really hard on the boy afterward. Too hard. It's obvious the boy was tricked into leaving his sister alone like that. Of course, he would think his mother took the baby inside. Why would he think it was somebody else who had her? It is too bad he didn't check to be sure, but he was under orders not to interrupt a music lesson and he was only an eleven-year-old boy. Anyway, even if he did, my daughter likely would have been long gone." He reaches for his glass. "Of course, I blamed his mother. How could she leave a boy in charge of a baby? I regret how I handled it very much. Of course, I was in pain, but I was too rough on Lin. It created a rift in our relationship that hasn't healed totally. I've tried, but he has a hard time forgiving me." His voice thins. "I don't blame him. That's why I agreed to meet with you."

At that revelation, I allow a pause in our conversation. I take a sip of lemonade to give Ben a little time to recover.

"What I know from that day I've read in the newspapers, police records and notes Lin's given me. As I said, we had an initial meeting," I say. "A lot of time has passed, but what can you tell me about the day?"

"It started like a regular day. I got up, had breakfast, and said good-bye to the kids and Jessica." His voice cracks a bit on "good-bye." "I went to paint the exterior of a house in town. Later that afternoon, one of the town cops showed up. He told me I was needed at home. He wouldn't tell me why, only that it was very important. All kinds of things were going on inside my head as I drove home. Did one of the kids get hurt? Did something happen to my wife? There were state cop cars outside my house. Now, I was really worried. The town's police chief pointed to where I could park. I went right up to him and asked what was going on. He said, 'Your baby daughter is missing.' It was like he was speaking in another language. Missing? My daughter? And from then on, nothing was ever the same."

Ben goes on about the drama that unfolded after he came home, his wife's uncontrollable fear and grief, and his young son's confusion. A State Police detective took him aside to question him. He had questions himself as he waited inside the house for any news. An organized search was held in the woods behind their home and their neighbors' yards. Ben wasn't allowed to join the searchers. From inside his house he saw reporters and TV crews on the sidewalk.

"I never felt so helpless," he says. "The cops decided Elizabeth was nowhere in the neighborhood. Jessica and I still held out hope. The person who took our daughter couldn't have done it for ransom. Each time the phone rang or there was a knock on the door … we even went on a TV station to make an appeal. Nothing." He shakes a finger. "The worst was when the state cops brought Jessica and me in for questioning. They were just considering all angles, but it was a horrible experience. They searched every corner of our house as if we had done something awful to her. They even questioned Lin. A situation like that would either pull a couple together or drive them apart. Our marriage didn't last long after that."

He taps the photo of his baby daughter in the album's last page.

I believe I have tortured this man long enough, but I have one more question, an important one.

"What do you think happened to Elizabeth?"

At the moment, the kitchen door opens. Linda is home, and Ben smiles slightly when he sees his wife.

"Did I come back too early?" she asks Lin.

"No, you're fine, Linda. We're just about done."

I repeat my question.

"Somebody wanted a baby and they planned it well," Ben says. "They had to know a little boy would be watching her and what it would take to distract him. That Tim Todd, whoever he was, had to be involved somehow. The cops claimed he wasn't after they interviewed him. They said someone probably had been watching when those students came and went at the same time every week. Maybe there were two people. One to let the dog go and one to take our baby. But how would they know about Elizabeth?"

"That's a good point," I say. "Lin believes he might have seen his sister. He showed me a photo he took in Luella's. What do you think?"

"I've seen the photo. It's not very good, but maybe it's possible."

Linda comes across the room and kisses the top of her husband's bald head.

I stop the recording app on my phone. I am done for now.

Next Jessica

My mother and I are early as usual, so we do our own tour of the streets and roads in Jefferson near Lin's childhood home and where his mother still lives. I am interested especially in the area behind her home, which is where the abductor might have come from. There's a farm on Proctor Road with large fields still used for growing, but it appears its frontage land was broken off into a few lots for ranch-style houses, either for family members or to sell outright for money during one of the housing booms.

"I thought it went okay last night, didn't you?" my mother says.

"I'll let you know after I get that call from Ruth later today," I joke.

We are, of course, talking about last night's dinner when I told the kids my mother and I will be living with Jack. Actually, Jack volunteered to do the telling, mighty brave of him, half-way through dessert. My granddaughter Sophie was on his lap as he told my kids he's asked us to move in with him and why. I laughed when Alex joked, "Does that mean Matt and I get free beer from now on?"

"I'll give you the family discount," Jack joked back, but then he got serious. "I love your mother and want to be with her. Of course, that means I will be a part of your lives more. I can't replace your Dad. I understand that."

They and I are aware of all the changes that need to happen, and I recognized relief on their faces when I said I wasn't selling the home. Of course, my mother's endorsement was key. But that's not my concern now. Right now, I'm trying to get a feel for this neighborhood in Jefferson.

And, yes, I did ask Alex about having Ben Pierce as a teacher. He said he was tough but it was easy to get him off track telling stories. That sounds about right.

Luckily, no one brought up, Ruth, to be specific, whether I had a new case. I have to watch what I say around Sophie, who at age two is aware of what we adults talk about. Besides, it doesn't seem the kids would expect me to have a case right away and telling them about moving in with Jack was enough news for one family gathering.

"Stop the car, Isabel," my mother says.

I come to attention.

"What?"

"See over there? It looks like a path through the woods."

That's what it looks like to me, too. There's even a small sign. But there's no time to explore the path properly. I'm just going to have to come back, maybe after this interview if my mother doesn't mind waiting in the car. I never missed a deadline as a reporter or editor, the same goes for an appointment. Typically, I am early thanks to my parents, who, if you recall, would come an hour before to get a good seat. And so I turn my car around and get to Jessica Pierce's house exactly when I said I would. Jessica is in the front yard of her Victorian tending to the flowers still in bloom. She's a thin woman, average height, and with straight shoulder-length silver hair, well-styled. I would describe her face as elegant, the same word Lin used to describe the woman he feels could be his sister. Her eyes, their different colors, would make anyone stare. Jessica must have been a knockout when she was younger. She still is.

Jessica guides us through the front door and into her living room for our interview, a break in tradition for me. The room is full of antique furniture, with ornate dark wood and classy upholstery, built-in shelves filled with hard cover books, mostly classics it appears, and framed paintings on the walls. The woman has taste. I am also guessing there is or was money in her family. Her original last name was Booker, one of the royal families of Jefferson, I recall.

A dog barks from another room.

"Don't worry. Ludwig's in the kitchen. It's better that way. I'm afraid he isn't a friendly dog. There, he's calmed down now."

61

Ma and I choose the couch as she takes a chair. I set my bag on the coffee table and get ready as she offers us something to drink, but we are fine without it.

"How do you feel about my taking this case?" I ask.

She doesn't answer right away. Her hands rest one on top of the other. I note her long musician fingers.

"Frankly, I didn't think it possible to investigate what happened so long ago," she says. "I've always believed someone took her that either lost a child or couldn't have one to raise as their own. Why they chose mine, I honestly don't know." She sighs. "My heart breaks still when I think about her. Ben might have told you she was unexpected. But I loved Elizabeth, and I hope whoever had her treated her well."

"Lin told me about meeting a woman he felt could be his sister."

"Yes, I heard the story. It might just be wishful thinking. And the photo isn't very clear." She pauses. "I've read about your success in the paper. And my son speaks so highly of you. So I gave my blessing even though this brings up painful memories. Believe me, I want to know what happened to my daughter."

"Lin gave me some notes that show me you tried to figure it out yourself."

She nods.

"I didn't get very far before I gave up."

I glance toward my mother. We had agreed during the ride here she would bring up the next question.

"Jessica, could you tell us about that day?" my mother asks. "Please give us as much detail as you can remember."

Like her ex-husband said, it started as an ordinary day, and then she gives us information I had already read in her notes and the clippings. Tim Todd was there for his lesson, so she asked her son to watch his sister. Having her on the front porch wouldn't do. She needed to be taken for a long walk in the neighborhood, so she would fall asleep, and if he came back earlier, he would have to wait outside and keep himself occupied.

"Did he take care of his sister a lot?" I ask.

"Only when Tim came. Once a week. Lin was on summer vacation from school. This wasn't his first time. He had been watching her six weeks. I had a plan that when he went back to school, I would bring Elizabeth to my mother's house for one day while I taught Tim and some of my other serious students. Mom had agreed she could at least do that for me."

Six weeks. That would certainly give someone enough time to observe the boy when he was outside with his sister. I wish I could hypnotize Lin and have him tell me what he saw those days. If only it were that easy.

"What happened when you went outside?"

"I had just finished giving Tim his lesson. After he left, I went into the kitchen to make myself a cup of tea and while it was brewing, I went outside to check on the kids." She pauses. "The tea. That's a detail I just remembered." She glances at my mother and me. "You two are very good."

"Did you see him get in his car and leave?" my mother asks, and I nod in recognition of her astute question.

"No, I didn't," Jessica says quietly. "We talked at the front door, and then I went into the kitchen. I know what you're going to ask next." She shakes her head. "I didn't check on Lin and the baby then. I went out later after I fixed myself a cup of tea. I didn't see Lin and when I went to the carriage, it was empty. I called to Lin. Maybe he had his sister with him although he wasn't supposed to take her out of her carriage. When I went to the side yard and yelled for Lin, he came home emptyhanded. I asked him where his sister was. He said, 'I thought you had her.' He told me about the dog running off, and when he came back, finding the carriage empty. He thought I took her inside. He didn't dare ask because he was told not to bother me during lessons." She heaves a loud sigh. "I cried out loud and went in the house to call the police."

I pause to give Jessica a bit of space before I proceed.

"How long had Tim Todd been gone when you went outside?" I ask.

She shakes her head.

"Ten-fifteen minutes at the most."

"I noticed Tim Todd's the only adult student you mention in

63

your notes that your son gave me. What can you tell me about him?"

"Many of my young students were from the school where I taught, or they lived in town. My older students had been with me long before. I did that for a couple of years for some extra money and for the challenge. They helped me be a better musician. Tim was one of those students. He was a skilled pianist, very passionate about it. In his early twenties. He wanted to be a solo pianist in a large orchestra. But as you can imagine, the competition was tough, but he worked hard at it and I kept challenging him to get better. I understood what he was up against. I had tried it myself but didn't make it. So I became a teacher instead."

"Did he become successful?"

"Yes, but not under that name. He goes by Robert Todd. Robert is his middle name. He thought Robert Todd was a better stage name. Have you ever heard of him?"

My mother and I both shake our heads.

"I'm afraid we don't follow that kind of music."

"I heard from my other students that he worked in a couple of large symphonies, even playing solo, and did some soundtrack work for albums and movies." She stops. "I imagine it wouldn't be hard to find where he now lives given the internet."

"So you lost contact with him?"

"I saw him only once," she says quietly. "I had stopped giving lessons altogether. I couldn't bring myself to do it anymore. Besides, Lin really needed me. He took it so hard, and his father didn't help the situation. He blamed me, too. You know Ben, don't you? I eventually went back to teaching in the school where I taught before. Our marriage only lasted a few years after our daughter's kidnapping. I never married again. That marriage was enough for me."

"Ben lives in my town as you know. When I met with him yesterday, he expressed deep regrets about his actions." I let that rest although it appears to have no impact on Jessica. "But back to Tim, you said you saw him another time."

"I went to a concert where he was in the orchestra. Oh, that was about ten years later. I thought he stole the show with his solo. I went backstage to congratulate him. He seemed surprised to see me. We spoke for a few moments. But he said he was too busy to talk, so I left."

The wall clock strikes the hour. We've been here that long. Now, it's time for one of those deep-breath questions, that is, you take a deep breath before you ask. I used to do it when I was a reporter who had to ask an uncomfortable question. Here goes.

"I am going to ask you a rather personal question. It's part of the job to clear up any loose ends. It's about Tim Todd. Your relationship was strictly as teacher and student?"

Jessica's brow tightens into a deep fold.

"I am shocked you asked that question. I was his teacher."

"I'm sorry. I didn't mean to offend you," I say although my apology doesn't seem to have an effect, and she didn't answer my question.

Jessica glares at me and then my mother, who is trying hard to be calm herself, but her mouth is open.

"I believe it is time you both left. This interview is over."

Jessica is on her feet and stepping toward the door to signal our exit as I gather my things together. I give my mother a hand to help her rise from the soft couch.

"Thank you for your time." I keep my voice cordial when we reach the front door. "If you want to talk again, you have my number."

"Don't expect it."

The Path

After Jessica Pierce kicked us out of her house, she stood behind the screen door watching us get inside the car and didn't shut the one behind it until I made a three-point turn and drove away. Now, I wait at the stop sign at the end of Carter Road for a pickup truck that has the right of way. We're not going home just yet but back to the entrance to that path in the woods we saw earlier.

"You sure struck a raw nerve there, Isabel," my mother says.

"It appears I did. You okay over there, Ma? You sound a little shook."

"I'm fine, really, Isabel. I'm just not used to these kinds of situations although it appears you are. You handled that well."

"Lin told me I should ask her that question myself. Since he didn't object when I brought it up, I'm figuring he had his own suspicions. I'm definitely going to ask him the next time we speak." I take a right onto Proctor Road. "Her response makes me wonder. She certainly didn't put it to rest, would you say?"

"Not at all."

I park near the trail's entrance, where there is enough space created off the road for a few cars to park although mine is the only one. A small sign gives its name: Lucas Biddeford Trail. I give my mother a quick study. She's correct that I am more familiar with difficult interviews, starting when I was a reporter digging for a comment or information someone didn't want to give. I had my share of "no comments," swear words, and hang-ups. Now, as a P.I., I've had to deal with uncooperative people of interest or suspects who a few times put my life in danger. My mother wouldn't have enjoyed my one-on-ones with ex-chief Thorny or the Beaumont brothers when they were suspects in my second case. As for Jessica

Pierce, things would have been hunky-dory if I hadn't asked about her relationship with Tim Todd aka Robert Todd, whom I'm itching to investigate online. What did Lin say when I asked him about his mother's relationship with her former student? "You'll have to ask her." But now my concern is with my mother who has been a real good sport assisting with my cases. I have to remind myself she is ninety-three.

"You sure you're going to be okay here by yourself? I could return another day."

My mother reaches into her purse and pulls out a paperback. Yes, she always comes prepared. She could put those scouts to shame.

"I'll be just fine, Isabel. Go right ahead."

"I'll make it twenty minutes tops. Just honk the horn if you need me back. Promise?"

My mother waves her hand in absolution, and then I am on my way. I stop briefly to check out the sign, which says the trail and forty acres around it are owned by a conservation trust, a gift over twenty years ago from a local family who wanted it preserved. People are welcome to use it but be respectful of the neighbors.

With a backward glance to the car, I begin my walk among tall trees. There is little underbrush, which means this is a rather old forest. I am five minutes in when I stop. If I estimate correctly, I could be behind the houses on Carter Road. I leave the path and walk through the woods until I reach the no-trespassing signs posted on the trees to show the boundary line and to protect people's privacy. Beyond them I glimpse one of the neighbor's homes, another Victorian with a distinctive color combination, this one a slate blue with white and burgundy trim. I believe I am three houses away, so I use the no-trespassing signs to guide me until I reach behind Jessica's. I am less than thirty feet, half the distance between telephone poles, from her back yard, including the side of the garage where the dog Patches was tied. It wouldn't take much for someone to come this way given the lack of underbrush to release the dog from its chain. Could the same person have taken the baby this way? Perhaps.

I move a little closer to the backyard to take a couple of photos with my phone, but I retreat when I see Jessica leave the side door with her unfriendly mutt Ludwig, which begins running free in the backyard. She's on her cell phone. Her face is as unpleasant as it was when our conversation ended badly. She speaks loudly but not enough for me to hear what she is saying and I'm not about to get closer. That dog is sniffing and yipping. It trots towards the woods but Jessica calls it back. She bends to pick up a ball and bounces it against the garage for the mutt to chase. This is my opportunity to get the hell out of here. I try to be as quiet as possible as I slowly retreat step by step until I am deeper in the woods and finally back on the path.

My mother glances up from her book when I reach the car.

"How did it go?"

"Mission accomplished," I answer.

An Unexpected Tip

We get back home just in time. Annette Waters hasn't arrived yet with her tow truck although she is due any minute. My mother has decided to give up driving forever although she will hold onto her license in case she needs to get me out of a jam. That's her humor not mine. It's a big decision for a woman who enjoyed putting the pedal to the metal, but since coming to live with me, she hasn't shown much interest in driving by herself. Once when she was going to the general store, she made a wrong turn and got lost. I went on a search to find Ma after she seemed to take an extraordinary amount of time for her errand. And she wasn't comfortable making the two-hour-plus drive back home, as she still calls it, which is why my brother Danny and I do an exchange on the Mass. Turnpike. Ma wanted to give Annette's son, Abe, her car since he recently cracked up his, but the Tough Cookie wouldn't hear of it. "We'll give you a fair price for it," she told my mother the last time we saw her. "He's gonna work it off."

I'm letting our dog, oh, let me rephrase that, Ma's dog, out as Annette's tow truck comes down our driveway. Abe is with her. She expertly positions the tow truck behind the car, which my mother insisted I have washed and waxed at the car wash before it passed hands.

"Hey, Ma, they're here."

Annette and Abe walk up the front path. This is a first for Abe, but Annette has been here before, when she hired me for my second case, plus another time with Marsha for my mother's birthday party, which shocked my daughter Ruth a bit but their appearance made for a lively event.

But this time it's for business. Annette nods at Abe and growls something under her breath I don't catch before he hands my mother a fat envelope filled presumably with cash, a figure the two of them arranged without my input. Ma bought the car from Annette after I totaled the one she brought here. Hey, it wasn't my fault. I had an alleged murderer trying to run me off the road.

"Do you want to count it, Mrs. Ferreira?" Abe's face reddens. "It's the amount we agreed to over the phone."

My mother and Abe had a telephone conversation? This is news to me. Ma has the car's title, plus a bill of sale I created on my computer ready.

"Here you go Abe," my mother says. "It's all yours."

Annette gives her son the evil eye. She's been working hard to train him to be a good adult in her own way, giving him a job and a place to live in the apartment behind the Pit Stop, the convenience store she co-owns. And now, he's the drummer in the Junkyard Dogs. I half expect her to slap his arm and grumble, "What do you say?" But Abe beats her to it with a genuine thanks to my mother as he takes the paperwork, gives my mother an awkward hug that startles my non-hugging mother, and with a quick bow of his head, he's out the door to get to work.

The Tough Cookie takes a seat.

"How's your new case goin'?" she asks.

"I'm just getting started. This one's gonna be tough."

She shakes her head after I tell her about my new case.

"Don't know anythin' about that one. Almost fifty years ago? Really?"

I'm not surprised Annette hasn't heard about the kidnapping. Given she's in Caulfield, a few towns north and west of where I live, she has access to a different set of locals. Caulfield and Jefferson have few if any connections. No one from one town would go to the other unless they had kin living there. And I would wager Caulfield has more natives percentage wise than Jefferson, which has become a semi-suburb of Hampton, the county seat.

But then again, Caulfield and the towns around it would be a great place for a man or woman with a past to hide out. Plus, she and her cousin, Marsha own the Pit Stop, the only gas station and convenience store for miles. She's lived there all of her life, and like a lot of the natives, she keeps tabs on the newcomers.

"You ever hear of a man named Tim Todd or Robert Todd? He is or was a musician. Plays the piano."

"There's a guy named Robert Todd who comes into Baxter's. Sometimes he plays the piano. He'll come in on a Sunday or sometime when there's not a lot of people. He seems rather harmless, quiet and kind of a loner." She stops and laughs when she realizes she just used a description for people who are often guilty as hell. "Anyway Dave lets him play. You should talk with him about the guy."

My mother chuckles. I can read her mind. I can't escape talking with Dave Baxter about a case it seems.

"What's he look like?"

"He's kinda old. White hair, lots of it. Not bad lookin' for his age." She shakes her finger. "And he has the longest damn fingers I've ever seen. He doesn't play the kind of music the regulars like. It's that highbrow stuff. You look excited there, Isabel. You, too, Maria."

I nod.

"He definitely sounds like the guy I'm looking for. Any idea where he might live?"

"No, I don't. You could ask Marsha if he comes into the Pit Stop for gas. She's there more than me. I bet Dave Baxter will know." She gives me a sly laugh. "He won't mind you askin'."

Annette is clearly alluding to the obvious crush Dave has on me.

"That might be a good time to tell him we're going to live with Jack," my mother says. "Fred's moving out."

"You two?" She snorts a laugh. "How come I don't know about this?"

I try to conceal my surprise. I don't want my mother to feel badly about blurting out the news, but some damage control is needed here.

"Uh, because it just happened and we haven't told anybody. There's stuff to work out. If you don't mind, Annette, could you keep it to yourself please? But when people start talking

71

about it, you can tell them you already knew. Okay?"

Annette leans back in her seat as she focuses on the living room window.

"Will do. Abe's got the car hitched up. I gotta check to make sure he did it right. I don't wanna lose the car on the way." She stands and knocks the table top with a fist. "Nice to see you both, and I'll make sure Abe takes real good care of your car, Maria. Gotta get back to the junkyard. Somebody's droppin' off a Crown Vic. I'm keepin' that one for myself for next year's demolition derby." She laughs. "This time I'm gonna make sure I win. Gary Beaumont better watch out."

"See you around," I tell her, and then I remember something I want to ask her. "When's your next gig at the Rooster? My mother wants to hear you play."

Annette smiles at Ma.

"You do, do you? Jack's kinda booked, so I hope soon. We're playing at Baxter's two Saturdays from now. Why don't you come, Isabel?" She makes a chuckle that contains a large amount of mischief. "I'm sure Dave would love it."

"I'm sure he would."

Email from Lin

Annette's gone and soon my granddaughter will arrive with her parents, who are celebrating their anniversary with a trip to Boston. They're staying in a swanky hotel, going to a play, and eating out at a high-end restaurant where I am treating them to a meal. We will have Sophie for two days. I used to watch Sophie for a couple of days each week, but that stopped when Ruth's job turned full-time and it made sense for her to find daycare. She's a fun kid, but I will have to keep a constant eye on her now that she's a toddler. Ruth made me promise I won't work on my case, yes, she finally found out I have one with my old boss, like doing surveillance or interviewing a suspect. I get it. She doesn't want her daughter in danger. Neither do I. Ruth doesn't know I took Sophie along when I was driving the backroads for one of my cases, and I don't ever plan on admitting it. I could hear the lecture now.

Ma's taking a nap. She said she had too much excitement today and needed to rest up before Sophie comes, which makes me feel guilty that I took her to that interview. I value my mother's opinion, but maybe in the future I will just leave her out. I don't have much time before Sophie's arrival, so I sit on the front step and check my phone for any email, scrolling quickly until I find one from Lin. Here's how it starts:

Isabel, my mother called after you left. She was very upset because you asked her that question. She wants me to call off this case. But I said no. I'll tell you the rest when we speak next.

I can hardly wait to hear what Lin has to say. Yes, I'm being sarcastic. He's the one who told me to ask his mother about her relationship with her student. Thanks a lot, coward. In the same email, he gives me the contact number for his longtime neighbor, Frieda Payne and the name of the convalescent home in Hampton for the other, Lawrence McGowan. There's also a new name and number: Randy Walsh, who was a town cop then, just a rookie. This isn't a long list of possible sources, but as what tends to happen, one can lead to another.

I scan the rest of the inbox and don't find anything that can't wait for my attention. Anyway, Ruth and Gregg have arrived. I am up, outside, and opening the back door to Gregg's car, where Sophie sits in her special kid seat, and smile as she greets me, "Gamma." And while Ruth and Gregg carry everything their daughter will need for two days into my house, I have her in my arms, and then let her down when Maggie the dog romps toward us from the woods.

Once inside, I get my last minute instructions from Ruth, as if I didn't raise three kids, just as my mother comes from her room. She jokes about the amount of stuff in our living room.

"Are you all moving in?" she asks. "All this for two days?"

"Speaking of moving," Ruth says. "I believe I might have found a good renter for the house. My in-laws, Anne and Phil. They'd like to live closer to us. They're planning to sell their house because it's too large. This would give them time to figure out what they would want to do next. Who knows? Maybe they'll even buy the house and it would stay in the family. What do you think about that idea?"

"It could work." I lift Sophie into my arms. "Now, you'd better get going if you want to make your dinner reservations."

Robert Online

Sophie keeps us all busy, including the pets, for the rest of the day. By time I'm done giving her a bath and reading three books aloud, it was past her usual bedtime, but I certainly won't be telling her mother. I check in with Jack, who says it's a busy enough game night for the card players. Too bad I can't come. I might actually win one with the group that's here tonight. Very funny, Jack.

So I bring my laptop to the kitchen table to do the only surveillance permitted while I have my granddaughter here.

"You doing that Google thing?" my mother calls from her chair in the living room.

"That's right. I want to see what I can find about this Robert Todd or whoever he is."

I try the name Tim Todd first, but don't find anything except for men with the same name living or dead in other parts of the country, and none fitting what little I have on the guy. Thank goodness Lin held onto those clippings that mention him. Next I hunt for his alleged new name, Robert Todd. Oh, hold on, I find a man by that name who appears to be a rather famous pianist. I've never heard of him before because I'm not big into classical music, but it appears lots of people have. He's been featured on various musical websites. The New York Times did a story about him, noting he was a self-made musician who achieved fame through hard work, talent, and a bit of luck. Hmm, I wonder about that last part. Robert talks about tours in Europe. He doesn't mention taking lessons with Jessica Pierce or that he was at her house when Baby Elizabeth was taken. The story says he has a home in Massachusetts. He looks dapper in that formal getup such serious musicians wear. There's no mention of a wife or romantic partner. His later photo is just as Annette described him: kind of old with lots of white hair and not bad looking for his age. Yes, he has long fingers. I don't find him on Facebook or Twitter, but he could be using an alias. I print a copy of the story for Ma.

"Here you go."

She skims the story.

"Interesting. I am curious what Dave will have to say about him."

"Me, too. I don't really want to wait until Ruth and Gregg get back, but it looks like I have to. How about lunch on Saturday?"

My mother smiles above her book.

"Sounds like a plan to me."

My cell phone rings. Lin's name pops up on the screen.

"I believe I may be disowned," he says when I answer.

"I didn't say you told me to ask her about her relationship with Tim Todd or whatever his name is. You know he goes by the name Robert Todd, don't you?"

"What are you talking about, Isabel?"

I repeat what Lin's mother told me.

"She never mentioned that to me."

"Turns out he's a well-known musician for his kind of music."

"I guess I should have kept looking. I'm glad you are."

"I hate to say this, but there might be more to his story than your mother wanted to tell you or me."

"I believe you're right."

"Anyway, I have a lead on a guy by that name who might live around here. Maybe. I'll fill you in when I find out more."

He ends the call with a quiet "Thanks."

Stopping By

We don't have many days left warm enough to go swimming or play by the shore of Redneck Beach, a place for locals. That's where I took my mother and Sophie for a few hours. We had the beach to ourselves. She and I played in the water and used the river stones to build stuff for her dolls while my mother supervised and napped in the sun. "Soak it in for the winter," I told Ma. "If only," she said. This will likely be my last time here. I note the leaves of the hardwood trees are losing their green. Very soon, too soon really, they will be red, yellow or gold, depending on the variety.

I can't really do much of anything for Lin's case with my granddaughter here although I did give my boss Bob a call this morning to fill him in on what I've done so far. No, he's never heard of Tim or Robert Todd, so I surmise the man hasn't been in trouble with the law at least when Bob was a lifer with the state cops. But he will ask around. Bob was amused about my meeting with Lin's mother. His reaction? "You struck a raw nerve." Hey, that's what my mother said.

Now, we're in my car heading back home. I deliberately take the long way around so we pass Jack's and the Rooster. He would love to see Sophie and vice versa. Actually, she's asked about him a couple of times. He's got his hands full right now, putting a new roof on the Rooster, a job he would like to finish today. He's got a few of the True Blue Rooster Regulars helping out. When Jack called last night, he said he was going straight home and to bed, that he was beat from roofing during the day and tending bar at night. "I'm gettin' too old for this," he half-complained. "When did you say you were movin' in, Isabel? I could use more help." Very funny. I heard the to-do list over breakfast recently. Replacing the roof was way overdue. Next year, he might upgrade the men's room, which is really a shit-hole, if you don't mind my vulgarity. The floor's a bit ragged and the plumbing is way overdue for a redo.

Just as I approach Jack's, a truck loaded with furniture leaves the driveway. I recognize Fred's pickup. After we exchange beeps of our vehicles' horns, I slow and come to a stop in front of Jack's farm. Home sweet home soon.

A few miles later, I pull into the Rooster's parking lot, far from any possible nails on the ground.

"Building inspector," I announce as I walk closer with Sophie in my arms.

Jack's down the ladder. He gives Sophie's cheek a gentle pinch.

"Jack, Jack," she says.

"Hey, sweetie, what can I do for a bribe?"

"You talking to her or me?"

"Uh, her. I know what you want."

Jack goes over to greet my mother, who's staying put in the car's front seat, and then he's back.

"Have you told anybody yet?" I ask.

"About you movin' in with me? I was gonna wait until Friday when you're there. I'll make the official announcement, maybe even have a toast. What'd you say about that?"

I smile at the suggestion of a celebratory toast.

"That would work. I saw Fred taking a truckload of stuff out just now."

Jack nods.

"He seems gung-ho about this woman. He should be." One of the guys on the roof gives Jack a shout. "I haven't told him yet about our plans. Uh, looks like there's a problem up there. Hey, honey, I gotta go."

"You do that, Jack."

Not Such Good News

It's one of those non-stop nights at the Rooster, snapping caps off bottles and manning the tap for those with a more discerning taste for beer. One of the True Blue Rooster Regulars complained, "Jesus, I wasn't expectin' the whole town to show up tonight, were you?" Jack doesn't mind. He needs to pay for the new roof and for tonight's band, the Lone Sums, which hasn't played at the Rooster for a few months. I was told the band broke up briefly after the lead guitarist found out the drummer was messing around with his wife, which got more complicated since they used to be best friends. So much for that friendship, and since the lead guitarist formed the band, the Lone Sums had to find a new drummer. So I imagine we have a number of Lone Sums fans here tonight among the usual Friday night revelers. In case you're wondering, they have the typical Rooster playlist down, that is, country, a little rock, and more country.

"And what can I get you tonight?" I ask one of the regulars.

"Do you really have to ask, Isabel?"

"King of Beers?"

"You got it."

And that becomes a typical exchange. When the band starts, we have to speak louder or resort to finger pointing and nods. Jack told me he was going to wait for the break after the band's first set to make the announcement. He plans to ask everyone to raise their bottle of beer as a toast. Jack grinned when he said, "Get ready for it." I am since I've never had this kind of a formal announcement about moving in with a man. Certainly, that didn't happen with my late husband Sam, the only guy I've lived with so far.

But the band's only started, playing Johnny Cash's "Folsom Prison Blues," the one about a guy stuck in prison cause he shot that man in Reno, rather a depressing topic, but that doesn't stop people from dancing. Plus, the band is keeping a decent beat. Gary and Larry Beaumont watch the action from a table they commandeered to the right of the Rooster's small dancefloor. I've never seen either of the brothers dance, but they appear to be having a grand ol' time pointing and laughing. They probably imbibed with some of the weed they sell before they arrived although any transactions of that sort are banned here and in the parking lot.

That's when Fred arrives, accompanied by his new lady love, Amy Prentice. He's grinning and has his arm around her when they enter the open door before she splits for the ladies room. She came into the Rooster long before she hooked up with Fred. I wouldn't label her a True Blue Regular although that will change if this relationship lasts. I'm guessing she's around forty, give or take a few years, wears makeup, and works on her hair that must have been blond when she was a kid. I believe she has a job in the office at a large construction company. She may have a couple of kids who live on their own, which would work because I don't see Fred as the father figure type. And just now, I've decided her nickname will be Lady Love. My mother will like that.

Jack is behind the bar with a tray of bottles he's snatched from the tables.

"Hey, I've got great news for you," Fred says.

"Yeah? You gonna be a father?" Jack jokes.

Fred rolls his eyes.

"Nah, I found somebody to move into my space right away. So now you don't have to worry about fillin' it when I leave."

Jack squints.

"What are you talkin' about, Fred?"

"It's Lisa. She needs a place to stay, so I told her she could take mine. She lost her job and it didn't work out with that guy in South Carolina, so she's coming back. It's only ... "

Wait a sec. Fred is letting Jack's ex-wife move into his house without telling him. As you may recall, they were married for a minute when they were kids, but not that long ago she made my life a bit miserable when she returned to town and tried to hook up again with Jack until Mr. Nice Guy finally told her it wasn't gonna happen and she high-tailed it back to South Carolina. Last I heard, at the demolition derby last month, she had a good job and a honey. I'm annoyed at Fred, who will retain his nickname el Creepo with this bonehead move. But I'll let Jack handle this. Fred's his cousin. He doesn't let Fred finish. He has dropped his typical Friday night jovial expression.

"Fred, I don't know what the hell you were thinkin' but you just call her up and tell her to make other plans. She ain't movin' in."

"I can't. She's packed up what she can and is on her way north. Lisa should be here tomorrow."

"Tomorrow? What about her house here?"

"Somebody's renting it. Got a lease. She can't exactly kick 'em out cause they've got kids in school. Sorry."

"You're not as sorry as I am." Jack's voice is loud enough the customers around us are watching. "You didn't even think to ask me if this would be okay?"

I keep my mouth shut and let the cousins duke it out. But now, people on this side of the bar are staring at Jack and Fred, whose standoff is a more interesting attraction than the Lone Sums playing a bad version of "Mamma Don't Let Your Babies Grow Up to Be Cowboys." I touch Jack's arm. He glances my way, and then at the people nearest to the bar. He jerks his head toward the front door.

"Let's take this outside. Now." Then he turns his focus on me. "I'll figure this out, Isabel."

Fred might be the clueless moron he demonstrated tonight, but he catches on from Jack's growl of a tone that he's messed up big time although from the way he sets his mouth, I am guessing he still has some fight left in him. I and everyone else watch them leave, and just to make a point this is a private matter, Jack shuts the front door behind him.

"Hey, anyone need a beer?" I ask to break the mood. "Step right up. The line forms in front of me."

Lady Love returns looking for Fred while I'm snapping the lids off Buds. I advise her to find a seat while he's outside with

Jack and hand her a beer I will put on Fred's tab. They may be a while, I tell her but that's all. She wasn't here for the exchange, and I'm not about to repeat it although the guys in line might enjoy it.

"Never seen Jack that pissed before," a True Blue Regular says as he drops a buck into the tip jar. Then he turns toward his pal beside him. "Oh, yeah, remember that time? Uh, never mind, Isabel. You don't wanna hear about that one."

Yes, I do, but this isn't the time as the door opens, but it's not Jack or Fred, but Annette Waters making a beeline past the waiting customers to the bar. There will be no stalling the Tough Cookie. She crooks her thumb.

"What the hell's goin' on out there?"

"I believe Jack is ready to murder his cousin." I glance at the next guy waiting for a beer. "Only kidding."

"I kept hearing Lisa's name and Jack's house. Aren't you and your mother movin' in with Jack?"

I hold a finger to my lips.

"Uh, there appears to be a little delay." I check the line of customers, who appear to be extra-attentive tonight. "Right now's not a good time to talk. I'll fill you in later." I hand her a beer. "Here, have one on the house."

It seems like forever when Jack returns with Fred, who has what I would call a sheepish expression. He can't even look me in the eyes. People clear a path as they approach the bar and come around to where I'm standing.

"Hey, guys, I did a stupid thing," Fred says to the bystanders. "I hope I didn't ruin your evening."

I can honestly say that Fred's stupidity didn't and it will likely be the height of their weekend. They'll be yakking about this one for sure, as in, "Remember that time Jack almost killed his cousin for letting his ex-wife move in next door? You know Lisa, don't you?" I can only imagine what they will say my part in the story will be. I bet the Old Farts will drill me about it the next time we meet.

After telling the next guy in line, "I'll be right back," I follow Jack and Fred into the dark kitchen.

"I'm real sorry, Isabel," Fred says without an ounce of the

insincerity or sarcasm he typically delivers.

Jack nods at Fred.

"He felt bad, real bad when I told him about our plans. I told my dumb-ass cousin I'll give her a month, and then she's outta there. I guess Lisa got herself into a real bad situation down there with this guy. And don't worry, Isabel, there's no way she's workin' here."

A month? I have to put up with that woman for a month? I'll bet good money she will be showing up here, expecting a free drink, and making a real pest of herself. It's not like I could move in right away, both sides of the house need work before that happens, but I just don't like the thought of that woman living there. I suppose she has to find a job, too. But I'm going to be the good sport.

"Okay, apology accepted," I say to Fred, who mumbles a thanks before I ask him to leave so I can talk with Jack. I wait until we're alone. "I'm not going to let this ruin our night. I say we go ahead and let everybody know about our plans."

Jack smiles back.

"Really, Isabel? You want to do that?"

"Of course, I do."

Jack wraps his arms around me.

"Aw, Isabel, that's why I love you."

At Baxter's for Lunch

Jack appeared to be in no rush to leave this morning, but then again, my mother and I will delay doing our errands until later this afternoon. The plan is to go first to Baxter's for lunch, so we can ask Dancin' Dave about Robert Todd or whoever the hell he is. Jack noticeably doesn't make any snide comments about Dave or his expressed interest in me. Besides, it's now official with last night's announcement and the toast of whatever drink anyone had in their hand that I'm moving in with Jack, which publicly solidifies our relationship. Jack took the microphone to tell the crowd, which drew a lot of cheers and back-slapping on Jack, of course, after that. He even got the Lone Sums to play Waylon Jennings' "Good Hearted Woman," the first song we ever danced to at the Rooster.

He's still dwelling over Fred's unintentional interference in our plans. Just to ease things a little, I told Jack it will give me more time to figure things out about my house and everything that's in it. Lisa living next door to Jack is another thing altogether. I trust Jack. I don't trust her. Not one bit. I wouldn't even like the woman if she wasn't his ex-wife. What is Lisa capable of doing? I will refresh your memory about the time she moved in with Fred while her house was getting worked on and I caught her sunbathing in the front yard, naked from the waist up. That's what. But when Lisa arrives later today, she will be informed that my mother and I are moving in after she moves out.

Ma knows what's what since she was still up when I came home first last night. Her reaction? "I'd like to give that Fred a good talking to."

When my mother and I enter Baxter's, I tell the woman at the door Dave is expecting us, but it is unnecessary since he is already making his way across the room. He gives us a big welcome, which for me includes a hug and a peck on the cheek. I catch my mother laughing behind Dave's back. Thanks, Ma. When I called Dave yesterday to tell him we were coming and why, he asked, "Couldn't you leave your mother home this time?" But Dave, a man of good country manners, doesn't let on as he cordially leads the way to the deck, where it is still warm enough to have lunch. We get the corner table, where I let Ma have the best view of the lake.

While we check the menu, the three of us get the how-have-you-beens out of the way. We chat a little about my last case which, if you recall, concluded on the day of Dave's big birthday bash. He hasn't seen Shirley Dawes, the woman who hired me to look into her grandson's death, since, which reminds me I need to check in to see how she is doing. Neither has he seen another of his customers, who got arrested, but for robbing houses, not murder.

"Isabel, don't forget to tell Dave how you and I will be moving in with Jack," Ma says.

Dave blinks as if he's been startled, which is likely what just happened, but he recovers when she continues, "And how we can't do that until his ex-wife moves out." I detect a slight smile at that bit of info.

Oh, brother, that news about the move is definitely in the category of the need-to-know-basis, but then again, anyone who was at the Rooster last night and will be at Baxter's tonight will likely blab about what happened. Perhaps it is better Dave hears it from us. I give him a brief but entertaining description of last night.

"So, you and Jack are getting serious then?" Dave asks as the end.

"Yes, we are."

His smile fades.

"I hope it works out for you. I mean it."

"Thanks, Dave."

"But the ex-wife movin' in does complicate things."

I roll my eyes.

"You could say that."

"So, if it doesn't work out, let me know."

I manage to resist rolling my eyes again.

"I'm sure you'll hear about it."

We take a pause as we give our orders to the waitress. I stick with the trout. So does Dave, who recommended it to me the first time I ate here. Ma gets the steak because I told her in the car this meal is a business expense although there is a good chance Dave isn't going to let us pay. But I'm not here for a free lunch.

"How can I help you with your new case?" Dave asks after the waitress leaves. "You said over the phone Lin Pierce hired you for this one. That it's personal."

My mother's attention is fixed on a boat speeding across the lake as I tell Dave about Baby Elizabeth's kidnapping and the lack of success finding her. Actually, I am certain Ma is listening carefully to my conversation with Dave, but she doesn't want to interfere. Later, I will ask for her input.

"I was in the Army when that happened, Vietnam actually. But I heard about it from my folks. Sorry, I can't tell you much about it."

"That's okay. I wanted to ask you about something more recent."

"Go ahead."

"I'm searching for a man named Tim Todd. He was the student who was with Jessica Pierce when her baby was stolen. He was one of the adults she taught in her house. He was a serious student hoping to have a career in music." I decide to leave out any potentially trashy stuff since that hasn't been verified. "I want to ask him about that day. Maybe he can remember a useful detail. It was a long time ago, but an experience like that has to stick with a person."

"Sorry, I don't know anybody by that name."

"How about Robert Todd? It's my understanding that's the name he might go by now. Robert is his middle name. He started doing that maybe to distance himself from the case or for another reason. I am guessing he must be in his early seventies." Ah-ha, I see a glint of recognition in Dancin' Dave's eyes. "Annette Waters told me a man with that name

86

plays the piano here once in a while usually on Sundays. Hold on. I have a photo I downloaded on my computer. See if this is him."

Dave's head moves in a small bounce when he sees the photo I printed.

"That's him alright. He came in one Sunday. I believe he was here for lunch, yes, that's it, and he spotted that upright Steinway I have in the back of the main room. It's been here so long, it's just part of the furniture. I heard him run his fingers across the keys. I get annoyed when people start pounding on the damn thing, so I went over. This Robert told me the date the piano was built after he lifted the top, sometime in the late 1800s, that it had some value but was badly out of tune. But he said it still had a good sound. I told him there were times I wanted to take it outside and chop it up cause it's in the way. I couldn't give the damn thing away. He told me he was glad I didn't. I remember him saying, 'Do you mind if I play?' I told him to go ahead. The piano might've been out of tune that day, but he played beautiful music although not my kind of music, or for most of my customers."

"What happened after that?"

"Robert ate at a corner table away from everybody else. When I went over to chat with him, he told me he worked in the music business for many years in orchestras and doin' recordings, even playin' solo. He said he missed performing." Dave stops to give a wave to a customer across the deck. "He asked if I minded him comin' in to play once in a while for free although he would welcome a dry martini." That draws a chuckle from Dave. "Next thing I know this Robert has a tuner come in to take care of the piano. The man said the tune would hold as long as I don't let little kids or drunks bang on it. And get this. Robert pays for it."

"Do you have a name for the tuner?"

Dave squints as he mulls my question.

"I dunno. He told me when he first came he was the piano guy, so that's what I call him. He just shows up when we're open. Usually on a day and time we're not real busy, like in the middle of the afternoon. Doesn't bother anybody. Just gets to work."

Piano guy? I guess that's the best I will get from Dave, who calls the waitress to refill our water glasses and get my mother another decaf coffee. Then he's back to it.

"Robert came the next Sunday and played for over an hour. I made his martini myself, and except for a few words, I left the man alone. It was late winter. We got a lot of snow that year, so there was a bunch of guys on snowmobiles here that day. I heard a few complaints from them about his style of music. My wife went over to unplug the jukebox, so they wouldn't get any ideas." He grins. "I'll give it to Robert. He told the guys not to pay any attention to him and go about their business."

"How long ago was that?"

He thinks.

"Maybe five, six years. My wife was still with me that first time."

"And he kept coming after that?"

"Yeah, about once a month, sometimes longer. I'd say he was overdue. He doesn't do much talkin'. I bring over his martini, I know exactly how he likes it, and we make some small talk about the weather or about the town.

"And how do you know he's coming?"

"He sends the piano tuner, so I'm certain he'll be here playing the next Sunday. I make sure I'm here so I can make that martini and also to keep an eye on the customers. Once in a while there'll be people who appreciate his kind of playin'. Usually newcomers. Robert doesn't like to take requests although he did once for me. It was after my wife died. He played the song 'Without You'." He sighs. "You know it?"

"The one by Harry Nilsson? It's a beautiful song." I give Dave a little space before I proceed. "Would you happened to have a phone number for Robert?"

"Let me check." He pulls his phone from his back pocket and scrolls through the contacts. "No, I don't have one. Maybe he gave it to me a long time ago. Could be in my office."

"That's fine. Could you give me a call the next time the piano tuner comes? Then I'll know he'll be showing up soon."

"Sure will, Isabel." Dave looks up as the waitress arrives with our tray of food. "That's enough business for now, wouldn't you say? I want to hear more about you and your mother."

I raise a finger.

"One last question, please. Do you know where this Robert lives?"

"Sort of but you should ask your buddies Gary and Larry Beaumont about him. I hear Robert doesn't live that far from them. They've mentioned him before when they've been here. I take it he likes his privacy. You can't see his house from the road, and there's a locked gate at the end of the driveway, so nobody bothers him."

"Does he live with anybody?"

Dave smiles as the waitress places his plate of trout in front of him.

"You said only one question, Isabel. It's time to eat. You'll have to come back." He mouths the word "alone." "Now, let's dig in."

And dig in we do. The fish is prepared well, as I tell Dave, but my mind is elsewhere. I will line up a visit to my buddies, as he called them, Gary and Larry. Let's just say I see another side of the two brothers than most people, especially after they helped me out of two sticky situations. They are definitely soon on my list. I'll see if my mother is up for that visit. She might be amused visiting their wreck of a house again. These guys are absolute slobs.

Right then, I realize Dave is trying to get my attention. He mentions the changing leaves across the lake. It's nowhere near peak yet, but it is an attractive view. Soon the city folks who don't have enough trees where they live and certainly not our views will drive out to the hilltowns to have a peep.

"Sorry, I was thinking ahead. But I will definitely be back after I do a bit more snooping."

Dave nods.

"You do that, Isabel."

Making a Pit Stop

Next we go to the Pit Stop, which isn't that far from Baxter's, not because I need gas although I will get some anyway but to quiz Marsha aka the Floozie. Marsha and her cousin Annette took over the place earlier this year, but being co-owner and the person most frequently behind the counter, she might know something about Robert Todd. It's likely he even gasses up there since the Pit Stop has the only pumps in this part of the hilltowns. Otherwise you have to pray you make it to a station near the closest city or plan way ahead before you go home.

Marsha is on the phone behind the counter, but she says, "I'll catch you later," to whoever is on the line and hangs up. She comes around to give my mother a hug, which surprises both of us since Marsha isn't the hugging kind and you know how my mother feels about it, and a slap to my arm, which is the Floozy's usual form of endearment to me.

"You two look like you're up to somethin'. Am I right?"

"Besides getting some gas, we could use a little info for my new case."

Now recovered from her hug, my mother says, "You were so helpful, Marsha, in the last one. Isabel is trying to track down a person of interest we believe lives around here."

Person of interest? Both Marsha and I smile at my mother using that phrase. I believe Marsha enjoys our visits although I make sure to spend some money. After all, she's manning or make that womanning a store in the middle of nowhere. I am very aware a customer could show up any time to buy gas, beer, or cigarettes, or all three, which will require her attention, so I plan to get right to it.

"Do you know a man named Tim Todd?" That draws a blank expression. "No? How about Robert Todd?"

I pull out that photo again. Marsha's lips scrunch up a smile as she nods.

"Yeah, I know the guy. Comes in for gas. Smokes, but only that American Spirit brand. The beer we carry ain't good enough. He laughed at that California wine we carry. I like to call him Bobby just to tick him off." She uses the tip of a finger to push up the end of her nose, a sign my own kids used to brand someone a snob. "And why in the hell are you interested in him?"

I have Marsha's full attention, but not my mother's as she walks around the store to check out what's on the shelves, when I tell her about the new case and how Robert Todd might be involved. Of course, she wasn't even born when the kidnapping happened. She says she had never heard about it before.

"Really? Something like that happened around here?"

"So, what else can you tell us about Robert Todd?"

"Doesn't say a whole lot. He'll ask how I am but that's about it. He's usually all business, gets what he wants and leaves. He pays for everything in cash, which is fine by me. Oh, and he has the longest damn fingers I've ever seen on a man."

"Did you mention that to him?" I joke.

"Sure did. I asked if he was a surgeon. He gave me a long look and said he was a musician." Marsha leans her backside against the counter's edge away from the display of magazines and newspapers. "I actually saw him play a couple of times at Baxter's. It was that high-brow shit. But he was really good. I'll give him that. The first time, I went over and asked if he knew any country tunes." She chuckles. "He said he didn't, but the next time I saw him, he played Patsy Cline's 'I Fall to Pieces.' When he was done, he looked toward me at the bar and said, 'There you go.' I thanked him the next time he came in here."

"That was nice. Dave Baxter told us Robert Todd lives near the Beaumont brothers. Do you know where that is?"

"It's on Laurel Road, I don't know the number, but you can't miss the big gate and the sign that says, "**NO**

TRESPASSING — BEWARE I OWN A GUN AND A BACKHOE.'"

My mother, who sets a box of cookies on the counter, and I glance at each other.

"I guess we won't show up uninvited," I say although I have decided for certain my mother won't be going even if I am.

Now, Marsha's attention is on the store window where a pickup has pulled up to the gas pumps.

"Hold on. I got a customer." She shakes her head. "Oh, shit, bad timing, Isabel. It's Buster Meacham. Heard he made bail, so there he is. Uh, Isabel, you might not wanna be here when he comes into pay. Buster always does cash."

"Too late I would say. He's gonna wonder why there's a car beside the pumps and nobody is in the store. He might even recognize my car."

Marsha makes a nervous chuckle.

"This could get interesting."

Buster's arrest was a bonus from my last case. It turned out I solved two: the death of young Lucas Page and a string of house break-ins. He was involved in the second although initially I had sound reason to think he was with the first. This would be our first meetup since Dancin' Dave's birthday party and that wasn't exactly a happy exchange. I glance at the large mirror installed above the counter so whoever is there can watch for thieving customers. My mother is checking out the pet food section.

We can't exactly march out there and hope Buster doesn't notice us. I have another idea.

"Hey, Marsha, do you mind if my mother hides out in your backroom? I don't mind facing him, but it might be too much for her."

"Go right ahead."

I move quickly, telling Ma my plan, and then ushering her behind the counter to the store's backroom as Marsha guards the door. I get no complaints from my mother. Besides, I tell her as I find her a chair in the back room she'll be able to hear everything. And after she's settled, I wait and watch Buster

92

drop down from his pickup. The rule here at the Pit Stop is if you're paying by cash, you have to do that before you pump gas.

As Buster ambles toward the door, he gives my Subaru a long glance. Marsha goes to her spot behind the counter and I position myself on the other side like we're having a friendly conversation.

"Sorry, I missed the action at the Rooster last night. I had to go to a stupid birthday party, but a couple of the customers were talkin' about it this mornin'," Marsha says, and then the door swings open with a ring of the bell above it. "Hey, Buster, how've you been?"

Under other circumstances that might have been an appropriate greeting for Buster Meacham but not today. His displeasure in seeing me is written all over his fat face. His mouth makes clicking noises as he drops and lifts his big bottom lip. I'm not afraid he's gonna slug me. He is on bail, and I am aware Marsha keeps a baseball bat behind the counter.

"You, bitch," he snarls.

I could be a wise ass and say, "Nice to see you, too, Buster," but my mother raised me smarter than that. So I step to the side to give him room at the counter and keep it to, "Hello, Buster."

The man pulls out his wallet, which is chained to his jeans, an interesting accessory considering this man is a thief, make that an alleged thief, since he may have been arrested and charged but he hasn't been convicted. Anyway, using alleged is a holdover habit from my journalism days.

"I'm getting twenty-five bucks worth."

"Sure, Buster," Marsha says.

Buster slaps bills onto the counter, grunts that it's all there, and whips around to face me.

"You got me into a whole heap of trouble," he growls.

But foolish or not, I ain't backing down.

"Buster, I believe you didn't need my help for that."

He glares. I stare. This is as much of a standoff that will happen between the both of us inside the Pit Stop because

Buster may be a crook, but he's no dummy. He's outnumbered and besides it wouldn't look good in court that he harassed the private investigator who helped the cops on his case in front of a witness, no less.

Marsha acts like she's not paying any attention as she scoops the bills into the appropriate sections of the cash register and then works the controls behind the counter.

"Okay, Buster, you're all set." She grabs a stack of paper towels from beneath the counter. "Let me walk you out to your pickup. I gotta make sure there's enough of these out there. Annette's kid, Abe, might've forgotten to do it. You know, kids."

Ma comes from the backroom after they leave. She's never met Buster in person but was with me when I first tracked him down at that trailer park in Rossville.

"That was one nasty man," Ma says. "I hope this Robert is nothing like that."

We watch as Marsha fusses with the paper towel dispenser while Buster pumps gas. They exchange some words, but I can't read their lips this far away. And then he guns the truck out of the Pit Stop's parking lot.

Marsha's back inside with the same stack of paper towels.

"Didn't need 'em. I just wanted to make sure he didn't do anythin' to your car."

"Like running a key along the side?" my mother asks.

"Yeah, somethin' like that."

"Thanks for looking out for us," I tell Marsha.

She gives my right arm a chop.

"Any time. Now, tell me all about what happened at the Rooster last night.

Don't leave anything out."

Snooping

I've paid Marsha, gassed up, and now I check the map app on my phone for Laurel Road where Robert Todd is supposed to be living. Marsha didn't have the street number, but that sign she described should be a dead giveaway, a fitting term for my line of work. We are already in Caulfield, a town I am not that familiar with as it is north of the coverage area for the Daily Star, the paper I used to run, and the only time I ventured into this county when I was a reporter was for a really big story. My phone has enough of a signal so I hit start.

"There goes that woman again," my mother says when she hears the mechanical voice giving me directions. Ma is a bit mystified by technology.

The app takes us down Caulfield's main drag, and then a right onto Birch and another onto Elm, which is the road where the Beaumont brothers live. We have lost a good part of the afternoon, so my mother and I have decided that we will forgo the Conwell Triangle today. We're okay for now on dog food and milk, so we can do it Wednesday. She might have one library book left she hasn't read. Like a lot of the towns, the library is open on the same days as the dump.

I slow then stop the car in front of Gary and Larry Beaumont's junk-filled front yard. The brothers appear to have a hard time parting with anything that's made of metal, even that car Gary drove in the demolition derby at the Titus Country Fair that is too damaged to ever be driven again.

"Maybe those boys should have Annette take some of that junk away for them," Ma says.

"I'll let you bring that subject up the next time we see them."

But there is no sign of life at Chez Beaumont. Gary's

pickup is gone, and if Gary is gone, so is his brother and sidekick, Larry. I have yet to see one without the other in public settings. Private? No thanks.

"In a quarter mile, take a right onto Laurel Road," the voice on the app announces.

"How does she know that?" Ma asks.

"Don't ask me."

Now, if I had the street number, the woman's voice would tell me how far to go, but my mother and I will have to count on finding that sign. We pass a few houses, a mobile home, and large stands of forest.

My mother points.

"That might be it, Isabel."

Just as Marsha described, a heavy-duty gate blocks the end of the driveway, and I have no doubt we are in the right place when I see the telltale sign about the gun and the backhoe. Its official number is 17, according to a small sign on a mailbox. The driveway cuts through a thick forest. I see no sign of life, so I pull ahead and to the side of the road. I let the car idle as I reach into the middle console for my binoculars.

"I'll be right back. Beep the horn if you see somebody coming."

Now, I'm on foot. Do I really believe the sign? I'm not about to find out although I seriously doubt Robert Todd the Music Man has a backhoe. Gun? Maybe. Yup, the Music Man is now his official nickname. As I walk along the road, I note wire fencing along the trees. It's not very high, I could easily climb it if I wanted to trespass, but the sign gives a clear message about this man's privacy. I stand a few feet away from the gate and use the binoculars to see where it leads. Unfortunately, a sharp curve in the driveway doesn't allow a view of the ultimate end, which naturally would be where his home is located. Did he build a home? Buy one? Inquiring minds, at least mine, want to know.

I stand and also wonder how much land the Music Man has and whether it abuts what the Beaumont brothers own. One question leads to another, but I am aware that standing here isn't going to yield any answers. I definitely will be giving the

Beaumonts a call. I head back to the car, give one last look toward the gate, and that's when I discover a camera high in one of the trees, then another. Does he really sit in his house watching a screen for potential invaders? Not on this road, which has not had a single vehicle pass by while we've been here.

"See anything?" my mother asks when I get inside the car.

"No, but I might have been seen. Looks like he has cameras at the end of his driveway. The guy sure likes his privacy." I reach in the backseat for my bag. "But he does have a mailbox. I'm going to leave him a note."

This is what I write on a page in a reporter's notebook I still use during interviews:

Mr. Todd,

I am a P.I. hired to look into the kidnapping of the baby Elizabeth Pierce 49 years ago. I was told you were at the home having a music lesson when it happened. I am hoping you might be able to share information or an observation that would help solve this case. My goal is to bring closure to the family.

Best,

Isabel Long

And after my mother gives it a read, I fold the note with one of my business cards inside. I slip them in between the envelopes already inside the mailbox. Then I give the camera a friendly wave as I make my way back to the car.

"We'll see if that gets me anywhere," I tell my mother.

I drive forward to find a convenient place to turn around but end up doing a three-point turn instead, carefully, to avoid the drainage ditches alongside the road. When we pass the Music Man's driveway, it is as empty as we first saw it.

So it's back home to Conwell, taking the most direct route since we need to let the dog outside. Luckily, that way passes Jack's house. When we get there, I slow the car to check his front yard, but I don't see Lisa's car. It's not at the Rooster when we pass the parking lot sparsely filled with the vehicles and Jack's pickup. I'll be coming later to meet with Bob Montgomery to talk about this case and to be there when Lisa will undoubtedly make her grand appearance.

"Looks like Lisa hasn't showed up yet," my mother says.

"I can hardly wait," I say with a great deal of sarcasm in my voice.

Saturday Night

I head to the Rooster after dinner. We used up the leftovers in the fridge since neither of us felt like cooking. Ma was glad to put up her feet and read afterwards. She is definitely not interested in participating in the nightlife at the Rooster although she wants a full report of my meeting with Bob and the pending arrival of Lisa Russell, the family name she took back after she got divorced from Jack. I have other names I could give her.

Bob is waiting at one of the side tables on the bar side of the Rooster's big room. No band is playing tonight, one never does on Saturday. If people want live music, they have to drive to Baxter's. But there is a decent crowd, largely because one of the True Blue Regulars is celebrating a milestone birthday, fortieth I believe, at the other end. The bar stools are only half-full, but the table Bob chose will give us more privacy.

Jack brings me a glass of beer from the tap.

"Here you go, honey," he says with a wink. "I can read your mind. Nah, she's not here yet."

"Who's he talking about?" Bob asks. "Oh, never mind. Lisa. I heard all about that."

"I'm sure you and half the town did." I roll my eyes. "So, how's Bob Montgomery P.I. doing?"

Bob nods.

"It's been a lot of work doing the required paperwork, but I have lots of time to do it. That's not a problem since I'm retired. I did bring your contract. Got it in my pickup." His fingers curl around his nearly empty bottle of Bud. "I've decided after all to rent that space where Lin had his old office. He agreed to give it a paint job and I have furniture lying around like a desk and other office stuff. Right now, I'm getting the word out, like with insurance companies. Lin's helping me with that, too. Maybe I'll reach out to that rag you used to run."

"The Star? Why not? They could interview you and Lin. Sorry, I don't know the editors there anymore."

Bob drains the rest of his beer, and then he has his hand up to signal Jack for another. I pull a folded sheet of paper from my bag and flatten it on the table in front of Bob, so he can read what I typed. While he professes he won't be a buttinsky when it comes to my cases, he does want to be kept informed. After all, he is the boss. I already told him about my meetings with Lin, his father and mother, and how those went.

"This the list Lin gave you?"

I nod and wait while he reads the names and their brief descriptions: Frieda Payne, Carter Road, Jefferson, who was a neighbor when Elizabeth was taken; Lawrence McGowan, a former neighbor who is now in a convalescent home in Hampton; Randy Walsh, who was a rookie town cop then.

"I will be in Jefferson tomorrow to take my mother to Mass at the Catholic church, so we're meeting with Frieda afterward at her home. Lin was supposed to line up our visit to Mr. McGowan afterward at the convalescent home, so we're all set there. I called the number Lin gave me for Randy, but he hasn't returned my message."

Bob nods.

"I know Randy. He was on the Jefferson Police Department for years. He's retired. Want me to give him a call?"

"It wouldn't hurt if you did. That way he knows I'm legit. The person that interests me the most right now is Robert Todd although at the time of the kidnapping, he went by Tim."

"Don't know the name."

I give Bob what I have on the Music Man and my efforts so far. I note an amused expression on his face as I give details about his playing at Baxter's and the surveillance done earlier this afternoon. No, I haven't gotten a response to the note I left in his mailbox.

"Of course, that'll mean a visit to Gary and Larry Beaumont," I say. "I am guessing their land might border his and I wouldn't be surprised if they've had not-so neighborly dealings."

"That's what I like about you, Isabel. You aren't afraid of talking with people like the Beaumonts. I see them in here and nobody says 'boo' to them."

I shrug.

"You gotta be friendly if you want people to talk with you. I learned that when I was a reporter."

"I just thought of somethin'. You should check in with Nancy Dutton, the Caulfield police chief, about this Robert Todd fellow. With a sign like that at the end of his driveway, I wonder if he's had some trouble there."

I met Chief Nancy Dutton on my second case, the one for Annette Waters' father, Chet. As I recall, Chief Dutton is pretty tough, but then she would have to be as the town's first woman cop.

"Great idea. I know how to find her."

"Oh, by the way, remember your old friend Jim Hawthorne?" He chuckles when he sees my sneer of recognition when he mentions the ex-police chief from Dillard aka Thorny. "He's now a part-time cop for Caulfield."

"Last I saw him, he was working as a rent-a-cop. I thought he and his wife were moving out of the area."

"I guess he changed his mind. Anyway, the town was having a hard time getting enough officers. You know the pay is crap. But he applied and they hired him."

I frown since Thorny got away with taking money on the side, but there wasn't any way to prove it. Plus, there was that business with Emerson Crane's aunt when they were kids. That guy sure knows how to abuse power. About all I could accomplish was for him to quit as police chief. Last I saw him was on the deck at Baxter's. Ugh, he managed to get himself a job on Caulfield's force.

"I take it they weren't going to ask me for references."

"Why? You got something on him?"

"Yes, I do, but now's not the time and place for that."

Jack walks over with Bob's next beer. I have barely touched mine as I've been too busy gabbing. He makes small talk with

Bob, but that stops abruptly when there is a commotion on the other side of the room. No, the birthday party for the True Blue Rooster Regular hasn't gotten out of hand. Lisa has arrived. She stands beside the pool table. Her arms are out. She's got a big smile.

"Hey, everybody, I'm back and glad about it," she shouts.

Speak for yourself, I say to myself, as Jack and I exchange glances.

"It'll be all right," he says. "Don't worry, Isabel. I'm gonna talk with her."

I watch as the locals greet Lisa.

"That who I think it is?" Bob asks.

"Yes, it is."

Mysterious Woman

Our meeting Sunday with Frieda Payne is a bust. I got a call early this morning as Ma and I were about to leave for Mass. Frieda said she didn't want to meet with us after all about the Pierce baby, as she put it. It's not like she claimed she wasn't home that day or didn't notice any strange cars on the street in the weeks leading up to the kidnapping. She said she had changed her mind and didn't want to be involved. She got off the phone as fast as she could. I didn't get a chance to ask about the Music Man.

I told my mother that Jessica Pierce must have had her hand in it. I don't believe Lin would have recommended talking with Frieda Payne unless he had a good reason. The same goes for Randy Walsh, the ex-town cop, who has not returned three phone calls. I am going to tell Lin my suspicions about his mother's interference, which makes me more wonder why. I have one more person to go on Lin's list, Lawrence McGowan. We will visit the convalescent home where he lives after Mass and maybe Jessica hasn't gotten to him, too.

As for what happened after my meeting with Bob was over, that was kind of a bust, too. No, I didn't go over to wish Lisa a happy homecoming with the others. I sat at the bar, nursing my second beer and keeping Jack company, when she made it to our side of the room. She and I went through the motions, but her purpose was to get a house key.

"We're gonna be housemates," she told Jack.

Jack's eyes shifted from her to me to her again.

"I need to talk with you about that."

She pockcted the key.

"How about later?"

Long after closing, when Jack finally showed up at my

house, he told me he found out when he stopped by his that Fred didn't tell Lisa she could stay for only a month. He had to break the news, which didn't make him or Lisa happy. Did she thank him for the month's stay, gratis, as pitched by Fred? Of course, not. And she had no clue that my mother and I will be moving in soon with Jack. El Creepo has been striking out a lot lately. I could chalk it up to being blinded by love or just being a jerk. Take your choice. I have mine.

But I put all of that behind me when I pull into the parking lot of the Hampton Heights Convalescent Home, only a few miles away from the church in Jefferson. It's a huge complex with a variety of options for old folks to live, from a small apartment to full-time care. Lawrence McGowan, Lin told me, is reasonably sharp, but he's had some serious mobility problems that make it too difficult for him to live on his own.

As my mother and I approach the front desk to ask for Lawrence, I notice her checking out the place. I bet she's thinking that if I wasn't able to have her live with me, she might stay in a place like this back home, as she still calls it. I've made it clear to my mother she is welcome in my home and soon Jack's after we get Lisa the heck out of there.

As he promised, Lin gave the staff at Hampshire Heights the heads-up we would be coming today. We are told to wait for Lawrence in a large reception area. We choose a couch across from a comfy upholstered chair. Actually, that would aptly describe all of the furniture here.

"Nice place," Ma says.

"But not as nice as mine. No cat. No dog. No cases to help me solve."

"You trying to make me feel better?"

"No, just that I want you to live with me."

"Yes, you do need my help."

Now, that makes me smile.

But this moment is disrupted when I see an aide escort an old man holding onto a walker come into the reception room and toward us. He's short and thin. His white hair is cut close to his head. His face has no distinguishing features. I swear I've seen a hundred old men like him.

"Lawrence, here are your guests," she says after she makes sure the man is seated.

"Who are you again?" he asks.

I introduce ourselves.

"Lin Pierce grew up near you. Do you remember him?"

"Oh, yes, Lin. I think we called him Little Lin when he was a boy."

I give my mother a questioning glance. How useful is this man going to be? Let's give him more time.

"When Little Lin was a boy his baby sister was taken from the family's front yard. He's hired me to find out what happened to her. My mother here is helping me on this case."

He's quiet for a moment.

"That was a long time ago. Yes, Jessica Pierce. She came here to see me. She wanted me to do something, but I can't remember right now what it was."

I bet I know.

"Lin says you were home. You had broken both your legs in a car accident so you couldn't work. You spent a lot of time sitting on your front porch because it was summer."

He smiles.

"Oh, yes, I enjoyed the piano music that came from the house. Jessica was a good teacher. I would sit there listening, especially when the older students came."

Ah, here's my lead.

"Do you remember a student named Tim Todd? One of her older students. He was a serious musician."

He nods.

"I met him once when Jessica brought him over to meet me. He wasn't a friendly fellow. He didn't say hi even when he parked in front of my house and I was sitting there. After a while, I stopped saying hi and just watched him get in and out of his car. But I did enjoy the music he played. There was one particular song I enjoyed."

"Mozart's Piano Concerto No. 21?"

He nods.

"Yes, that's the one."

Lawrence appears to be in a good place for more questions.

"You must have seen people coming and going, cars on your street."

"I did. I believe I spent a good deal of my summer on that porch. It was hard getting around with two broken legs. We even ate our meals on the porch. If it had been screened in, I might have slept there. My wife would get me a stack of books from the library. I was a big reader."

My mother nods in agreement.

"So am I. I am a big mystery fan," she says, as I note she leaves out the smutty romance novels she also reads. "What do you like to read?"

And for a few minutes, the talk veers into books, mystery writers they like and don't like. Food. Then it's music. My mother is not a classical music fan, but she fakes it nicely. I don't really mind if it helps Lawrence remember. Good job, Ma. But it's time to steer the conversation back into interview mode.

"So, Lawrence, while you were reading, did you ever notice any people you didn't know walking on your street."

"I used to see the little boy pushing his baby sister's carriage. Oh, that was Lin. I knew him." He pauses. "People I didn't know? A few times this woman came with that musician you mentioned. She waited in the car, but she also walked up and down the street while he was inside. I saw her in the yard across the street. She looked like she was checking out the gardens on the side of the house."

"You're talking about the Pierce home?"

"Yes, that's right."

I have the same feeling I see written all over my mother's face. Here is something useful.

"Do you remember what she looked like?"

Lawrence thinks for a bit.

"She was good looking. Tall. Dark hair. Nice figure."

"That's helpful," I say although he could be describing most anybody. "What can you remember about that day the baby went missing."

"As I was listening to the music, I saw the boy push the carriage up and down the street. Then he was reading in his front yard. Then I saw him run off and leave her. I remember a woman near the carriage. I don't know where she came from. I thought it was Jessica coming to check on her baby."

"This woman. Could she have been the one you saw before?"

"Maybe. I don't know. I wasn't wearing my glasses. It could have been that teenage girl who lived next door. No, she was older than that."

"Did you tell the police about it?"

"I must have," Lawrence says. "They never found her, did they?"

"No, that's why Lin hired me."

The attendant returns to the reception room to tell Lawrence it's time for lunch.

"Thanks for the visit," he tells us as the woman helps him with his walker.

"Lawrence, you had a phone call in your room, but I told the woman you had visitors and to call back later," she tells him.

My mother and I talk about the mysterious woman Lawrence saw on our way back to the car. This is a bit of information I don't recall reading in any of the papers Lin gave me. I will have to check them again.

We are in the row where I parked when I notice a woman charging on foot as if she's on a chase from the other side of the lot.

"Ma, get inside quick before she sees us."

"That who I think it is?" my mother asks.

"Yes, that's Jessica Pierce."

Inside the safety of my car, we watch the woman go through the front door, presumably to see Lawrence McGowan.

"You would think she would want to know what happened to her child. I certainly would."

"Yes, the whole thing is strange. Oops. Here she comes again."

Jessica is on the sidewalk as she scans the full parking lot. I slide down in the driver's seat. My mother can't, so she unbuckles her seatbelt and bends forward. But after a while, Jessica gives up and returns to her car, fortunately on the other side of the lot, then drives away.

"I believe we need to have a serious talk with Lin about his mother."

"If you don't mind, I'd like to be there for that one."

"Then let's go. I bet he's home."

Stopping at Lin's

Lin's wife tells us we can find him in the barn and that's where he is, mucking the stalls for his horses that are out in their corral. He wears overalls, rubber boots, and a black Stetson, looking more like the cowboy he wishes he could be than a guy who once did investigations for insurance companies. He stops what he's doing when I call out to him and drops the pitchfork against the stall's wall. Lin appears to have recovered nicely from his broken hip.

"My favorite detectives," he says as he removes his work gloves. "Hope you don't mind if we don't shake hands."

"Not at all. We came to talk about your mother running interference in this case."

Lin drops his smile.

"Oh, that. Yes, we need to talk."

We follow Lin to the house's side porch that has wicker furniture with cushions. My mother takes the chair with the sun shining on it.

"We just came from visiting your old neighbor, Lawrence McGowan, at that convalescent home. Spry old guy. Luckily, your mother hadn't gotten her hooks into him like she did Frieda Payne and it looks like that town cop. I guess she called while we were there. And then she showed up just as we were leaving."

My mother laughs.

"We had to hide inside the car, so she wouldn't catch us," she says. "She looked madder than a wet hen. Wouldn't you say, Isabel?"

"That's a good description or maybe even a raging bull. I was surprised she didn't go searching for us in the parking lot. They must've told her inside she had just missed us."

"I'm sorry," Lin says.

"Your mother is making it very difficult to solve this case if she won't cooperate or she's asking other people not to. What's her problem?"

Lin sighs.

"I wish I knew."

"Tell him the good news, Isabel," my mother says.

"You have some good news?"

"It turns out Robert Todd plays once in a while when the mood suits him at Baxter's. Dave said the only way he knows he's coming is when he sends over a tuner for the piano. He's going to let me know the next time that happens. Anyway, we did find out where he lives. It's in Caulfield."

"Caulfield? Really? How did he end up around here?"

"I found information about him online. I can forward you the links. But nothing turned up on social media like Facebook or Twitter that matched the musician, Robert Todd."

"You should see the sign at the end of the driveway's gate. No Girl Scouts will be selling cookies there," my mother chimes in.

I show Lin the photo I took with my phone.

"My goodness. You're not planning to jump the gate?"

"And call his bluff? No, but I did leave a note and my card in his mailbox. He hasn't reached out yet. Maybe he won't." I shrug. "But the visit to Lawrence did yield one good clue. Since he was stuck on his front porch that summer with two broken legs, he saw the comings and goings on your street. He mentioned Robert Todd, he was called Tim then, bringing a woman who would sit in the car and walk around the neighborhood while he was getting his lesson, and then seeing a woman near your sister's carriage that day. He couldn't tell if they were the same woman. He didn't have his glasses on. She could've been just a friendly neighbor."

"That's something."

From inside the house, Lin's wife calls his name, and when he answers, "Out here," she appears on the other side of the screen door. She opens it wide enough to hold out a phone for him to take.

"It's your mother," she says.

I nod.

"Go ahead." I mouth the words. "We'll be quiet."

Lin reaches for the phone and greets his mother. He doesn't have to put the phone on speaker. I can hear her yelling from where I'm sitting. Jessica Pierce is definitely pissed as she talks about the case, me, and stirring up a painful history, as she puts it.

"But, Mother, don't you want to find out what happened to Elizabeth? You already agreed to be a part of this investigation. Why the change of heart?"

"Somebody took Elizabeth and made her their daughter. You don't need to hire that woman to find that out."

"Yes, I do. I want to know what happened to my sister, what kind of life she had, why nobody could find her. And I'm sorry you feel that way."

"I'm telling everyone to not talk with her."

"You were too late with Lawrence."

"I heard. Who else did you tell her to talk with?"

"Isabel is smart enough to find her own sources," he says. "Frankly, I'm shocked you feel this way. Is it because Isabel asked if you were having an affair with Tim Todd? Well, did you?"

The only answer Jessica gives is to hang up the phone. Lin appears a little shook. I am perplexed as well his mother doesn't want us to find out what happened to her daughter. My guess is that if it was something really bad, she doesn't know if she could face it. She certainly has considered all of the scenarios, including the absolute worst.

I check on my mother, who gives me that oh-so-slight nod of encouragement. I can read her mind.

"Lin, do you want me to keep going or drop the case?" I ask. "It's totally up to you."

Lin raises his chin.

"There's something really fishy here. And I'm going to have to deal with my mother. It's long overdue. Sorry about all of that," he says. "No, I don't want you to stop. What happened to my sister has never left me. When I saw that

111

woman at Luella's, I was convinced she is living somewhere, maybe even around here, and unaware of who she really is. It wasn't until I started working with you that I felt I found a P.I. who would have the guts and instincts to solve this mystery. I've seen firsthand what you do. It's too bad you couldn't have started earlier being a P.I."

"I don't think I could have done that raising three kids. Besides, the best training I got was being a journalist. You've heard all of my slogans."

He makes a low chuckle in acknowledgment.

"Yeah, yeah, checking the traps and working the beat. What's that new one you told me? Following the lead," he says. "And after my mother's call I really want to know what happened fifty years ago. So please keep going and keep me informed."

"Will do."

Two Ideas

I am quiet on the way back to Conwell, taking a long dirt road I could never attempt during spring's mud season, but driving it lets me enjoy one of the features of living in such a rural area, that is, a road with no asphalt and absolutely no traffic. I've got a lot to think about between Lin's case and Jack's ex-wife moving in, and the only thing I have to worry about at this moment are wild animals crossing the road. Actually, I hope they do and I'm ready to admire them as I let them pass. Ma has seen plenty of deer since she moved in with me, but only one bear so far, and she was beside herself when that happened. A moose? Not yet. They've moved down here from way up north but still aren't plentiful. I can count seeing a mountain lion once when it crossed a field blackened by fire.

"Isabel, I just thought of something," my mother interrupts me. "Don't you have connections with the newspaper in that city with that nice restaurant we went to?"

"You're talking about the Berkshire Bugle."

"Maybe you could call that helpful reporter and ask him to do a story about your case. Someone might come out of the woodwork with useful information."

I smile at Ma's choice in words, but she is right. Sean Mooney, a reporter with the Bugle, was very helpful with my second case, the one about Chet Waters. Of course, I've made myself available for comments when he called about my others. Good reporters like Sean are always on the hunt for stories. I met him when he was an intern at the Daily Star, the paper where I slaved away at until the ungrateful new owner wanted me to reapply for my editor-in-chief's job and I said I'll take a pass. Unfortunately, we didn't have a full-time opening for a reporter then, so Sean went to the Bugle which covers the western most part of the state. It was a loss for the Daily Star.

"That's a brilliant idea, Ma. I'll give him a call."

I slow the car when we reach a swampy section along one side of the road. The trees here are fully decked out in reds and yellows. The area's wet spots are typically the first to turn color. I point that out to my mother, who only gives the scene a passing glance. She has something else on her mind it appears.

"Isabel, I have another idea. This one's about Lisa."

"Like hire a hit on her?" I joke.

"No, Isabel," she says in that motherly tone I heard when I was a kid up to no good. "You told me Jack's place needed to be cleaned out and painted before you move in."

"It's long overdue. I bet nothing has been done since his parents died. Likely before."

"So why don't you start on Jack's side? That would send a clear message to Lisa you'll be moving in."

I laugh.

"Yes, it would although that means I would keep seeing her. Maybe that would annoy her enough to move out sooner. I'll make sure of it." We reach the end of the road. I take the left since it will pass by the Titus Country Store. "How about we get something to eat first. Then we can talk with Jack about your idea."

"And we can check up on Lisa."

"That, too."

Monday Night at Luella's

Jack surprises me with a dinner date at Luella's. I believe he feels a little guilty that he's got a soft-headed cousin who invited his ex-wife to share his house. Jack also ended up helping Lisa unload the stuff she packed in a U-Haul trailer she towed behind her car all the way from South Carolina. I will give Lisa kudos, although I hate to admit it, for her ability to manage that on a busy highway, certainly not part of my skill set.

Ma and I were even cordial when we stopped by Jack's house yesterday on the way back from Jefferson although I did have to remind Lisa to call me Isabel and not Izzie. I am a hundred percent certain she didn't forget, she was just being Lisa. And nicer person that I am, I even suggested if she's going to stay in the restaurant biz to contact Dave Baxter for a job. He's always looking for help. What's that saying about restaurants? As soon as you hire somebody, they're walking out the door. I am definitely not encouraging her to work at the Rooster. She did that when Carole, Jack's cook, had emergency surgery, and I am going to make sure that woman stays in tip-top health. Besides, Jack assured me that he would never hire her again. I told him I would cook for him if it came to it.

"Isabel, I might have to hold you to it although I don't know how the regulars would like the change in menu," Jack joked.

"It'd be good for them to eat more vegetables," I joked back.

"Course, you'd be too busy to be a private investigator if you did that."

"Don't count on it," I told him.

And now, as we walk inside Luella's, Jack is the attentive companion, holding the door. He's wearing a dress shirt and tie, only the third time I've seen him with one, and the others were for two funerals. I chose a short, black dress for the occasion. We make a good-looking couple out for fun on a Monday Night. Jack was all compliments and teasing on the ride here. He pulls out the chair and makes sure I'm comfortably seated after the maître d' leads us to our table. Jack, I found out, asked for this specific table, tucked in the corner and with a great view of the Berkshires at sunset out the window, when he called for a reservation. Hmm, my suspicious mind has moved into second gear. Jack must be up to something. Oh, stop it, Isabel, and just enjoy the evening.

The waitress lights the candles on the table and points out the day's specials on the printed menu before she takes our drink orders, a pinot noir for me and top-shelf scotch for Jack, which might mean I will be driving his pickup home if he keeps drinking it. The waitress gives me what my mother would call a funny look. No wonder since I recognize her as the woman who waited on us when Ma and I pretended we were restaurant reviewers. We even dressed like we were rich folks up for the weekend from New York City. It was all a ruse to talk with Luella's luncheon chef, a suspect in my last case who kept avoiding me. Sometimes I have to work harder to get people to talk and that was the case with him. The same goes for this one. I have yet to approach the Music Man, but considering the fortress he has in Caulfield, I will need what I used to call a reporter's good luck to have our one-on-one, especially since he hasn't responded to the note I left in his mailbox. One of the worst things that happened for me as a journalist was when people got cell phones although in the hilltowns that came much later because internet service was so poor. People didn't want ugly cell towers popping up in their town and spoiling the view. Even now, when I drive through a few towns, I get the "no service" message on my phone. But when people only had landlines, we got a new phone book listing their numbers every year, except for those who paid extra for an unlisted one. Anyway, Dave didn't have the Music

Man's number and never thought to ask him for one.

The waitress makes a smirky smile.

"Are you here for another restaurant review?"

"No business. Just pleasure tonight," I smile back but keep the smirk in check since I am technically off the clock, especially with Jack present.

"Fine. I'll be back with your drinks."

Oh, screw being off the clock, especially since I just spotted a grand piano on the other side of the dining room. In my uneducated opinion, it appears to be a lot more elegant than the piano at Baxter's where Robert plays although that upright is a Steinway. It's a longshot but sometimes those pan out. I wait until the waitress brings our drinks.

"I have a question. Do you ever have music here, say on a Sunday afternoon?"

"We do but not very often. A man comes in to play the piano from time to time."

"Is the pianist's name Robert Todd by any chance?"

"I don't usually work Sundays so let me ask. Is he a friend of yours?"

"No, he's just somebody I would like to meet." And then I slip into my slightly deceptive mode. "I hear from his fans that he's very good." Oh, I find myself slipping further into an outright lie. "I'd like to hire him for a party I'm planning, so if you have his phone number that would be great."

"I'll see what I can do," the waitress says, and then she's really gone.

Across the table, Jack catches on fast since by now he's familiar with my tricks. He waits until the waitress is out of earshot.

"That the same guy you say plays at Baxter's?" he asks.

"I guess we'll find out."

"And what kind of a party were you planning?"

I raise a fingertip to my lips.

"None really. She'd be suspicious if I outright asked it. Dave doesn't even have his number."

We raise our glasses and make a celebratory clink.

"To us," Jack says.

117

"Yes, to us."

Jack sets his glass on the table.

"Now about repainting my place," he says. "I have an idea about that."

"Go ahead," I say as I watch the waitress talk with the maître d' near his station.

"I like the colors you chose, but I think I'm gonna hire someone to do it. This guy's run up a sizable tab and he can work it off painting. When he's caught up, I'll pay him or he can start a fresh tab. What do you think about that idea?"

Jack mentions one of the Rooster True Blue Regulars who's been down on his luck lately. Leo Silver's wife dumped him. Then he lost his job at a local garage because his boss was the man his wife left him for and he's only been able to find odd jobs here and there. He's rooming with his married brother but doesn't know how long that will last. Then there are the two kids he never gets to see. Believe me, I've heard it all while tending bar, and the poor bastard's life had turned into a sad country song. I would say the nickname the Sad Sack would fit him, but I keep that to myself. Jack doesn't know the name game my mother and I have going, like the Old Farts and more.

"Will he do a good job?"

"I'll make sure," he says. "Besides, you and your mother can drop by to keep an eye on him."

"You can count on it."

Jack shakes his head, and when I look, I realize he's signaling the waitress, who stops her approach. He pulls out a small velvet box from his jacket pocket and places it on the table in front of me.

"This is for you," he says.

I smile. I can't help it as I open the box to find a cameo pendant attached by a simple arrangement to a gold chain, which definitely appears to be quite old. I glance up. For once, I can't think of anything to say but, "Oh, Jack, thank you."

"It was my mother's. I wanted you to have it. You know, to celebrate you movin' in with me."

I let Jack talk as I work the clasp and the chain so I can

118

wear it.

"How do I look?" I ask Jack when I'm done.

"Beautiful as always."

We can't kiss in a restaurant so I reach out to clasp his hand. He's smiling. I'm smiling. I know what we'll be doing when we get back to my house later.

The waitress is here to take our order. Jack's going for the steak, naturally, and I will order the salmon. He even wants to splurge on appetizers. I note she doesn't write down our order but commits what we say to memory. Yes, Luella's is that fancy a restaurant.

"I asked about that piano player," the waitress says. "You were right about the name. Robert Todd. Sorry but we don't have a phone number. He made an arrangement with the owner long ago that he will send someone over to have the piano tuned, and then he'll show up on the next Sunday afternoon. I've been here when the tuner shows up. We don't even pay him. But the maître d' says it's been a few months since this Robert has played."

If Dave and the owner of Luella's don't have his phone number, I'm hoping neither does Jessica Pierce. And then I find myself smiling because I just got a brilliant idea.

"Do you happen to remember the piano tuner's name?"

She thinks for a moment.

"I remember his first name is Martin. One time I called him Marty, and he corrected me. I bet there aren't too many piano tuners who have that first name."

I smile. I'll make sure we leave this waitress a good tip.

"I bet you're right."

Gary and Larry

A dog barks and paws at the front window of Gary and Larry Beaumont's house as Ma and I make our way through the junked vehicles and plain old junk to the front door. I swear there is more stuff here than the last time we came earlier this year. That's when Gary hired me for a case involving his late brother, Cary. On her previous visit here, my mother joked about finding the kitchen sink among this mess. No sinks but I do see an old kitchen stove and washer.

"Those boys really should take care of this mess," my mother says with a click of her tongue. "People driving by this place would think it's abandoned."

"Perhaps that's their motivation all along."

Larry, the beta brother, comes onto the front porch, carrying his little pooch Ricky that was yapping in the window. He walks down the steps to give my mother first dibs to pet the dog, which makes happy little yips. Ricky is one of those terriers whose role here is to make Larry happy and to bark like crazy when anybody shows up. Nobody will be sneaking up at Chez Beaumont.

"Ricky, did you say? He looks like a nice little lap dog," Ma tells a grinning Larry, who usually isn't the center of attention.

"He's mine. Gary got him for me."

Gary, definitely the alpha brother, comes through the open door. He wears a Jim Beam tee-shirt, which goes nicely with Larry's Budweiser shirt, and I have indeed filled that order many times on a Friday night at the Rooster. Both brothers have freshly groomed mullets. They even have shaved.

"Come on in, ladies," Gary says. "Would you like some coffee? I made a fresh pot."

Fresh pot? The last time Ma and I were here we were offered

instant coffee, which I can't tolerate even for a case. The boys are moving up, I'd say. And it appears, they did some cleaning in our honor or perhaps they've reformed. Dishes are piled in the sink, but the kitchen is nearly as clean as the one I have home. The rest of the house? I've never gone further than the kitchen. I didn't even want to attempt using the bathroom no matter how badly I needed to go, so I have no clue about the conditions in there. Am I brave enough to use the bathroom this time? We'll see.

"We'll take a cup. Right, Ma? Milk if you have it for me. Ma likes it regular, milk and a little sugar."

Larry chuckles.

"Course, I know what regular means. I'll let you fix it the way you like."

Ma nods as she sits. Our aim on these info gathering visits is to make people feel comfortable so they start blabbing without realizing it although by now, the brothers have become somewhat old chums and they know my methods. I smile as I watch Gary pour us coffee and boss his brother around to bring the milk and sugar to the table. Ricky sits in the corner away from their feet.

"You said over the phone you wanted to ask us about that guy Robert who lives near us. What's that all about?"

I take a sip of coffee, which isn't half bad, and compliment the boys before I clue them in about the Baby Elizabeth case and how his neighbor might have some involvement. The brothers sit forward as they pay close attention to what I say.

"Robert appears to be a rather secretive fellow," I say at the end. "Lucky for us, he turns out to live near you two."

"How'd you find that out?" Gary says.

"Marsha at the Pit Stop."

Gary's head bobs.

"Yup, she must know everybody's business that goes in there. I just hope she's not too much of a blabbermouth about us."

"She only told me because I asked," I say.

My mother sets down her cup.

"Tell him about the sign at the end of his driveway," she says.

I do one better. I pull out my phone and show the brothers the photo I took, which makes them chuckle.

"That's a new one, eh, Larry?"

"Better than the old one he had. That one just said '**KEEP OUT**." It was after the one that said "**NO TRESPASSING**." He keeps the chuckle going. "Maybe he got rid of 'em cause of all of those bullet holes."

"Hmm, no idea how they got there," Gary says with a chuckle. "Anyway, his land and ours bump into each other along the back."

"He's got a fence along the road. Is there one there, too?" I ask.

"Nah, he ain't rich enough for that," Gary says. "Just the front and a little ways on each side."

"Dogs?"

"Nah, he uses cameras instead." Another chuckle. "Course, they're not high enough to catch a drone."

"You have a drone?"

"Uh-huh, bought one last year. Nice way to keep tabs on our property and his. So we know for sure he ain't got a backhoe. A gun? Dunno about that." He snorts. "Plus, we get a kick outta flyin' it."

"I see. When did Robert move there?"

"Hmm, let me think. He bought the land some years back. It might've even been in his family." Gary shakes his head. "No, that's not it. To tell you the truth, I wasn't paying that much attention." He grins. "But it gets more interesting. Five, six years ago he had this house built underground with stones in front. Looks like some goddamned elf lives there. Right, Larry?"

That gets Larry laughing.

"I call it the hobbit house. You know after that movie."

"You wouldn't happen to have a photo of the house?" I ask without correcting Larry that it was first a book.

"Course we do," Gary says, signaling his brother. "You know where they are, right?"

"Think so."

And then, Larry is gone.

"Did you paint the kitchen recently? It looks brighter than the last time I was here," my mother asks. "That's a nice, light yellow."

Gary smiles.

"We did. Room hadn't been painted since we moved in here. I told Larry I was sick of livin' like a slob. No women are gonna spend any time here. Not the ones we want to keep around longer than one night."

Uh-oh, I believe I can predict what's coming next.

"Gary, I bet Annette Waters could haul away some of the metal you have in the front yard," Ma says. "She could have it crushed like she does to those cars that get too junky for her to use for parts. You could get a dumpster for the rest."

Ma goes on about how it would impress women if they had a nice clean yard. Meanwhile, Gary sits back in his chair, staring with what I will call a look of amusement at my mother, who I believe is the only person who could get away saying any of this to him.

"I'll keep it in mind, Maria," he says.

"Got it," Larry says from the other room.

Larry is back with a manila file folder, which makes me believe Gary is far more organized than he puts on. But then again, he does have a business although not a legal one, if you catch my drift. Larry hands the folder to his brother, who removes a short stack of 8-by-10-photos he places on the table in front of my mother. He and I stand on either side of her.

Gary points.

"That's the crazy house Robert had built." He points to the first photo, and then goes through the pile for another. "This one's a better shot. See how it's buried underground, except for the front."

Gary goes through the photos one by one so we get a good impression of the Music Man's homestead, which appears nicely landscaped. And, yes, the house could be a home for J. R. R. Tolkien's characters.

"Wow. He has an inground swimming pool," Ma says. "And look at that large garage."

Gary has that chuckle going again, and then Larry follows suit.

"I saved the best for last," he says.

In that photo, a white-haired man appears to be flinging his arms and screaming, presumably at the drone flying overhead. What's even better is that he's naked. A towel, presumably he had been wearing, is on the ground.

"That's him?" I ask.

"Yup, that's Robert Todd in the flesh," Gary jokes.

"Has he ever come over here?"

"Once after he first moved in." Gary snorts. "Let's say it didn't go too well for either of us. He didn't like us riding our ATVs in the woods or our snowmobiles. He claims we were on his property."

"Were you?"

"Nah. He just didn't like the noise." Gary looks at his brother. "What did he tell us?"

"He said it ruined his peace and quiet. That's why he moved to the country."

The brothers laugh.

"I told him I didn't like listening to piano music. That's why we live here in the country."

Ah, the Music Man is typical of a lot of newcomers who move to the country and expect it to be the paradise they imagined. No chainsaws early in the morning or any kind of engine sounds for that matter. Well, good luck with that. But I wonder how Sam and I would have felt if we had built our house next to slobs like Gary and Larry. Thank goodness, we didn't.

My mother goes through the photos again, one by one, but stops mid-way.

"Isabel, take a look at this one." She hands me a photo. "There's a woman in it."

Hot damn, it has a woman getting out of a car.

"Let me see the next one, please." Ah, in this one, she's looking up, probably because she hears the noise of the drone. It still is too far to get a good view of her face to tell how old she is. She has dark hair, but it could be dyed. "Would you mind if I borrowed these two photos? I want to show them to Lin, the man who hired me."

Gary lips pucker into an amused smile.

"Go right ahead, Isabel. If you think it will help."

"It just might."

The Interview

My mother and I get home in plenty of time before Sean
Mooney, the reporter from the Berkshire Bugle, shows up for
our interview. I offered to meet him at a coffee shop in
Mayfield, where the paper is located, or even the newsroom if
it would be more convenient, but he said over the phone he
wanted to see me in my work environment. I assume he means
my office, where I have a portion of one wall devoted to a new
map for each case, plus photos and any other relevant papers. I
recently expanded the cork bulletin board because I like
standing in front of the wall in hopes that what's pinned there
will inspire me. I will want to have a similar arrangement
when we move in with Jack. He did say I could use the extra
bedroom for my office after we clear out the junk he has
stashed there. I also requested putting a bed in there for when
Sophie sleeps over, an idea that made Jack smile since he
loves that "Li'l Sweetheart," as he calls her. The feeling is
mutual.

My bulletin board contains the two photos Gary Beaumont
took of the Music Man's backyard, the one with the woman,
not the one of him naked and screaming although I have it on
my phone. I detected Gary and Larry are amused to be part of
this investigation. They promised to call if they discover
anything more from their neighbor. My mother told them,
"Boys, please don't get yourself into trouble," which drew a
snicker from the brothers.

On second thought, it's probably a wise decision I remove
those photos since they were given to me as a favor and likely
in confidence. I stash them in my desk drawer until this
interview is over.

I leave my other recent addition, a printout of the homepage for Martin James's website for piano tuning services. Turns out his business's name is Piano Guy, which is what Dave Baxter called him. No wonder. At least I got the name Martin from the waitress at Luella's. I waited until Jack hit the road this morning to meet the beer truck to log onto my computer. Considering the places where the Music Man plays in Mayfield and Caulfield, yes, the founders like adding field onto their towns' names, I guessed the tuner might live in the area, and lucky for me, there are only three, which made it easy to narrow it down to Martin James. He didn't answer his phone, so I left a rather vague message requesting he call me back. Too bad Jack doesn't have a piano at the Rooster that needs tuning.

I give my desk a once-over and decide a little messy works as I head downstairs after my mother announces Sean's arrival. When Sean was an intern at the Daily Star, he was eager to write investigative pieces. Like a lot of young reporters he had the Pulitzer in his headlights although as I explained, that's something to shoot for, but first he needed to start out learning to write a lede, which is the opening sentence to a news story, spell people's names correctly, quote them word for word, and ask the right questions. As I've said, I wish the Daily Star could have held onto Sean because it was clear he was a rookie with skills. I even let him tag along with our top reporter when she was working on an investigative piece about a local nonprofit, so he could see firsthand how it was done, a much more meaningful experience than hearing about it in a college classroom. As I tell new hires fresh out of college, welcome to grad school.

Sean has done well at the Berkshire Bugle, even snaring a few awards, including an investigative piece about a corrupt city official. But like a lot of papers whose staffs continue to shrink as circulation and ad revenues drop, he has to do a variety of stories, from covering fires to town meetings, as he told me on the phone. I didn't have to work hard to convince him to do this story when I called although my case began in Jefferson. I pitched the angle that I was trying to solve a case nearly fifty years old and that my focus is on finding sources in the western-most part of the state, those Berkshire towns New Yorkers love to visit and claim as their second home. Anyway, the Berkshire Bugle and my old paper, the Daily Star have an agreement where they share stories gratis. Maybe the new editor-in-chief at the Star will be ticked off I went to the Bugle first, but my loyalty to that paper ended a while ago, like when I lost my job. Besides, I always take their calls for stories, so there shouldn't be any complaints.

I step outside to greet Sean, who's slim and of average height. His fair looks are a tribute to his Irish heritage. He's wearing what I would call a typical reporter's costume these days, a plaid, buttoned-down shirt and chinos. When I was the editor, I never expected my reporters to wear a tie or suit jacket if they were covering a local event. Dressing like that would scare off the country folk. But they couldn't be slobs. Sean passes that test.

After we get past the usual greetings and intro with my mother, who has decided to bow out of this interview and eavesdrop while she reads in the living room, we head to the kitchen table, where else. I tell him we will go up to my office later, but this table is where I've done a lot of my research and talk over my cases with my mother, plus a few people of interest if I feel they're safe enough to bring home. He's got a pad, pen, and phone out. Sound familiar? I smile when the only refreshment he will take is water from the tap.

"I've already spoken to Lin Pierce, his father Ben, and your boss Bob Montgomery over the phone for background," he starts. "Isabel, that's quite the case you've taken on although all of them said they were confident you would solve it."

"Yes, that's why I called you. I need to get the word out."

"Lin filled me in and I did a little research, but why don't you tell me about the challenges you are facing."

I smile.

"It's only a hunch, but I think it's a strong possibility that whoever took that baby could have raised her in the western part of the state. Probably a very rural area. It would be easy to get away with stuff back then. Communication was pretty primitive. People only had a landline, a couple of TV or radio stations if they lived up high enough and had an antenna on the roof of their house. Maybe they got the local newspaper delivered." I pause. "And there's a chance she could still be living there. Did Lin tell you about seeing a woman who he thought was his sister? Good. I'll show you the photo he took although it's not very good. But I believe Lin, or I wouldn't have taken his case." I pause again. "One thing I learned from being in the news business, people are nosy, damn nosy, especially in these little towns. The trick is getting them to talk about it. I'm hoping somebody saw something and is willing to meet with me about it. It's been fifty years. What do they have to lose?"

Sean lifts the pen from his pad.

"You brought up a good point, about using what you learned as a journalist to solve cold cases. Could you be more specific?"

I am more interested in talking about Baby Elizabeth, but I humor Sean with anecdotes about those useful transferable skills, such as conducting interviews and maintaining a network of sources. I also have what I call my bullshit barometer. I can tell when someone isn't being truthful with me. We touch on my previous cases, how those worked, and the risky situations I got myself into. I've even gotten hurt and had an attempt on my life. But, I tell him, the results have been worth it.

"I'm not in it for the money," I say.

Sean chuckles.

"I guess neither am I."

"And unlike my job at the paper, I have my mother to advise me. She's helped a great deal."

"You are being too modest," my sharp-eared mother says from the other room.

Sean laughs.

"Not too many P.I.s have a partner with, uh, so much life experience."

"Yes, that comes from being ninety-three," I say. "Anyway, it's great sharing my cases with my mother. She comes up with ideas to consider, plus having her along has helped open doors."

"What's her background?"

"She's read a lot of mystery novels."

"I see."

After that diversion, we return to the case. I refocus on the possibility that the woman Lin saw and spoke briefly with could have been his sister. There were so many similarities between the woman and his mother at that age, especially with their eyes.

"Their irises have different colors. One brown, one blue. It's a family trait."

"That's interesting."

"Why don't we go upstairs and I'll show you more."

Up in my office, Sean heads right to the bulletin board, gives me a quick grin, and then he's busy studying what I've pinned there, going left to right, which is how I post stuff.

"That the woman?" He moves closer to the wall. "Uh-huh, too bad it's such a lousy photo."

Sean studies the photos I have of Baby Elizabeth and her family.

"I'm trying to find a way to meet the man who was having a music lesson during the time the baby was taken," I say. "He was one of the mother's adult students. A pianist."

He flips back several pages on his reporter's pad.

"Wait a sec. Here it is. Is his name Tim Todd? From the news stories I read he was with the baby's mother when it happened. By the way, when I called Jessica Pierce, she declined to speak with me for this story. I'm being nice about it. She wasn't."

"Perhaps it brings back too many bad memories," I say, trying to be nice as well.

"His name was Tim Todd, but he goes by Robert. I prefer you don't mention his name in your story. He hasn't done anything wrong as far as I know. I don't want people to think he has, and you know what kind of trouble that would bring you and your paper." I point to a photo I took of the sign at the end of the Music Man's driveway. "As you can see, he appears to value his privacy. I'm working on a cordial way to meet him."

"Cordial? And you think Robert Todd is key to this investigation?"

I pause, thinking how much more I want to tell Sean since

there is no way I will read the story before it runs. I never allowed that when I was an editor or reporter, which used to tick some people off, but as I would tell them, it's a standard operating procedure for journalism.

"I have a couple of leads on how to reach him without getting shot and my body buried in the ground," I joke. "But I prefer you not include that in your story until after I solve it, if I do solve it. I promise to give you first shot at the story if that happens. I don't want to jeopardize this case."

"No worries."

My mother calls from downstairs. A woman is at the front door who says she's a photographer from the Berkshire Bugle. Sean had warned me. Minutes later, the photographer has me turned in my office chair with my back to the desk and the bulletin board. We try it a few ways. In a couple I smile, looking friendly but not too friendly. We go for something semi-serious.

I'm just hoping this story will lead me to the right person.

Paint Job

I knock on the front door of Jack's side of the house and shout, "Building inspector," before I enter. My mother is outside feeding treats to Jack's mutts. We're here to see how far Leo Silver aka the Sad Sack got today. My understanding is that he would be painting the living room first in this nice shade of gray I thought would complement the fir woodwork, which we will leave natural. Jack agreed.

As I make my way past the couch and other furniture moved into the kitchen, the only sound I hear is one of those new country stars singing on the radio about driving on the highway and looking for trouble. Jack is on a ladder with a roller in his hand.

"How's it look?"

"Great. But where's your helper?"

"Uh, next door, helpin' Lisa."

"I didn't think helping her was part of the deal."

Jack climbs down and drops the roller in the pan.

"She said she had some sort of problem with the kitchen sink, that it was clogged, so he went over to help. Better him than me. My damn cousin must've been a slob washing his dishes, letting food go down the drain." Jack waves around the room. "He got most of the painting done. I was just doin' a little touch up. What'd you think?"

"He did a nice job."

"Your furniture should look really good in here with mine."

"That's the idea, I believe."

"How did your interview go with that reporter? Was it weird to be on the other end?"

"A little. I know how people feel when they ask to see the story before it runs, you have doubts about what the reporter will use, especially when you get relaxed and start blabbing stuff, but I will have to trust the guy. Sean says the story should be in the paper later this week. I told him to print my landline number in case somebody wants to call me with a tip."

Out the window, I see my mother talking with Lisa. Ma has that what's-what look on her face I've seen before. Now, they are walking onto the other side of the house. I could ask Jack if Lisa has found a place to move into yet, but she's only been here a couple of days. I just don't want her getting too comfortable. The same goes for a job.

"Tough time of year to be looking for a place to live," Jack says as if he's reading my mind. "Winter will be here soon."

I turn toward Jack. He'd better not be getting soft. If so, Lisa might not be in any rush to move out, and then before I know it, he'll be hiring her part time. Stop it, Isabel. Don't be hard on the guy.

"Lisa's very resourceful. Plus, landlords wouldn't want an empty house through the winter, having to heat it so the pipes don't freeze and all that."

There's a knock on the door separating the two sides of the house. When Jack goes to unlock it, my mother's in the opening, smiling.

"I was just telling Lisa what I plan to do with the place when we move in, so she'd better hurry up and find someplace to live," she says.

"Oh, you were," Jack says with a chuckle, as he shuts and locks the door again.

Next the Old Farts

The Old Farts have a visitor today. It has happened twice when I've showed up at the Conwell General Store's backroom, which on both occasions earned mixed reviews on my part. In one case, the Visiting Old Fart, the official name I use, thought he was more of a know-it-all than those in the group, but he was dead wrong. Let's face it, he would have to be peeking into people's windows to know more about what's happening in town than the Old Farts, in particular their ringleader, the Fattest Old Fart. Another Visiting Old Fart, who I would nickname the Clueless Old Fart if he became part of the group, had a gazillion questions so the conversation that day, about somebody's bankrupt company, took so much time he sucked the life out of it.

I don't recall ever meeting today's Visiting Old Fart. Maybe he's a newcomer who just stumbled onto the backroom or a recent retiree who's kept a low profile in our town. But he does look awfully familiar. I study the faces of the Old Farts after they settle down about my arrival and I have a cup of crappy coffee in my hand. No, it's neither an espresso, which the Old Farts call expresso for laughs, or a cappuccino, the other joke. Okay, who is he related to in this group? Come on, guys, I'm waiting.

"Isabel, I don't believe you've met my brother, Alex," the Bald Old Fart, aka Ben Pierce, says. "He's visiting for a couple of days. He lives near the New York border."

"Nice to meet you, Isabel," Alex says. "My brother's told me a lot about you."

The Fattest Old Fart barks a laugh.

"And we can fill in what he left out. Isabel's visits are often

134

the highlight of our week."

Ben clears his throat.

"Uh, Isabel, I want to thank you so much for pissing off my ex-wife. She called me. I hadn't heard from her in years. I got an earful after you and your mother visited her. The words that woman used."

I raise my coffee cup.

"Any time," I say, which will be the end of levity here if we proceed with news about the case.

"So, how's the case going?" Ben asks.

The laughter stops. The faces on the Old Farts turn serious.

"Slow but sure. I did track down the man who was taking lessons from your ex-wife at the time, you knew him as Tim Todd, but getting to actually meet him will be tough. Robert, that's the name he goes by now, doesn't appear to be a very friendly guy. Here. I'll show you."

I work my phone to bring up that photo of the sign at the end of his driveway and pass it around the group. Each looks up at me after their turn.

"Uh, be careful," Ben says as the Fattest Old Fart hands me my phone.

"I believe his bark may be worse than his bite. I met a couple of his neighbors. Plus, I have some solid leads on how I can meet him." I say, keeping that photo of the Music Man naked and screaming to myself although I can imagine the uproar it would generate. Oh, yes, indeed I still have it on my phone. It's a keeper. "And I did an interview with one of the reporters from the Berkshire Bugle for a story about the case." I turn toward Ben Pierce. "You spoke with that reporter, Sean Mooney."

"I did. Thanks for letting me know ahead of time, so I was prepared. We talked for a while."

"Isabel, why did you go with that rag and not your old one?" the Old Fart with Glasses asks. "You still ticked off you got canned?"

"I didn't get canned, as you say. I just didn't reapply for my job," I correct him. "I chose the Bugle because I have a hunch there's a strong connection for this case in its coverage area.

I'm hoping somebody remembers something useful. So much time has passed, but people were just as nosy back then as they are now, maybe even more since they didn't have so many distractions."

"Did you mention us for the story?" the Fattest Old Fart asks.

"What? And divulge my most valuable sources?" I smile. "I wouldn't want to put any of you in danger."

"Danger? I could use a little danger in my life," the Serious Old Fart says. "My wife complains I've gotten too boring."

And that comment leads to a brief discussion about one of the Serious Old Fart's in-laws who got nabbed driving after drinking over the legal limit. No, he wasn't coming home from the Rooster. Jack's pretty watchful about who's drinking and how much. I've even seen him take the keys away from someone close to the limit and drive him or her home himself. "I ain't losin' my liquor license cause somebody was stupid enough to drink too much," he once said.

But Ben brings the conversation back to my case with a comment, "I was telling my brother about the case, and he had something interesting to share. It's the first time he's told me." He nods at his brother who sits beside him on the school bus seat. "Go ahead, Alex."

"My brother showed me a copy of that photo Lin took of that woman he saw at Luella's. It's kinda lousy but there's something really familiar about her. He told me about her eyes, how they are blue and brown. I swear I've seen her before."

After a little prodding, I find out Alex Pierce lives in one of the state's smallest towns, Booker, no field in this name, located in the state's upper left corner, and until he retired from his office job, he worked in downtown Mayfield. Is that where he saw this woman? Or was it in his town? How long ago? But luckily, his brother gets to it.

"Come on, Alex. Tell her what you told me."

The brothers have everybody's attention.

"I honestly didn't make any connection to my missing niece. I had seen her once before she was, uh, taken. Darling, little baby. And those eyes. Just like Ben's ex." He glances at his brother. "I can't be certain, but over the years I've seen a woman with features similar to her mother. That's when we lived in Mayfield. I was working at the electric plant there. I hadn't seen Jessica in years, only a few times since she and Ben got divorced, for family gatherings. Elizabeth was born the same year as my youngest son."

I read the expressions on the Old Farts' faces. They want him to get to the answer faster. Me, too.

"Anyway, I was in a hardware store in Mayfield when I saw that woman. She was maybe in her twenties. She was there with an older woman. Over the years, I saw her again a few more times, once in a coffeeshop, sometimes with that woman, sometimes a man. She changed over the years, got older, but you can't hide those eyes."

"When's the last time you saw her?"

"Maybe ten years ago. It was at an outdoor concert. An orchestra was backing up this singer my wife wanted to see. We had great seats up front." He mentions the name of a singer big in the fifties and sixties known for pop standards, music my mother would like, and then in his older years, getting renewed respect from audiences. "This woman was in the orchestra. She played the piano."

"Piano?"

"She was very good as I recall. Even had a solo part. But it wasn't until my brother told me that Lin hired you for this case that I remembered. I hope it helps."

I smile.

"Thanks for sharing."

I glance at the clock. I figure Jack must be up and having coffee with my mother. I stand, ready to give my good-byes, but the Fattest Old Fart tugs on my arm.

"Think you can get away from us so fast, Isabel?" he says with a snort.

"Why? What's up?"

"How about you and your mother moving in with Jack Smith? How come we didn't hear about it directly from you?"

I sit back down beside the Fattest Old Fart.

"If you had been at the Rooster on Friday night, you would have heard the official announcement. After that, I knew it would get back to you. I bet it's already been a topic of discussion here. Right?"

Their faces affirm my answer.

"So, what about Lisa?" the Fattest Old Fart says.

I don't plan to go into the kind of juicy details the Old Farts crave, like the stupid mistake Jack's cousin made or the fact it might not be easy for Lisa to find another place to rent around here.

"I'm sure you've heard what happened to her in South Carolina. Anyone here know of a place she can rent or a job opening? No? If you do, please let her know, so you can get her out of my hair." I get the response I expected with that last comment. I'm back standing. "Anyway, until next time, fellas."

"Hey, you can't leave us just yet," the Fattest Old Fart complains.

I smile.

"Oh, yes, I can."

The Piano Guy

Today, Jack and I are painting what will be our bedroom sometime in the near future. Leo the Sad Sack didn't show and Jack didn't hear from him why. The phone went to voice mail when he called. So Jack gave up and called me, begging me sort of, to help him paint, not long after he left my house. When I returned from visiting the Old Farts, I found he had fixed my mother and himself breakfast, eggs and toast, which made me smile that he feels so at home. I don't mind painting. That was the original plan after all. Plus, working on Jack's side of the house gives Lisa the clear message she had better get off her ass and find another place to live.

At least, the Sad Sack helped yesterday to move the bedroom furniture into the wide hallway, the bed pieces, a bureau, plus a ratty upholstered chair that will be getting the heave-ho if I have any say about it. I don't care if it came on a wagon when his parents' grandparents moved here, which I doubt. It's just another bachelor piece of funky furniture. The good stuff, which was in his sister's side of the house, got stashed away in the attic, Jack told me, after Fred moved in there. The only art on the walls was an oil painting an uncle did of an ocean scene long ago and a family portrait with his parents and sister. Jack must have been around ten when it was taken, an awfully cute little boy I told him.

When I arrive, Jack kneels on a drop cloth spread over the floor while he uses a screwdriver to open a can of white paint. The ceiling and walls are already washed, something he also had the Sad Sack do before he left yesterday. Any holes were filled with spackle. Jack must have had a premonition.

"That's what I get for being a nice guy," Jack tells me. "I guess I'll just have to ban Leo until he pays up. Too bad, he actually had worked off half of his tab and I was gonna start payin' him soon. But if he doesn't work off what he owes, he won't ever be comin' back and I'll have to chalk it up to a loss."

"That happen often?"

"Nah, but it will send a message to anyone who wants to try."

"How much did he owe you?"

"You don't wanna know, Isabel. Anyway, unless he has a damn good reason he didn't show up today, he can find another place to drink like at your buddy, Dave Baxter's place. He takes in all of my rejects."

Yes, Jack does have a list of banned customers, handwritten, which he keeps discreetly near the register, as if I would forget and serve any of them. Actually, Jack has two. One is the six-month list and the other is for the permanent outcasts. You can make the first list by being a real jerk, starting a fight, or showing up too drunk to be served or drive there, so Jack has to bring that person home. Having sex in the parking lot is another no-no although Jack doesn't patrol the cars. Usually, he gets a report from an observant customer about that.

At the end of the sixth month, the person is allowed back as long as he or she meets the Rooster's standards of decent behavior. But two strikes and you are out for good. "This ain't baseball, so you don't get three," Jack once told me. Besides not learning your lesson the first time, some folks have made the permanently banned list right away with a fight involving blood and damage to the place or selling drugs, which is how the Beaumont brothers got rejected until I begged mercy for them. After all, they did come to my rescue two cases back. Their names are the only ones crossed off the permanent list. By the way, it doesn't count if you show up with somebody else's wife or husband, as long as it doesn't lead to the above-mentioned fight or sex in the parking lot.

Jack is right about Dancin' Dave taking in the Rooster rejects. But maybe they behave themselves because after that there's no other place to drink and hang out except at home,

140

which is why they like going to bars. Of course, there's that dive bar, Red's in Dillard, which I visited during my second to last case.

Just like tending bar at the Rooster, Jack and I are a good team painting. We get the ceiling done in no time and then work on the walls. He's on one side of the room and I'm on the opposite. The radio in the kitchen is cranked to Jack's favorite country station and I made sure it is loud enough to bother Lisa, who I note doesn't appear to be in any rush to be looking for work or a place to live at least today. Her car is parked outside and I saw no sign of life earlier. It seems my mother's friendly warning didn't have an impact. Perhaps I need to have a woman-to-woman talk with Lisa.

My phone buzzes in the back pocket of my jeans. I always check when that happens in case my mother needs me, but this call is from Dave Baxter. Dave wouldn't call unless he had a good reason. I climb down the ladder.

"Hey, Dave, what's up?"

"Isabel, you might want to get here. The Piano Guy just showed up."

I look at how much Jack and I have left to do, which is one more wall. We also want to do a second coat this afternoon after lunch, which Ma is making for us.

"How long does he usually take to tune the piano?"

"Hour, maybe hour and a half. But he showed up when I wasn't here, so I don't know how long he will take. I'd ask, but the fussy bugger doesn't like to be disturbed when he's tuning." I imagine Dave shaking his head when he says that. "Look, Isabel, I can bribe him with somethin' to drink to keep him here a bit longer. Too early for beer. Maybe he'd like a cup of coffee on the house. But sometimes he flies out of here if he's got another client. Are you gonna make it?"

"I'll be right there," I say, and after I hang up, I tell Jack, "I hate to do this to you but that piano tuner I've been trying to get a hold of just …"

"Yeah, yeah, I heard. Go ahead."

"I promise I won't be long."

He raises the paint roller.

"Isabel, if we're gonna be livin' together, I gotta get used to this kind of thing. Just leave the roller and brush in the pan. I'll take care of it. We were gonna do the second coat later anyway."

I blow him a kiss and head out the door, grabbing a rag to wipe the paint from my hands before I toss it onto the floor of my car. I figure it will take me about thirty-five minutes to get to Baxter's if I don't get stuck behind a logging truck. But I can count on Dave to keep him there.

Jack would be proud of my driving skills, as I actually pass a dump truck and go a little over the speed limit, but then I am not expecting the local cops to have a speed trap on one of the back roads on a Tuesday morning. Who would they be trying to nab? A silver-haired P.I. on her way to interview a person of interest? Besides, I know enough of them that I would try to talk my way out of a ticket.

I arrive at Baxter's as the Piano Guy is packing up his tool kit. Except for the fuzzy white hair, he's a nondescript old guy, real old, like in his eighties, certainly not what I expected. I give him credit for sticking with something this long. I note a pronounced limp I suspect is permanent since a wooden cane with a curved handle leans against the piano bench. Dancin' Dave sits at a table near the piano, presumably to keep an eye on him so he doesn't get away. Thanks, Dave.

"Mr. James?" I say as I introduce myself. "I left you a phone message."

He looks up from his tool case.

"Sorry. I've been awfully busy. You have a piano you want tuned?"

"Uh, no, I wish I did." I pull a card from my bag. "I'm a private investigator. I'm trying to reach one of your clients."

The Piano Guy squints at the card, then me.

"Private investigator? I'm sorry. I don't understand."

At that moment, a waitress sets a cup of coffee on the table where Dave sits.

"Here you go, sir. Milk, one sugar like you want it," she says.

Dave gestures toward a seat at the table.

"Take a load off. I've asked Isabel to join us. She's a good friend of mine and she's helped a lot of people."

Martin James looks at Dave, me, and then Dave again. Perplexed might be an apt word to describe the expression on his face. He shuts the lid on the case and sits. He's clearly outnumbered. I take the seat beside his.

"My understanding is that you tune pianos for a musician named Robert Todd," I say.

"Yes, I do."

"Mr. Todd's not in any trouble. Let me be clear about that. He just might be able to help me with a missing person's case I have. It's a very old case. Almost fifty years." I continue as I have the man's full attention. "I know where Mr. Todd lives, but it appears he, uh, values his privacy, so I'm not about to knock on his door like I do with other people."

Martin James lips form an amused smile.

"I'd say that was a smart idea."

I am not going to divulge what I saw in the photos Gary Beaumont took with his drone, so I will pretend I don't know what's beyond the gate and that sign about the gun and backhoe.

"Dave says the only way he knows Mr. Todd is going to show up to play here is that he sends you over to tune the piano first. When I was in Luella's for dinner, I heard the same story from the waitress there."

Martin presses his lips together.

"I don't know if I should be talking about a client with you, especially one who values his privacy as you just said. Robert pays me very well to tune those pianos and the one at his home. Other than that, we don't have much contact. He calls to tell me when he wants me to tune. At his house, Robert knows when I'm arriving, so he leaves the gate open and lets me in the door. He goes into another part of the house, or if it's warm enough, somewhere outside. A few times, he actually watched me at work. He hands me a check when I'm done. Robert is not one for talking, but that's okay. He's a very serious musician. I remembered when he played with an orchestra at Greenwood in the Berkshires."

143

"Would you be willing to give me his phone number?"

"Oh, no, I couldn't do that." He frowns. "What's this case about anyway?"

I give him a brief version, and even though I detect he is interested, I'm not convinced I've won him over. I decide to change tactics. I'm not even going to ask Martin to give the Music Man my phone number. Robert Todd might not show up here on Sunday after all. Perhaps, it was a mistake to come here today. Think, Isabel, think fast. The Piano Guy hasn't touched his coffee.

"Mr. James, my reason for taking this case is to bring closure to the family after all these years. Do you have children? Yes? Me, too. Even so, I can't imagine how the family felt with that baby stolen, and despite so much time has passed, they still do." I pause to let that sink in, hopefully to the Piano Guy's heart. "I understand about protecting your client's privacy, especially with Mr. Todd. I respect that." I place my hand over the card. "I am sure I will find another way to speak with him. In fact, please forget we had this conversation."

"Forget? I can do that."

With a grunt of a bye, the Piano Guy grabs his tool kit and leaves. Dave and I don't speak as we watch him leave.

"Sorry, Isabel. That was a waste of time," Dave says.

Actually, I wonder if instead, I jeopardized my chance to meet Robert Todd. Maybe Martin will warn him so he doesn't show up Sunday. Crap. But I don't want to drag Dave into this. He was only trying to be helpful, and I did ask him to call me when the piano got tuned.

"Hold on, Dave. He's coming back."

Martin James's cane taps the floor as he limps toward our table. He stops and picks up the card.

"I thought about what you said. I bet Robert would want to help. He's a quiet guy, but a decent one. Let me see what I can do. He would want to be prepared."

"Thank you for doing that."

"No trouble. No trouble at all."

144

Chief Dutton

I turn down Dave's offer for lunch because I have one waiting at home. Besides, I promised to be back so I can help Jack paint. "You'd better hurry up before I eat your sandwich, too," he joked when I called to say I was on my way. Actually, he's already had lunch with my mother and plans to bring mine to his house since he's raring to go. I would love to have eavesdropped on that conversation between my mother and him. She loves hearing the local gossip even though she may not personally know the characters involved. Of course, I've filled her in on what I hear in the backroom of the store from the Old Farts. "People back home didn't do those kinds of things," she said after I told her about the latest breakup and hookup. Oh, yes, they did, Ma. It's just much harder to hide that stuff in a small town like Conwell.

I am nearly to the line dividing Caulfield and Titus when I see police lights strobing in my rearview mirror. I glance at the speedometer. No, I'm not driving over the limit. My inspection and registration stickers are up to date. But I pull over as soon as I find a wide enough shoulder to park. The cruiser does the same behind me, and I smile when I see Chief Nancy Dutton in uniform, strolling toward me. She's a big-boned gal with dark hair cut short, a style that makes her full face appear fuller. She has a strong stride that shows she means business to anyone she would stop, except for me because I know why she stopped me. She got the message I left on the office phone.

I roll down my window.

"Is there a problem, Chief Dutton?" I joke.

"Uh, you were driving a little too slow there, Isabel," she dishes it back. "Got your call. So, you want some info on Robert Todd."

At my invitation, she walks around my car and gets in the front seat.

"What can you tell me about him?"

"Funny guy. He's called me a few times about his neighbors. You know the ones, Gary and Larry Beaumont. He didn't like they were flying a drone over his property. I met with him in person at his house. Now that's a weird place. Have you seen it?"

I could tell her I've seen the photos that the drone took but decide to withhold that bit of info and come up with something neutral.

"Haven't been there yet. I'm trying to figure out a way."

"The place looks like somethin' out of that movie with the elves. You know the one. All stone and in the ground. Not my idea of home sweet home," she says. "Mr. Todd really didn't like it when I told him there was nothing illegal about it. He complained it was an invasion of his privacy."

"I've driven by there with my mother. We saw the locked gate and sign."

"Those are kind of recent. I heard he put up cameras, too. Years before that, he had an alarm system installed and that gate. That was after somebody broke into his house, so I understand why, although he seems to have gone overboard."

"What can you tell me about the break-in?"

"I can since it's public record. He was playing music somewhere when it happened. You know he's a musician? Thought so. Nothing of value like jewelry or art was taken. Someone did break the lock on the file cabinet in his office and went through his papers. They made a mess in there."

"They went through his papers? And nothing was taken? That's odd."

"I thought so, too. I advised him to get a safe or safe deposit box at a bank if he had any papers of value. Or get a dog like everybody else around here."

"So you went inside his house."

"I wasn't the chief then. Just an officer on the force. It was a Sunday. The guy who was chief sent me so he didn't ruin his weekend. His family was having a cookout. Robert had really

146

nice things. Guy definitely has some bucks. He wasn't alone when I met with him. A woman was there. Middle-aged, I guess, but in good shape."

"Let me guess. She had two different colored eyes."

Chief Dutton blinks fast as she makes a half-laugh.

"How did you know?"

"Just a lucky guess," I answer.

"What else can you tell me about her?"

"Why? Is she part of your case? Oh, I can tell she is. She was an attractive woman. Very quiet. Didn't say a word when I was there. Actually, she went into another room."

"Her name?"

"Now that you mention it, he didn't tell me. I wasn't there to interview her and I was still kinda new at being a cop, so I didn't pursue it. Too bad, eh?"

"Yes, too bad." But now I have something else to ask the chief. "Heard you have a new officer. Jim Hawthorne."

"Yes, I do." Chief Dutton's eyes shrink a bit like she's sizing me up. "Jim told me you and he have some history."

"You could say that. I met him in my fourth case when he was the chief in Dillard. Last I saw him, he was doing security at the Titus Country Fair on demolition derby night. I thought he and his wife were going to leave the area."

"I guess they changed their mind and are sticking around. Anyway he heard I had an opening. Actually two. One officer retired. The other got a full-time job in Mayfield. It's hard to find someone with the right training to work part-time for a small town like ours." She shakes her head as if she's agreeing with herself. "He said he missed being an officer."

"He does have the experience. I'll give him that."

"Doesn't sound like you're a fan."

"Yes, you could say that."

Making the Front Page

I run upstairs to my office after I get a text from Sean Mooney that my story, as he put it, would be on the front page of tomorrow's edition of the Berkshire Bugle, but it's already been posted online. His editor also reached out to my old paper, the Daily Star to see if it wants to run it, gratis. My mother was having a pre-dinner snooze in her chair, but my excitement wakes her. "The story's on the Bugle's website. I'll print you a copy," I tell her.

I don't have a subscription to the Bugle, but I haven't used up the four free stories the newspaper offers each month, so I'm good. The closest store where I could buy a print copy would be at the Pit Stop, which might make it worth the trip, that and to see if Marsha has heard any interesting tidbits or perhaps the Music Man has been in recently to gas up or buy smokes. I wonder if it would be helpful to find out what make of car he drives. The Floozy would know.

Sean Mooney's story is published in the top box of the homepage with this headline: **Sleuth's next case: Baby stolen 50 years ago.** I give the editor an A- for that headline because he used the word "sleuth," but I'll gladly take the publicity. And although the story, which has a photo of me at this desk, doesn't show it, the print edition might have a drop head that goes something like this: **P.I. seeks public's help.** Of course, if the editor wrote that, then the copy editor would have to make sure "public" was spelled correctly.

Here's how it starts: **CONWELL — Private investigator Isabel Long is onto her next case — discovering who stole a sleeping baby from her family's front yard 49 years ago.**

Elizabeth Pierce's kidnapping took place in Jefferson, but Long, who has had a successful string of solving cold

148

cases in the hilltowns since she started nearly a year ago, believes individuals in the state's far western county could help solve this mystery despite how much time has passed.

"I was hired to find out what happened to her and to bring closure to the family," Long said. "Law enforcement and even family members tried hard to find Elizabeth. But communication and access was different 49 years ago. I've made a good start but I am looking for people who may have information that might make the difference."

The story has a concise summary of the case, including comments from Lin and my new boss, Bob, plus a "declined to comment" from Jessica Pierce. Ben Pierce aka the Bald Old Fart offered this: "I would love to know what happened to my daughter. Maybe she doesn't even know who she really is. Please get in touch with Isabel if you have any helpful information." Besides my photo, the story has one of Lin and some vintage shots he supplied, including the one with him and his baby sister. I note the one with the empty carriage is not one of them.

Sean does give some color about me, including how my mother is my unpaid adviser, a term we agreed upon so I don't get in trouble with the law. He quickly mentions my cases. Of course, there are a couple of paragraphs or grafs, if you're a journalist, about my former career at the Daily Star although thankfully, he skips the circumstances of my leaving. He even mentions I tend bar Friday nights at the Rooster. Jack will like that.

As I requested, the story tells people how they can reach me, via my landline. I honestly believe anyone who has information will call the day the story appears in print and maybe a couple of days more, given the Star likely won't run the story on the same day. Ma and I have already discussed how we will handle this. She at first volunteered to answer the phone when I am not home, but we end up deciding to let them all go to voicemail so we can screen the calls. If the call sounds promising and the person doesn't sound like a total screwball, she or I will pick up or I will call them back. Plus, it would drive us both nuts sitting around the house waiting for phone calls. Anyway, here's my new message: **Hello. You've reached the number for private investigator Isabel Long. If you have information for my current missing person's case, please leave your name, number, and a brief message. I will call you back. Thanks.**

I print a copy of the story and bring it to my mother, who practically snatches it from my hand. I watch her read, her lips moving, and wait for her comment.

"Let's hope it works," she says afterward.

"Me, too."

First Calls

The first call is not from a wannabe source but Craig Nowak, the current editor-in-chief of the Daily Star, who sounds agitated when I answer or maybe he just has a naturally grumpy voice. I took the call because I recognized the number that popped up on my cell phone's screen. I was expecting somebody from the Star would call and decide to just get it over with. I've never met the new editor-in-chief since the publisher decided this time to hire from outside the company instead of within the ranks, which can bring new energy to a newspaper but sometimes the wrong kind if the new hire doesn't understand what its readers want. The verdict is still out, I hear.

"Isabel, I was rather disappointed you reached out to the Berkshire Bugle instead of your old paper for this story," Craig says. "After all, the kidnapping happened in one of our towns."

Hmm, I could say I was rather disappointed the paper's new owners expected me to reapply for the position of editor-in-chief I had for fifteen years, but I don't. What would be the point? He wasn't involved in that decision or even working for the Star at the time. So I decide on a more tactful approach.

"I wasn't disrespecting my old paper." I pause to make a point. "But while the crime took place, as you said, in the Star's coverage area, I wanted to broaden my reach to the Bugle's because as I pursue this case, I suspect I will find persons of interest there. And besides, I am aware the Bugle and Star share stories all the time, so I hope you are planning to run it. I could use all the help I can get for this case."

We end the conversation cordially. Craig says the Star will run the story soon. He talks about how tough the news

151

business is these days, the usual worries about the loss of advertising revenue and circulation. He's had to make a few cuts in the editorial department. I offer my sympathy. I listen to that "digital first" mantra I've been hearing for years about the future of newspapers.

The second call comes when I am already in bed. Jack, tuckered out from painting with the Sad Sack, yes, he showed up today saying he had car and phone trouble the day before, and tending bar, snores lightly beside me. The snoring isn't keeping me awake. My thoughts about the case are. Damn, it's after midnight. Even my mother is in bed. I hear my voice on the house phone's machine, and then I quickly slip out of the covers. I am halfway down the stairs when I hear a gruff voice say, "Keep your nose out of it if you know what's good for you."

I'm glad Jack's snoring away upstairs as I make my way to the phone. No number is on the screen. It simply says: **Private.** How clever.

Jack stirs when I get back in bed.

"Everything okay?" he asks.

"Uh-huh, go to sleep," I say, hoping I will be able to do the same.

Taking It Out

I take Lin's call when Jack and I are finishing our morning coffee. I'm dressed in my painting clothes because I plan to help today. Leo the Sad Sack promised Jack he would be there, but I'm not counting he will show up two days in a row. Yesterday, the two of them finished painting the bathroom and hallway. Today's project is the dining room Jack never uses because the furniture, including the large table and chairs built of white oak that has been in his family forever, is too formal for everyday use. But he likes the idea it would give my family enough room to get together for meals. Jack says one of the benefits, his word, of our relationship is that he inherits a ready-made family. The trim around the windows and door are still natural wood, fir, I believe, so all they need is a long overdue cleaning. After the dining room, there's the second bedroom filled with accumulated junk, the kitchen, and, of course, what will be Ma's side of the house, which we can't touch until Lisa gets the hell out of there. A little heart-to-heart with her is on my list.

"Glad you told me the story was online. We don't get the Bugle in the store down here," Lin says. "Maybe that'll stir things up."

That's the idea.

"Are you going to tell your mother about it? She wouldn't talk with the reporter when he called."

"I suppose I should," he says. "Didn't you say it's going to be in the Star? By the way, I got those photos of that woman you emailed me. It's too hard to tell if she's the one I saw at Luella's that time. Sorry."

Later, as we are washing the walls in the dining room, the Sad Sack finally shows up just when Jack and I had given up on him. His hang-dog face almost makes me feel sorry for the guy. He's from a reasonably old family here in Conwell, none of the money crowd though, but people who worked hard for it. He's just having a tough time although he tells Jack he has a tip about a garage that's looking for a full-time mechanic, but he'd like to finish the paint job for Jack now that's he's getting paid.

"Sure, buddy," Jack told him.

I am less interested in the Sad Sack's tale of woe and more on whether that story in the Bugle has generated any more phone calls. I am guessing not since Ma hasn't called me. She doesn't know about the late night call, and I wasn't about to play it with Jack around this morning, so he would get all worried about me. I may be used to people who are unhappy that I am pursuing a case, but not him. Besides, I had excellent training when I was a reporter, then an editor, dealing with people who wanted to keep their names and news out of the paper or felt we got the story wrong. Still, I wish I could have played the message again. Now, I am wondering if the caller was a man or a woman pretending to be one. I will definitely need my mother's opinion on that.

I step outside and sit on the porch's front steps to take a break in the sunshine since the guys inside don't need my help right now. Actually, at this stage, I am in their way. I admire the trees on Jack's property. The leaves of the ancient maples that line both sides of the driveway and the woods beyond are on fire with those fall colors of red and orange. The fields have long rows of cut stalks from the cow corn a True Blue Rooster Regular grew. Jack didn't charge him much to lease the land since he was more interested in keeping the fields open and useful. When his parents and sister Eleanor were alive, they grew enough food for themselves and to sell at the farmstand that was at the end of the driveway. I used to buy vegetables there when Sam and I first moved to Conwell.

But never mind about that. The door to the other side of the house opens and out comes Lisa. This will be our first one-on-one since she returned. Our brief encounter at the Rooster when she made her grand appearance doesn't count. Lisa looks a little dolled up, even wearing makeup and a modest dress, so I'm guessing she's on the job hunt today. She stops when she sees me. It would be particularly rude, even for Lisa, not to since she has to pass within yards of me to get to her car. I play friendly and ask how she's doing.

"Got a job interview today, actually two," she says. "You were right about Baxter's. Dave's got a couple of possibilities. Don't know if I wanna be stuck in the kitchen. But he did mention he needs a part-time bartender, too. I am definitely not interested in waitin' on tables."

"Don't blame you. What's the other job?"

"Just another restaurant. This one in Mayfield."

"Luella's?"

"How'd you guess?"

"Just lucky, I suppose. Nicest restaurant there." I glance behind me. "We're making progress with the paint in there. Only two rooms to go."

Lisa gives me a smirk.

"Don't worry. I'll be out of your hair as soon as I can manage it. If I had known how hard it would be to find a place to rent, I might've stayed in South Carolina."

I smile and nod, but inside I say, "Too bad you didn't."

"Good luck to you," I say instead.

Lisa continues walking but after several steps, she does a reverse so she's standing in front of me again.

"Isabel, you'd better face it. Jack will never love you as much as he did her."

"Her."

"You know who I'm talkin' about. Adela Collins."

I am well aware of Jack's relationship with Adela since her disappearance was the subject of my first case.

"Adela has been gone a long time, almost 29 years now. She was important to Jack, but he's moved on."

"Huh, that's what I thought when we got back together." She makes a snarky laugh. "Oh, Jack didn't tell you about that? I guess it was probably before you found Conwell and moved here. Or maybe after and you didn't hang out with the locals like you do now. Anyway, I found out Jack had only enough space in his heart for one woman." She takes a finger. "Do you really think he forgave you for what happened to his sister?"

"I don't believe you understand the relationship Jack and I have."

There goes that laugh again.

"I guess you're gonna have to find out the hard way like I did. Anyway, don't sell your house anytime soon. You might need to move back." She tips her head back. "Don't worry. I'll be out of your hair soon enough. You and your mother."

I don't say a word as Lisa walks to her car and backs it fast out of the driveway as if she's proclaiming herself the top female here. She just can't get over that Jack could be happy with me. She certainly tried to get him back, for the second time it seems, if she's not lying through her teeth. Still, I never heard that she and Jack tried to rekindle their relationship. I need to ask him about it at the right time.

I hear footsteps behind me.

"You and Lisa talk it out?" Jack asks.

"I guess we did."

Who Calls

I leave Jack and his helper to pick up the lunch my mother is making. I asked her to make a couple of extra sandwiches for the Sad Sack since it is unlikely he brought any food. Leo could go to the Conwell General Store to get a sandwich, but as my mother taught me, you don't eat in front of other people if you don't have enough food to share. Besides, I bet the guy doesn't have a whole lot of money although he does buy cigarettes. The plan this afternoon is while the Sad Sack paints, Jack and I will begin hauling junk, and I mean junk, out of the spare room outside to the yard and barn. There's not enough for a dumpster, so Jack plans to make a couple of trips in his pickup to places that take junk like furniture too ugly to repair, old car parts, and even snow tires for a vehicle he hasn't owned in years. Then there are piles of old clothes and boxes filled with other broken crap. Of course, I'm dying to find out what response, if any, that article has generated. It took a lot of effort not to call my mother, but then again if one had generated a huge revelation, she would have contacted me.

When I arrive home, my mother is bagging the sandwiches, turkey with mustard and mayo on wholewheat bread, plus the vegetable fixings, which will merit a comment from Jack who still isn't used to my choice in bread. Neither is my mother although I try to buy the softest store-bought version. The dog Maggie stays near my mother, hoping for meat scraps, which I am sure she's indulged.

"Has the phone been ringing off the hook?" I ask.

"I'd say we've gotten a few calls, but I don't know how much they will help," Ma says as she folds the top of the paper bag. "You can hear for yourself."

"Anything good?"

"I believe your best bet is somebody who says she used to be a teacher and another person who lives in this town I never heard of. One is from a TV station who wants to interview you. That would be good, don't you think? That man you call the Fattest Old Fart called. There were a few hang-ups like the person chickened out or maybe they were calling about something else. Oh, I heard that call from last night. I believe the person called again today."

"What do you think? A man or a woman pretending to be one?"

"Hmm, I'd have to listen again. By the way, one person says she's a psychic who could help, for money, of course."

"Of course."

"Nothing from Robert Todd?"

"No, nothing from him."

"Did you get any calls on your cell phone?" Ma asks.

"Uh-huh, Sean Mooney, that reporter, and Lin. I'll call them back."

It appears the Music Man was not moved by the note I left in his mailbox.

I glance at the clock. I believe I have enough time to listen and take notes. Jack and his helper may be hungry, but I can't let these opportunities pass. A pad and pen are ready on the counter.

The first is indeed from the Fattest Old Fart, who demands my appearance in the backroom after Ben Pierce aka the Bald Old Fart brought them a printout of the Bugle's online story. His son Lin emailed him the link because the Conwell General Store stopped carrying the newspaper a few years back, or maybe the Bugle dumped the store because it wasn't generating enough sales. Anyway, the Fattest Old Fart prefers print to online. Actually, hearsay is more to his liking.

"We will expect to see you bright and early tomorrow morning," the Fattest Old Fart says.

Next. The psychic makes her pitch, claiming she believes she can see where Elizabeth now lives, that she needs my help since she's been a prisoner all these years. It's an intriguing message, but I'm not desperate or naïve enough to go this route. I bet others have. I jot down her info anyway.

Next. "I saw your story in the Berkshire Bugle. My name is Mrs. Marian Brown. I was a teacher at an elementary school in the town of Davis. I am retired now. But I remember teaching a little girl who I wonder could be the one you are looking for. The story mentions her eyes had different colors. I taught a girl like that, oh, it had to be over forty years ago. I have a book with the group photos of all the classes I taught you might want to see. Funny, I always wondered about her parents since she didn't look like either of them. I thought she was probably adopted."

My mother and I lock eyes across the room.

"This one's a keeper."

"Try the next one," Ma says.

A man who identifies himself as Pete Baker says he lives in the town of Davis. His voice wobbles a bit, so maybe he's old.

"I saw the story in the paper. I knew a girl like the one you are looking for," he says before he gives his number and name again. "Her family used to live near me for a while. I think I know where they are now."

Okay, Pete you make the list.

The last message doesn't have a number and the voice is the same one I heard last night.

"You got my message, didn't you? You'll stop this case if you know what's good for you," the person says.

My mother asks me to play it again. This time she closes her eyes.

"I honestly can't tell if it's a man or a woman," she says. "I'll try to pick up the phone if I hear that voice again."

I smile. All right, Ma.

"Whoever it is obviously has access to a computer and knows how to use it. Or someone they know."

I check the clock. I need to get those lunches to Jack and the Sad Sack, but first things first. I need to call Marian Brown and Pete Baker to set up an interview. The Fattest Old Fart? I'll just keep him in suspense.

Clearing the Junk

Both Marian Brown and Pete Baker are on board for a meeting tomorrow. Since they sound like normal people over the phone, I warn them I might be bringing my mother, which doesn't bother them. "Isn't she your unpaid advisor?" Marian asked, which makes me believe she read that story in the Bugle very carefully. Pete sounds like he's also up there in years. He told me he used to be on the Davis Selectboard, which is typically three people who make executive decisions for the town. It appears he is also a nosy neighbor and has his suspicions about a family. I guess I will find out if it's a load of bull when I meet him. The psychic? If she's really one, she will know I won't be calling her back.

"Isabel, look at the time. Jack must be starving," my mother says.

"All right, all right, I'll get going."

Jack and Leo the Sad Sack are sitting on the front porch when I arrive with the basket of food. Each has a glass in his hand. No beers. Just water.

"I hope I didn't keep you guys waiting too long," I say.

Jack grins.

"My stomach wouldn't stop growling," he says although I can tell he's kidding me. "I was beginning to wonder if you forgot all about us."

"Fat chance that would happen," I kid back.

I set their sandwiches, bags of chips, and pieces of leftover apple pie, the first of the season, on the porch's table. Jack brought out the Adirondack chairs plus the table, all built of cedar by his father that was stashed years ago in the spare room and forgotten. He told me his parents used to sit with his sister on this porch, taking in the view of the farm. I told him

160

we can do that together.

Of course, there's the matter of the story Lisa told me about Jack and her, but with the Sad Sack munching on his sandwich, this is not the time. I've finished mine, so I go inside to assess their progress in the dining room, squeezing between the furniture now piled in the kitchen. The sage green paint I chose for the walls works nicely. Leo is actually a skilled painter, and I tell him that when I return.

"Your mother makes good sandwiches," he says with his mouth full.

"Yes, she does. Ask Jack."

Jack has finished his sandwiches and is onto the pie.

"I'm gonna get spoiled living with the two of you." He slaps his gut. "And fat."

"Gonna?" I joke.

And so it goes. Jack, of course, brings up the phone calls. Leo perks up a bit when I give a brief report, which also means I have to give him a version of my case. I don't mind. There's always the remote chance he's related to or knows somebody connected to the case. After all, his family has lived in Conwell almost forever and perhaps members migrated to the other hilltowns due to marriage, mischief, or just a change of scenery. His head gives a slight roll back and forth as I talk.

"Davis? I've got family there," Leo says. "Want me to ask if they've heard anythin'?"

"Please do. Here's how to reach me," I say, stretching for my bag that I had dropped on the porch. I find a card inside and hand it to the man, who will deserve a name change if he is indeed helpful to my case. And now that he's caught up with his tab and is actually getting paid by Jack, I can go one step more. "Or you can find me at the Rooster on Friday night."

Lunch is over, so the Sad Sack is back to painting, and Jack and I get to work in the spare room. I've never lived in a house that had a junk room like this, a junk drawer, yes, where I've thrown odd ends and parts of stuff I didn't know where else to put them. Jack's plan of action, as he described it to me earlier this morning, is to divide the stuff into three piles in the empty barn: large junk like broken furniture and pieces of metal that

161

will go into the open container at the town dump; true trash, again for the dump; and anything useful to donate, say to the Salvation Army. Make that four piles. If there is anything of value, we will set that aside. Someday we will tackle the attic, Jack warned.

"What about the tires?" I asked.

"The dump will take them, but I gotta pay for that. I should've gotten rid of them when I sold my mother's car."

His mother's car? His dear sweet mother has been dead over ten years.

I slip on my work gloves and pick up the tires. Jack is behind me with two more. They go into the junk pile. For the next hour, we lift, carry, and drop items into the appropriate pile in the barn. The smallest pile has anything of value, which so far includes a vase, a kerosene lantern with its glass chimney remarkably in perfect shape considering I found it in the corner of the floor, and clay flower pots. We also found boxes of clothing that had been his father's, the last of his parents to die, but none of it fits Jack who is a good foot taller and has more heft to him than his old man.

But we are making good progress. The room is half emptied. Jack goes into the kitchen to get us water and we rest our butts on a sawhorse he's planning to keep. Now's the time.

"I had an interesting conversation with Lisa earlier today," I say.

"What about?"

"You and her. I didn't know you both tried a second time to live together. She said it happened before I lived here or maybe just after."

Jack nods.

"Yeah, we did," he says in a tone like he just remembered. "I guess I should've mentioned it before."

"It's okay. I was just surprised I hadn't heard it from you. She probably decided to bring it up since I'm moving in with you." I wait for Jack's acknowledgement, a nod and a half-smile. "But what she said next kind of bothered me. She told me it didn't work out because you were still in love with Adela Collins."

The half-smile fades.

"No one knew what happened to her then. Not until you solved that one. I didn't know even if she was still alive and took off somewhere. Yes, I did love that woman very much."

"Lisa says you'll never love any other woman like you did her." I pause. "She says I'm fooling myself to believe you would. She told me not to be in any rush to sell my house."

Jack shakes his head.

"And you believe her?"

"I don't want to," I say.

"She's right I should have told you Lisa and I tried living together again. There just wasn't that spark between us to keep it going. I guess I put it out of my mind just like all the other women I've been with. I'm sorry about that." He makes a brief pause. "But she's wrong about Adela. I did love her. But what we have is different. Just like it was with you and Sam. He was your first love, a long one. You'd still be married to him if he hadn't died. I didn't father any of your children. But I sure love being with you at this time in my life." He slides his hand around my back. "What about you, Isabel?"

"I feel the same. I just wanted to hear it from you."

I suppose this is the time to seal this with a kiss, but that potentially sweet moment is disrupted when the Sad Sack walks into the room. He hooks a thumb behind him.

"All done in there," he says. "I'm gonna clean up. How's it goin' in here?"

"Just fine," Jack says. "Right, Isabel?"

"Yes, just fine."

Mrs. Brown and Peter Baker

Mrs. Marian Brown opens the front door to her unit in the town's senior housing, Maple Acres, to greet us. She's a rather large woman. Actually, everything about Mrs. Brown, which she doesn't correct when I call her that, is large: the frames for her eyeglasses, her facial features, and certainly her body. She wears a loose-fitting top and pants with an elastic waistband like my mother wears for the comfort and ease, as she puts it. Mrs. Brown is up there in years although not as old as my mother. By the way, Ma backed out last minute, saying she wasn't up to it. She complained she is starting to feel her age, which concerns me, but fortunately, she has a doctor's appointment tomorrow.

"Come in, come in," Mrs. Brown says before she leads me to a couch, something of heirloom quality, while she takes a nearby chair built also for comfort and ease. "Could I get you something to drink? Coffee? Tea? Water?"

I politely turn her down. I am more interested in hearing what she has to say about her former student than quenching my thirst, and it appears Mrs. Brown doesn't need encouragement. I go quickly through the interview routine before I set the phone on the coffee table, taking a moment to check out the environment. From my knowledge of construction, I would classify Maple Acres as a higher end development with well-built units reflecting the local architecture. Mrs. Brown's furnishings and art are tasteful, including a painting of an American Indian woman, Navaho, I believe, and when I remarked about it, she says, "Oh, yes, that's an original R.C. Gorman. I bought that one in New Mexico when nobody knew him."

Mrs. Brown rambles a bit about her travels with the late Mr.

Brown. I humor her a bit before I turn the conversation around to my case with an introductory summary I now have down pat.

"On the phone you mentioned you thought of one of your students after reading that story in the Bugle," I say.

"That was an interesting article about you and this case," she says. "I do remember a little girl who fit that description and from the article I would say the timing matches. Plus, she is the only student I ever had with those eyes. The condition is called heterochromia. I looked it up. It's supposed to be hereditary, but when I met her parents neither had it. Perhaps it was a recessive gene in the little girl. But highly unusual, wouldn't you say?"

Recessive gene? How about a stolen child? But I don't bring that up.

"Yes, I agree it is unusual. What grade did you teach?"

"Oh, fourth, the highest grade in our school, Davis Elementary, when it was still open. I loved teaching that age group. Anyway, that's when we had enough children to have our own school and it wasn't so expensive to educate them. Now, Davis sends their children to another school in our regional system. I'm not happy about it."

"That's true, a lot of towns have lost their schools. I'm glad mine still has one." I pause. We could be here a while and I am chomping at the bit to hear what she has to say. I have to keep this woman on track. Besides, I will be meeting Pete Baker next. "So, about the little girl you mentioned. What can you tell me about her? I don't believe you've said her name."

"Oh, sorry. I don't get many visitors," she says. "Her name was Anna, Anna Robbins. I recall she liked that her name spelled the same forward and backwards. Smart little girl. Pretty, too. And those eyes." She smiles. "But very shy. She was content to play by herself on the playground. That was a small class that year, and since the students had been together since Kindergarten, they were close, so she was a bit of an outsider although I tried to fix that."

Ah, finally a name. I try to contain my excitement.

"Was this Anna's first year at the school?"

"Yes, I believe so and her only. I'm not sure where she went to school before that. Forgive me. It was a long time ago and I've had so many students."

"You are doing just fine. Do you remember her parents?"

"Vaguely. They had the same last name as hers, but I don't remember their first names. They came once for a parent-teacher meeting and they showed up at school events we held in the cafeteria. The school didn't have an auditorium. So the tables folded up and the janitor would set out chairs. There was a portable stage."

"Did you see the family around town?"

"Not really."

"Do you remember where they lived?"

"I believe they moved to Davis that summer. I can't tell you from where. Sorry. They bought this old house on one of the back roads. Beautiful place. Really grand. The couple must have had money although I don't know from what to buy it. It used to be the home of a famous writer. He called it The Aerie."

She mentions the name of an author known as a recluse, M.T. Grant. He had a strong following after "Locked in Step," a coming-of-age book he wrote in the fifties, although he didn't care much for the adulation. He wrote others but they didn't have the pizzazz of that one. I remember reading a savage review of one that called the author Empty Grant. Ouch. But in the case of M.T. Grant, one book turned out to be enough to make him famous. Too famous perhaps. He's been dead a while now.

"Do the Robbinses still live there?"

Mrs. Brown ponders.

"Oh, no, it's a museum now as it should be. The Robbinses lived there for a while and sold the property to a historical group who turned it into a museum. The house comes with considerable acreage. It is nicely restored, including the grounds. The museum is open during the warm months. I can give you the exact address if you like." She nods. "As I said, they didn't get involved in our town. I lost track of Anna Robbins after fourth grade. I don't believe she went to the fifth grade at the region's middle school. Perhaps she went to a private school although she was too young to board. There were excellent opportunities around here. Or homeschooled although that wasn't popular then. You had to go through a lot of legal hoops to do that. It's much different now, I understand."

"What else can you tell me about Anna Robbins?"

"Let's see. Anna never took the bus. One of her parents always drove her to school and picked her up, or she had a driver. I brought it up with the woman one day in case they didn't know Anna could get a ride on the school bus. The woman told me a strange thing. She said she was worried her daughter could get kidnapped while waiting for the bus."

"That is strange."

"I apologize that I'm not being more helpful. But at least I can show you a photo of her." She pulls an album from the side table next to her chair onto her lap and flips slowly through pages containing group photos of students posing in rows with Mrs. Brown. "These are all the classes I taught. Oh, here it is. That's her in the front row in the blue dress. Why don't you take the book."

I hold the book on my lap. Anna Robbins has long blond hair with bangs across her forehead. She doesn't smile for the camera. Yes, she has those telltale eyes. Do I see a resemblance to the Pierce family? I'll have to show a copy to Lin. I snap a photo before I hand the album back.

"So, the Robbinses sold that home. Do you know where they moved?"

"Sorry, I don't."

"That's okay. I'm meeting Pete Baker next. He called me," I tell her. "Maybe he will know."

"Pete Baker. Here in Davis. Are you sure, dear?" she says when she sees me nod.

"He said he used to be on the Board of Selectmen when he called me. Like you, he read the article in the Bugle. He said he was a neighbor of the girl I am looking for. He had a voice that wobbled a bit."

Mrs. Brown gives me a look she must have done with her

students, as in wrong answer, try again.

"Isabel, Pete Baker has been dead at least five years. That awful cancer. And there are no other Pete Bakers in Davis. He did live on the road near The Aerie, but I'm unsure if it was when that family lived there." There goes that look again. "It appears somebody may be trying to trick you."

My mouth drops open. The woman is right, and somebody went through a lot of trouble to fool me. Or throw me off their trail. I recall the friendly conversation I had with the alleged Pete Baker. Shame on me for not checking online or I would have seen his obit.

"Then I wonder who he really is," I say.

"Where were you supposed to meet him?"

"He said he was a neighbor, and he gave me this address." I search through my reporter's notebook and read the address aloud. "It's 42 Old Post Road."

"That's the same road where the Robbinses lived. So did Pete Baker when he was alive. Are you sure you want to go all by yourself? I am getting an uncomfortable feeling about this. Somebody is obviously lying to get you there."

Me, too. Now I wonder if I should go anyway and check the place out. Or be really brave and meet whoever is pretending to be this Pete Baker.

"Don't worry, Mrs. Brown. I've been in tricky situations before," I say for her and my benefit.

"There will be signs for The Aerie. But let me at least draw you a map of how to get to Old Post Road."

I could respond there's already a map on my phone but don't. She's just trying to be helpful like she has been this afternoon. So I thank her as she gets up with considerable effort and goes to the high-top desk in the room. She is busy scribbling away on a pad as she once again warns me about the possible danger awaiting me. I take a peek when she hands me the paper.

"Thank you."

Mrs. Brown watches me from the front porch of her unit as I back my car out of the driveway. Then I am on a tour of Davis, following her map, until I reach Old Post Road. Long ago, this used to be the main route to deliver mail in the town's very early days. So, this maple tree-lined road connects two other towns on either side of it, definitely a stellar drive for the fall foliage, but that's not my interest today. I am checking the street numbers, another more recent addition to homes, for 42, which will be on the right side of the road. Conwell got street numbers finally in the eighties when it was no longer practical to say someone is one down the road from the Randolph place, especially since the last Randolph hadn't lived there in ten years and sold it to some newcomer. Besides, it wasn't helpful for the firefighters and EMTs to find a place fast. After Sam and I moved to Conwell, we eventually encountered other changes, like we could no longer just use the last four digits of a phone number to call somebody in town. We had to dial the entire number. Yes, we had those kinds of phones back then.

Enough of that history. I am concentrating on the numbers I see on mailboxes and front doors at Old Post Road in Davis. The houses are spread far apart so there are gaps: 2, 10, 16, 22, 26, 30, 36, 40, 48.

There is no 42 Old Post Road.

I get it. Between 40 and 48 is a cemetery. I back my car to the front of the entrance and take the short gravel drive that forms a loop inside. Nobody is here. Maybe somebody will come. If so, I'd rather be on the road than trapped in a cemetery. Or more likely this was a prank after all.

I wait along the side of the road for fifteen minutes. Nobody and nothing.

I continue on Old Post Road to the address Mrs. Brown gave me. It's not hard to find The Aerie. A sign at the end of the driveway says: **The Aerie Museum.** It lists the nonprofit that owns it and notes it was the former residence of author M.T. Grant. Another sign lists that it is open from May 1 to Nov. 1, plus the days and hours.

It is a grand house as Mrs. Brown said, colonial style and maintained well by the historic group. The front of the property has a high fence of brick and iron, plus a large gate to keep out adoring fans of M.T. Grant perhaps, and certainly anyone looking for a stolen child. I note several vehicles in the

169

visitors parking lot.

I sit thinking on the side of the road. This trip has been worthwhile. I have a name, a photo, and other information from Mrs. Brown. And that bit of trickery about Pete Baker tells me I may be on the right trail. I turn the car around and park on the side of the road across from the Davis Cemetery. There is still nobody here. I take my bag and lock the door before I follow the driveway until I am standing on its middle. I grab the eyepiece Sam and I used for birdwatching to scan the cemetery. I smile when I see a piece of paper attached to the top of a headstone and as I get closer, I see it is held there by a rock. I pluck the paper and read what somebody wrote with a black marker in a boxy print: **You will never find her. So stop.**

I glance around. Nobody is watching unless they are in the woods behind this cemetery and I don't believe I will check that out. I nod when I see the markings on the gravestone. It's the spot where Pete Baker is buried. Very clever. My mother will be amused when I tell her. I also know what else she will say, "Isabel, it looks like you are getting closer." Thanks, Ma.

An Apology of Sorts

My mother and I are in the waiting room at the doctor's office for her annual physical when I get a call I want to take. I see the name "Jessica Pierce" on the screen because I had entered her number into my contacts. I figure I should go outside the office to answer it in case she plans to ream me out again. After all, Sean Mooney's story appeared in the Daily Star today. The people sitting in the other chairs might find it amusing, but I don't plan to find out. I show my mother the screen.

"Go ahead," she says. "I'll be fine."

I answer before I reach the door so I don't lose her.

"What can I do for you, Jessica?" is the best I've got right now.

There's a slight pause on the other end. Maybe this was a misdial.

"Isabel, I saw that story in the paper this morning about your case. I was wondering if you had any time this afternoon to talk." Her voice is as cordial as it was at the beginning of our conversation when we met what seems to be a long time ago. "I would like to clear a few things up. I also want to apologize to you and your mother for my behavior. I believe I got a little carried away. You taking on this case has brought back painful memories for me."

"This is not the first time it's happened. I frequently encounter emotional situations when I investigate cases."

"That's what my son and, uh, ex, told me. Are you available, say two?"

"Yes, we are."

"I will see you then."

My mother talks with a nurse when I return.

"This is my daughter," she tells the nurse, and then she asks

171

me, "Everything okay?"

"We'll be meeting Jessica at two. She wants to go over a few things."

My mother smiles.

"I'm ready to see the doctor now," she tells the nurse.

I watch my mother leave. So, Sean Mooney's story got Jessica Pierce to rethink our stance about this case. Maybe we've gotten other calls on our landline. I did return Sean's. He wanted to know if his story yielded a response. The TV station wants to shoot a segment in front of Jessica Pierce's house. I said I would have to get back to them on that. I can't do it without Jessica being on board, which I thought would be impossible until I just got this call.

Our plan is for Ma to have her exam, and then I will join her and the doctor when he's finished. I'm no doctor, but I'd say my mother is doing fine considering her age. Her mind is sharp. Physically, she's not active, but she was never a go for a long walk kind of mother. She will stroll around the yard to supervise what I've done and to toss things for the dog Maggie to catch. But that's about it. She has said a number of times, she's looking forward to the move. It's probably the best situation to have her own space but be connected to Jack's and mine after we get that damn Lisa out of there. Tonight, Ma's coming to the Rooster. Jack had a last minute cancellation, a chainsaw accident by the drummer with the scheduled band, a new one called the Hilltown Haymakers. The band bills itself as "country music with a punch." Well, that punch will have to wait until the drummer's leg heals. And lucky for Jack, Annette Waters' Junkyard Dogs was available and willing to pinch hit. My mother is already their biggest fan and she hasn't even heard them play.

The reading material available in the office doesn't interest me, so I pass the time going online on my phone.

"Mrs. Long?"

I glance up when the nurse says that to me. I can't think of the last time somebody called me that.

"Yes?"

"The doctor's ready to see you."

172

Meeting Jessica Again

Multi-taskers that we are, my mother and I squeeze in a few errands before we venture to Jessica Pierce's house. By the way, the doctor says Ma's doing well for her age although he was glad she gave up driving. What did my mother reply? "I like being chauffeured around although my daughter could drive a little faster." Thanks, Ma, for keeping that joke going. Jack would be proud.

Jessica is waiting on the front porch when we arrive. As she leads us into her living room, she has a pleasant smile and uses much friendlier words than when she kicked us out.

"First, I want to apologize to both of you for my behavior during your recent visit," she starts the conversation. "As I told you, Isabel, your investigation has brought up a lot of painful memories and, uh, feelings. But it really bothered me that you would question my integrity. I would never sleep or have sex with a student. That my baby was stolen because of it horrified me. But my son and ex have helped me understand why you asked that, Isabel. Something about following a lead and asking tough questions nobody else would have the nerve to ask."

She raises a hand teacher-like as if she anticipates I will speak.

"Tim began studying with me when I left the school after I found out I was pregnant. I stuck it out until about six months. Working with students, a lot of the time on my feet, was wearing me out. So I started doing private lessons in my home right up until Elizabeth was born and then resumed a month after I had her. We needed the money since we lost one paycheck, plus I enjoyed teaching. Tim was such a special student. He was a young man who had ambition and dedication. I knew he would excel if he had the opportunity. I see that he did under a different first name."

Jessica sighs.

"Elizabeth was such a good baby. Never fussy. Not like her brother when he was that age. At first, she stayed in the music room when I was teaching a student. She would lie in a bassinette I kept there and often the music put her to sleep. Or she would just listen. The students, even Tim, got a kick out of her. It was so easy to get her to smile." She sighs. "By time school was out for the summer, Elizabeth was getting a little fussier. It wasn't an issue for my young students. I would just hold her in my lap or pace with her. But that didn't work with my serious students, so I tried to time their lessons when she was taking a nap. Sometimes Lin would watch her in his room if she woke up. But it was different for Tim, who paid more by the way. I started having Lin take care of her. He got paid an allowance, so there was an incentive."

She sighs again.

"Did Tim come and go at a set time each lesson?" I ask.

"Yes, he did. The lesson would start exactly at ten and he would leave at eleven. I could set my clock by him."

"And that day?"

"Yes, the same. Wednesday."

"Could he have had anything to do with your daughter's disappearance?"

She takes a pause.

"I don't believe he took her. But I wonder if he was used somehow to steal my daughter. Someone figured out when I would be inside the house with him and how they could distract my son."

"The police did question him."

"I wasn't there for that, of course, so I don't know what he told them. He wouldn't be lying if he said my baby was taken while he was inside my house having a lesson."

"I saw you wrote his name in the notes your son gave me."

"I wanted to talk with him to see if he might have seen a vehicle or a person that day. The police tried their best to find Elizabeth, but then they gave up when the case went cold." She shrugs. "I tried myself for a little while. I was heartbroken that I lost my baby daughter. But Tim wouldn't see me when I tried once. He was going by Robert Todd and making a name for himself in the classical music business. I was told he was too busy. I even wrote him once, but it came back in the mail."

"Your neighbor, Lawrence said a few times Tim came with a woman, who sat in the car and walked around the neighborhood while he was having his lesson. That was the summer he had two broken legs, so he spent a lot of time on his front porch. He remembered seeing your son pushing the carriage and then running off. He saw a woman near the carriage afterward. He couldn't tell who she was since he wasn't wearing his glasses. He thought maybe it was you or a girl in the neighborhood. The timing was a bit fuzzy."

Her mouth drops open.

"I hadn't heard of this before," she says. "Have you spoken with Tim yet?"

I glance toward my mother.

"I'm working on it. He's a rather reclusive person, but I believe I've found a way to reach him. What about your neighbor you told not to talk with me?"

"I'm sorry about that. I don't believe Frieda would be useful. She reminded me she was on vacation at the Cape all that summer. Her family has a place there. I don't know why Lin gave her as a contact. I read the story about your investigation in the Star. You said you wanted to find closure for our family."

"I hope to do better and actually find Elizabeth."

Junkyard Dogs Return

I am trying to be patient as the man in front of me, definitely not a local, ponders the Rooster's selection of beers bottled and on tap. As the man told me, he and the missus who are from Boston are staying at a bed-and-breakfast to enjoy our lovely fall weather, foliage, and the local color, as he put it. I take it he means mixing it up with the locals by that last part. Anyway, I wish he would choose a beer since the line is getting longer and I see a lot of hurry-the-hell-up expressions on some of the faces. Word got out fast that Annette Waters and the Junkyard Dogs are making a return appearance tonight, so the Rooster is at capacity although the weather is still decent enough for anyone to hang outside. With the windows and doors open, the music does carry.

The band is already set up and the Tough Cookie is working her crowd of admirers, all guys, of course, although I saw her chatting with my mother. My mother came specifically to see Annette's band, so I reserved the best table in the house for that. Ma doesn't drink beer or rarely anything else with alcohol, so she's on her second diet soda after she finished dinner, Jack's treat. She was glad to see ribs were on the menu, one of Carole's specialties. My mother smiled like she had won big at Bingo as she ate.

But I act my best country friendly to the out-of-towner.

"You said Budweiser is the house beer," he says.

"Not in so many words, but I would say it's our most popular brand. Right fellas?" I say, which draws several uh-huhs and, oh boy, a few choice words for the man to order. "But the beer on tap comes from a local brewery. If you are a fan of IPAs, I would go with that one."

Thankfully, that works and after the visitor carries his pint glasses to his wife who sits at the table beside my mother's, the line moves on. Eventually, Fred aka el Creepo and his Lady Love step up to the head of the line.

"Is that your mother sitting alone over there?" Fred asks as I fetch them Buds. "Do you think she'd mind if we sit with her?"

I could easily say something really snarky about his bonehead moves as of late, but I believe my mother would welcome the company. My sons, Matt and Alex, sat with her earlier, but now they are chumming it up with some high school friends on the other side of the bar. I imagine I will get a lot of questions and comments from her later about who is here. Jack and I don't expect she will last the entire night, so I will have to bring her home at some point, but then again my mother continues to surprise me.

"That's a good idea," I say as I hand him back his change and he slips a buck into the tip jar. "Why don't you go ask her."

Jack is back. He's pretty proud he's finished clearing all the junk out of that spare room and Leo got it prepped for painting. Ma and I checked out the progress on our way back from meeting with Jessica Pierce. Leo will finish the second bedroom, my office, tomorrow. We were informed that so far, Lisa, who I expect will be here tonight, has not found a place to live. Ma was the one who asked, not nosy me, and as I suspected she gave Fred and his girlfriend her blessing to sit at her table. Fred and my mother are talking.

"Maybe we should make the Junkyard Dogs the house band," Jack tells me. "I'd love it if we had a crowd like this every Friday night."

Just then, Abe Waters makes a loud roll of his drums to get the crowd's attention. Annette gives her son a nod as she clutches the microphone. The woman has dressed for the occasion with a Western-style shirt and jeans so tight I believe the only way she could get them on was by lying on a bed as she pulled them up. The black and turquoise cowgirl boots, Lucchese, she told me earlier, are a nice touch.

"Thank you all for comin' tonight. And thanks Jack for

havin' us. I'm gonna dedicate this first tune to a special woman here tonight. Maria Ferreira." She points toward my mother, who never gets this kind of attention. Ma may be smiling, but I can guarantee she's squirming inside. "Shania Twain sang it first, but here's how the Junkyard Dogs do it."

Then Annette and the Junkyard Dogs tear into "Man! I Feel Like A Woman," which draws hoots and hollers from the crowd. Oh, that Tough Cookie gives a great show.

But back to earlier in the day, or rather this case, which unfortunately for Jack is a bit of a distraction for me or perhaps a focus these days, I got another warning call from that pissed-off person. My mother and I still can't figure out the caller's gender. And, oh, the psychic called again. She claims she knows exactly where I can find "poor Elizabeth," her words, not mine. My mother joked maybe she was the one who took her. The Fattest Old Fart, of course, checked in with yet another reprimand for not visiting the group with an update. "We deserve to be the first ones to hear any news" is how he put it. I got a couple of calls from Daily Star readers wishing me luck. Oh, Randy Walsh, the retired Jefferson police officer who appeared to be ignoring my messages, did call to say he got the green light from Jessica Pierce to talk with me, but actually he didn't think he had much to offer since he was only directing traffic that day. My mother and I agreed that it wasn't a total loss since the story's appearance on the front page prompted Jessica to get in touch with us.

On the other side of the room, the Junkyard Dogs are onto their next song, "Jailhouse Rock" by the King himself. The Rooster dancers know what's up when they hear the guitarist play the song's opening chords. None of them here will be as classy as Elvis, but my side of the room has cleared somewhat for those who want to try, except for the guys who have claimed barstools and are not about to give them up even for a great number like this one.

I am behind the counter, filling cartons on the floor with Jack's latest delivery of empties when I hear my name. When I stand, Leo is on the other side with a bunch of singles in his fist. Not only did he work off his tab, Jack paid him with the promise of more since he did such a good job. Leo also landed the mechanic's job with that garage, he starts Monday, so things are looking up. Next on his list is to find a place to live. All of this came from Jack last night.

"The usual?" I ask Leo.

I get a nod as I pull a cold Budweiser from the cooler and snap the cap, which makes a nice clink when it hits the can on the floor.

"I talked to my cousin in Davis, like I said I would. He told me somethin' you might find interesting."

I can't help smiling after he says that.

"You did? Well, I'm all ears."

"He told me about these rich people in the next town over. Morrisville. Used to live in a museum but they sold it and moved. It's a big ass place. High on a hill. Actually it's only a woman now. The old man died. They moved there years ago. But they never have anythin' to do with anybody in town. I heard she even has servants."

"Did you get a name?"

"Gloria Robbins." He pulls a paper from the pocket of his jeans. "Here. I wrote it down and the road where she lives."

And just like that, Leo is no longer the Sad Sack in my book.

"Thanks. You can put that money away. This beer's on me."

Moments later, after the Junkyard Dogs rip into Garth Brooks' "Friends in Low Places" to the crowd's approval, Jack is back clutching empties in both hands and with a questioning expression on his face.

"Did he pay for that beer?" Jack asks although I know who "he" is.

"Not that one. I am. It's his reward for giving me a great tip for my case."

I reach into the tip jar to remove enough bills to cover the beer, but Jack tells me to put them back.

"No need for that. What did he tell you that was worth a free beer?"

"He has family in Davis who gave him a name and address of someone who might be linked to this case."

"A person of interest?"

I smile when Jack uses that term.

"Yes, or a suspect."

He tips his head toward my mother who has her eyes and ears on the Junkyard Dogs.

"You taking your mother?"

"That might not be a good idea. She got upset when Lin's mother went off on us. The woman has since apologized, but Ma got shook that day. I don't mind getting told off or being put in a little danger. So I'll just go alone tomorrow."

"No, you ain't, Isabel. I'm comin' with you."

"Aw, you don't have to."

"I know but I want to. There's a difference. Besides, it wouldn't be the first time I did. Remember when we met the guy with the missin' arm?"

I laugh. That was for my first case when Jack accompanied me to meet a suspect I was a little nervous meeting, but it turned out the man had a good alibi. He had been in an accident and hospitalized after his arm was amputated.

"Okay, you're hired," I say, noting I have a couple of thirsty customers waiting to be served. "Now, let me do my job before my boss fires me."

"Fat chance that'll ever happen, Isabel."

Perhaps a Discovery

Ma and I made quick work of the Conwell Triangle this morning while Jack tended to his mutts back home and checked on Leo's progress painting the spare room, so he and I can head to Morrisville later. She gave her unabashed approval that Jack will take her place. I told her about the tip from Leo and Jack's offer as I drove her home last night after the Junkyard Dogs finished their last set with a rousing rendition of Lynyrd Skynyrd's "Sweet Home Alabama." Ma said she thoroughly enjoyed their performance, especially when Annette sang the old country tunes. I could say she was the Tough Cookie's number one fan, but she'd have a lot of competition from the men who were at the Rooster that night. I returned to help Jack close up, which took longer than usual since nobody seemed to want to leave last night despite last call. Even this morning, Ma was relieved she wouldn't have to meet a person we know nothing about and who might be pissed off, my words, not hers, that we invaded her privacy.

During the drive to Morrisville, Jack is in a jubilant mood after a profitable Friday night thanks to the Junkyard Dogs. For this trip, we're taking my Subaru instead of his pickup although I let him take the wheel. He tells me at one point, "It seems funny to be driving this low to the ground."

I put the address Leo gave me in my phone and let the voice from the map app tell us where to go, which still mystifies my mother that can happen. In the old days, as she put it, you used a paper map. Jack's never used one either. Ha, he says the same thing today.

"How does that thing work?" he asks.

"Don't know, but it does most of the time."

All that I have on the town of Morrisville is what I found

181

online. Part of the Berkshires, it's a haven for up-scale New Yorkers who want to get away to its hills, now in fall color, and a large rolling river. It has a museum filled with famous art that a rich couple, now dead, bought a long time ago, plus a private college and a charming downtown. There's a whole lot more going on here than in the one-store, one-church, one-school, one-stoplight town where Jack and I live.

The voice on the phone takes us up a hill overlooking the town, up, up, until we reach Fair View Road, which is really an understatement about what we can actually see of the Berkshires.

"Here it is," I tell Jack just as my phone announces we have reached our destination.

Jack stops the car at the end of the driveway that forms a half-circle in front of a grand-looking mansion. Somebody put some bucks into what I would call an impressive piece of art with its long porches and peaked roofs.

"These people are sure loaded," Jack says.

"My guess, too."

But it's time to stop gawking and do some knocking. We discussed a plan on the drive over. I don't want to overwhelm whoever answers the door with two people on the other side. If I am successful getting inside, I will ask if my associate can join us. I also set some ground rules. When my mother comes, she typically is quiet, so people often forget she is with me or maybe they dismiss her as just some old lady, which is a mistake because all the while she is soaking in everything they say and do, including the expressions on their faces when I ask a question. Once in a while she asks a question just to stay in it. So, I advise, and I am being nice here, that Jack do the same. Be friendly, but not too friendly. Let me do most of the asking and talking. But if he hears something that should be pursued further, he may ask a question. We even practice that on the ride if I can convince whoever answers the door to allow us both inside. If I can't bring Jack with me, he might have to wait a while in the car. But please don't start walking around outside casing the joint. We could get in trouble for that. Besides, they might have guard dogs.

"Ready?" he asks.

And with an okay from me, Jack drives through the open gates between two stone pillars and stops the car in a shady spot not far from the front door, where someone would have to step onto the porch to see him waiting in the front seat or peek outside a window. This time I will break my rule and use the front instead of a side door since it seems fitting for such a grand house. After a "Wish me luck," I am up the stone steps and pressing the doorbell beside the large wooden door that triggers a melodic series of chimes inside. As I wait, I hear someone playing something classical on a piano. No one comes, so I hit the doorbell again.

Minutes later, a middle-aged woman opens the door. She's dressed simply in a white blouse and semi-dress black trousers. She could be working in an office with that attire. Or maybe she works here as one of the servants Leo mentioned, except she has one distinguishing feature. Her eyes, one blue, one brown. And there is certainly a familiarity to her face. I try not to stare.

"Can I help you?" she asks politely.

"Yes, I was hoping to see Mrs. Gloria Robbins."

"Uh, do you have an appointment with her?"

"No, I don't." I say my name as I hand her my card. "I am a private investigator and I believe Mrs. Robbins might be able to help me with my case. It involves a missing person."

The woman, who does not give me her name, studies me. I would describe her gaze as cautiously interested.

"Missing person?" she finally says. "What would that have to do with her?"

I honestly don't know how many details I should give this woman, but I need to win her over.

"People I have met for this case say Mrs. Robbins might be able to help with information. I would have called first but I don't have the number for here."

That's not true, but I have to admit it's getting easier for me to lie for a good cause like solving a case.

"Please, wait right here. I will see if she's available."

"You can tell Mrs. Robbins I promise not to take too much of her time."

The woman leaves the door half-way open, so I could easily step inside the foyer, but that would be too intrusive. Instead, I use the opportunity to observe what I am able to see like the staircase climbing against a wall to the second floor. These are the kind of stairs that would make a person feel as if they were making a grand entrance or exit with the wide steps, dark wood, perhaps mahogany, and no fooling, a swan carved above the newel post. Large framed and matted photos are arranged on the wall. I bet if I moved forward a little more or poked my head inside, I would be able to see more, but I don't want to get caught. I have a better idea. I take out my phone, thrust my arm as far as I can so I have a better angle and take shots of whatever the phone can catch, namely what is hanging on that wall. I move fast.

I don't have enough time to check how I did because I hear a familiar voice, a loud angry one to be specific, coming from another part of the house. The first time I heard that voice, it was on my phone when the message said, "Keep your nose out of it if you know what's good for you." The person called once again and each time my mother and I couldn't tell the gender. Now, I am sure it is a woman.

This time, the woman, I presume Gloria Robbins, yells, "Make her go away."

I wait but not too long before the woman returns. She steps closely as if she's guarding the doorway, so I don't enter. My card is still in her hand.

"I'm sorry but Mrs. Robbins is not available," she says in a quiet voice devoid of any emotion. "You will have to leave."

"Could I make an appointment to see her at another time?"

"I'm afraid that won't be possible. I'm sorry."

Okay, Isabel, take a chance.

"Thank you, Anna," I say.

Her lips part.

"How do you know my name?"

I try not to smile. Quick, Isabel, come up with something.

"I met a teacher you had long ago, Mrs. Brown. Do you remember her? She called me after she saw the story published in the Bugle about this case I'm pursuing." Now, I slip into half-truth mode. "She mentioned your family and thought your mother might be able to give me some helpful information."

"Yes, I had Mrs. Brown as a teacher. In fourth grade. I still don't understand."

I keep a deep sigh in check and pursue ever so carefully.

"The person I'm looking for was stolen from her family's front yard. Her name was Elizabeth Pierce. She was just a baby sleeping in a carriage while her mother gave a piano lesson. That was nearly fifty years ago." I slip my phone from my bag and scroll quickly through the photos avoiding the ones I just shot. "Here's a photo of Elizabeth before she was taken. Let me enlarge it for you, so you can see her better."

Anna is silent as she studies the phone in my hand. I let her absorb this image, which clearly shows the baby's two-colored eyes.

"Pretty baby," she says finally. "And she was never found?"

She continues to study the photo, and then ones of Elizabeth with her parents and her brother. I explain who's who before I return to the original photos. Anna's full concentration is on that screen.

"Not yet," I say. "Her brother Lin Pierce hired me to find out what happened to her. He was just a little boy when she was taken. Of course, Elizabeth wouldn't have any idea. She was only a baby."

The woman in the other room calls again. I wish I had a way to take Anna's photo but that's impossible. She glances again at my phone's screen. Too bad I don't have a paper copy to give her.

"I really need to go," she says. "I'm sorry I couldn't help you."

Oh, but you have.

The door shuts and I walk down the porch steps toward the car. But, dammit, Jack is not in the driver's seat. I don't see him on the driveway or anywhere else. Crap, if he's going to come with me to interviews like this he's going to have to follow those rules I told him in the car. I panic a little, hoping we're aren't being watched from inside the house. Then finally, Jack strolls around the corner to the car in a casual gait

185

as if he's a welcome guest, which he is definitely not.

"Jack, where were you?" I ask once we are both inside my car.

"I got kinda bored waitin' for you, so I decided to check out the place. I didn't see much, except for the cars they drive. A Mercedes and a Lexus, would you believe it? I think I was able to take a photo. Here, see for yourself."

He shows me what has to have been the first photo Jack ever took with his phone. I text it to mine.

"This might be useful, Jack."

He gives me a satisfied grin.

"So, I got you somethin' good," he says. "What about you? Did you get to talk with Mrs. Robbins?"

"No, I didn't. But I believe I may have met Elizabeth."

"What? Who?"

"The woman who answered the door."

Calling Lin

We get back with plenty of time for Jack to open the Rooster. Carole is already in the kitchen working on tonight's menu. While there won't be any music, except for what plays on the jukebox, it should be a busy enough Saturday night. All the way home, Jack kept asking me about the case and every little detail about our reconnaissance mission. I told him nicely that what we did today remains top secret and not a topic of conversation at the Rooster tonight. He can blab away after I solve it, or rather if I solve it. But my reporter's instinct that once told me I was onto the makings of a good story is kicking in that I am on the right track with this case.

"Leo was a big help," I tell him.

The first thing I do when I get home is to download the photos from my phone onto my computer. The angle is a bit weird, but thankfully, my long arm was able to stretch that phone so it captured a number of photos, all of people, many of them of the woman called Anna and the people who were her alleged parents. A couple are of her when she is a baby, which I try to compare to the ones I have of Elizabeth. Frankly, it's too hard to tell if they are the same child.

That's what I tell my mother when I give my full report. She's in her usual spot in the living room, her comfy chair as she calls it, with the cat, Roxanne in her lap and a pile of books on the table beside it. The dog, Maggie who followed me inside rests near her feet.

"You had a very good day," she tells me. "But Jack can't be wandering around like that. I hope you set him straight, Isabel. I would never do something like that."

I almost laugh. Ma sounds a little jealous she didn't come, and frankly, if I had showed up at the door with her, I might have had an easier time getting inside. People aren't threatened seeing my sweet old lady of a mother. Plus, when we do meet people, they forget she's there or maybe they think she's not really there, if you understand what I mean, but they would be, oh, so wrong.

"I didn't have enough proof to tell Anna who I think she really is. Maybe if that woman hadn't been in the house." I stop. "Funny, she didn't say Mrs. Robbins was her mother. At first, I actually thought she was her servant."

"She could be both."

I sigh.

"Maybe my story and her seeing those photos will make her curious enough to begin asking questions. Anyway, she has my card."

I suppose I should check in with my boss Bob, but the next person to talk with is Lin. The missus says she would have to call him in from the field, but I tell her it would be worth his while if she did. He definitely will want to hear this update.

"How's it going?" Lin asks a little out of breath. "You have some news?"

"I believe so. I don't want to get your hopes up, Lin, but there's a good chance I met your sister today."

There is silence on the other end of the line.

"Say that again?" Lin finally says. "You met my sister? Where? How?"

"Please keep this in mind, Lin. I have no proof the woman I met is actually your sister, but my intuition says it's her. It happened today in the town of Morrisville. If it's her, she appears well. And I am guessing she has no clue that she was the baby I was describing."

"What about her eyes?"

"She had different-colored eyes, but that could be a coincidence."

"Isabel, please tell me more."

I do tell Lin more about my field trip to Morrisville although I leave out the part about Jack doing unauthorized snooping.

"Lin, you need to trust me on this one," I say. "I've only

188

made an initial contact and that was very brief. The person I was there to question didn't want to see me. But the woman who answered the door was really interested when I showed her those photos you gave me that I have on my phone. Maybe I planted a seed today and she does know how to reach me. Can you trust me?"

"I guess I have no choice," he says.

"Besides, I have another angle to pursue. I got a tip that the man you knew as Tim Todd is playing piano at a certain location tomorrow," I say purposely withholding the fact the Music Man will be at Baxter's. I don't want him showing up even if he hired me to take on this case. "I plan to question him if I can or at least set up a time when we can do it."

"You believe this man has something to do with the case?"

"I sure do."

Nosy Drinkers

It actually turns out to be a semi-slow night at the Rooster likely because the local fans of the Junkyard Dogs are at Baxter's tonight. I joked last night to Annette that she and her band are on the hilltown tour this weekend. "What's next? Red's Corner Lounge in Dillard?" I asked. I am keeping Jack company at the bar. The man can hardly contain himself about our trip earlier today to Morrisville. He says he wishes he was available tomorrow when I go to Baxter's to meet this Todd guy, which is what he calls him, but he's got to open the Rooster. That's okay with me. I prefer to be alone when I corner the Music Man. Ma initially wanted to go but changed her mind. She said it would make more sense that I be alone when I do corner him although since it is happening at Baxter's I won't exactly be alone. I just hope Dancin' Dave isn't too much of a pest.

"I'm beginning to understand better why you like doin' this P.I. stuff," Jack says after the True Blue Regular one stool over goes to the men's room. "All that sneakin' around."

"Uh, I wouldn't call what I do sneaking around. You were the one doing that and you weren't supposed to."

"Yeah, yeah but I got you a good picture of their cars. You can even read the license plates. You told me you put it on your phone."

I shake my head and laugh.

"Yes, you did. Detective work is a matter of finding the pieces and putting them altogether. But there are rules, at least in my book. I had to be upfront today about who I was and what I wanted. It's what I did when I was a reporter."

"You never went undercover?"

Okay, Jack, you've got me there. I did pretend to be a

190

restaurant reviewer in my last case, but I was desperate. And when I was working for Lin and his stupid insurance cases, I had to park outside people's home and take photos to show they either were faking their injuries or not.

"Yes, I did, but I'm not proud of it like you are."

Now, Jack is the one laughing.

When he returns to his stool, the True Blue Regular asks what's so funny, but Jack blows him off with a joke he heard from the guy who drives the beer truck, the one about a man's pet chicken I've already heard and isn't worth hearing again. Instead, I slide off the stool and head to the jukebox to play some music. The Rooster is just too damn quiet.

I am making my choices from the juke's selection of country and more country tunes when I hear a familiar barking laugh at the open side door.

"Isabel, I thought we'd find you here," the Fattest Old Fart says before he bellows outside, "Come in, fellas. We finally tracked her down."

And as the juke plays my first choice, Roy Orbison's "You Got It," one by one the Old Farts walk into the Rooster. Each one gives me a "Hello, Isabel" and a sneaky smile. Then the Fattest Old Fart is bossing the others to slide two tables together and gather enough chairs for everyone including me, I rightfully presume as he points to one.

"That's where you're sitting, Isabel," he says with the authority he typically uses in the backroom of the Conwell General Store. "And you thought you could keep avoiding us."

"Oh, you guys," I say as I sit.

The Fattest Old Fart is on the chair opposite mine as if he's going to interrogate me, which is probably his intention. As the others take their places, I weigh how much I can say that will satisfy them without giving away too much, especially with Ben the Bald Old Fart's connection to this case. I will skip my online research on Anna Robbins and her alleged mother, Gloria Robbins. Anna is or was a musician who has played in prestigious orchestras but didn't strike out on her own. I find a brief obit for her husband, who was also a musician. No children are mentioned. All I found about Gloria

191

is her address in Morrisville and an obit for her late husband, William. No profession is mentioned but it appears he was a generous benefactor to the Ivy League college where he graduated. A building is named for him.

Their heads are turned. I even catch a raised eyebrow from the Silent Old Fart I suppose to encourage me.

"I bet you're all wondering why I called you here," I say, which as expected gets the group laughing. The other drinkers in the Rooster all look our way when they hear that reaction and wonder what the heck is going on. I raise my hand. "I apologize for not taking you up on your invitation, but I've been a little busy."

"That's okay," the Fattest Old Fart, always the group's spokesman, says. "Now's the time to catch us up."

But thankfully I am spared answering right away because Jack has joined us. He's heard about my morning meetings with the Old Farts although he doesn't know my mother and I call them that, or their individual nicknames, so he uses their true names to welcome each one. He gives me a wink. He understands why they are here.

"What can I get you fellas to drink?" he asks.

Jack takes their orders and splits for the bar. I will wait until he returns to give my report or we will have another interruption. Besides, the Serious Old Fart and Old Fart with Glasses are reminiscing about the Rooster's former owners who sold the bar to Jack. That was when they were just kids and their fathers would make a detour here after the dump run. Turns out the owners were related to the Serious Old Fart. Who isn't related in this town, either by blood or marriage? They likely are if they're a native and their families go back far enough.

"Ah, the stories these walls could tell," the Silent Old Fart says as Jack returns with their beers and a couple of mixed drinks.

Just then, the Skinniest Old Fart leans forward as he crooks a thumb toward the Beaumont brothers who are entering the front door.

"Jack, you let those two drink here?" he asks in a low voice as if the brothers could hear him across the room.

"He does now," I say with a smile.

"How did that happen?" the Skinniest Old Fart asks for the group.

"Isabel begged me to take them back, but one slip-up and they're outta here for good," Jack says in a voice loud enough that if the Beaumont brothers are paying any attention could hear across the room. "I'll let you guys be. Isabel, you gonna tell 'em about today? That was somethin' else."

I shake my head ever-so-slightly, so Jack gets my message to curtail his enthusiasm. The Old Farts are nodding and grinning. They want to hear all about it, I'm sure.

"Uh, maybe," I say.

Jack glances at the bar, where thankfully a few customers besides Gary and Larry are waiting to order.

"I'll check back later," he says before he's gone.

The juke is playing "Harper Valley P.T.A." by Jeannie C. Riley, which is fitting background music considering the subject of the song has to deal with a bunch of nosy people in a small town. The difference here is the Old Farts aren't hypocrites, just a bunch of guys who seem to know everybody's business and talk about it, but they never cross over to meanness.

"Gentleman, may I have your attention?" I joke.

"Do you really have to ask?" the Fattest Old Fart jokes back.

"You all will be pleased to know that I've made progress since the last time we met." I give Ben Pierce aka the Bald Old Fart a nod. "Your brother's story made me decide to look further west. That's why I contacted that reporter from the Bugle. I didn't get a lot of response but one that was worthwhile, actually two if I include your ex-wife who apologized."

"She apologized? That's a first," he says.

"A psychic called twice but I'm ignoring that since she wants to be paid and I believe she is full of shit." Naturally there is a group laugh on that piece of information. "Then there was one caller who played a trick on me, sending me on a bit of a wild goose chase."

All eyes are on me as I tell them about my experience at the cemetery. I skip the threatening calls I am certain now were made by Gloria Robbins. Was she the one who also set up that wild goose chase with that dead man Pete Baker that ended in the graveyard? If my betting mother were here, she would say the odds were good that she did. But somebody else made that call for her.

"I want to be cautious here, I believe I have a lead, a really strong lead, actually two, but I need to keep them to myself for now." I look directly at Ben Pierce. "I did share some of that information with your son since he hired me."

"Do you think you've found my daughter?" he asks.

"I believe I have found someone who might be," I say, deciding to withhold my meeting with Anna Robbins. "I wish I could tell you more. But I need to be very careful because if it is her, I don't believe she has any clue she was taken. I hope to change that in a subtle way. And if she isn't, then I've reached a dead end." I raise a finger. "And I do have an important meeting tomorrow with a person of interest. I believe he might be a big help."

I see nodding heads and serious faces among the Old Farts, who appear to have absorbed the gravity of the situation. This reminds me of the not-so-old days when I was a reporter on the trail of a hard story. I wouldn't share details ahead of time to anyone outside the newsroom, and I pledge to do the same as a P.I.

"Don't worry. When this case is solved, I will spill all in the backroom of the store," I continue. "Right now I can't."

"So, do you think you will solve this one?" the Serious Old Fart asks.

"God, I hope so."

Waiting at Baxter's

I am on my third glass of water and second hour waiting for the Music Man to show up at Baxter's. Of course, I'm not alone. Dancin' Dave keeps circling back to my table, which has the best view of the piano and hopefully my white-haired, long-fingered person of interest. Dave sits for a conversation, starting with the Junkyard Dogs' successful premiere last night, gets up to tend to some business with the staff or his customers, and then returns for the next round. I believe he's enjoying my wait much more than I am. He has offered wine or beer on the house, which I declined because it is too early for that and I want to keep my wits about me. The same went for a late lunch although I accepted a mug of tea. He didn't bother asking about the plate of appetizers he brought to the table. Dave is just happy to have my company. He also gave me an update on Lisa, who he hired as a cook for a couple of shifts, including Fridays, which is why she didn't show up at the Rooster that night until the end of the Junkyard Dogs' last set, and Saturdays and Sundays, which means she is likely already in the kitchen. I don't plan to check.

"Lisa seems to be gettin' the hang of it fast. She is experienced," Dave says. "Whether she sticks around, that's somethin' else. She told me she was having a second interview at Luella's. More money there. Eh, I try not to get too attached to my kitchen help. By the way, I still need a bartender. Know anybody who might be interested?"

I ignore the wink.

"Sorry, I don't."

Dave chuckles, part of his routine with me. But our conversation is interrupted by the arrival of Annette and Marsha.

"Fancy meetin' you here," Annette says. "Jack know about this?"

I refrain from rolling my eyes as Dave chuckles.

"Of course, he does. Hey, I heard you and the Junkyard Dogs were a big hit here last night."

Annette gives my arm one of her playful slaps.

"We sure were. Now I'm gonna spend the money we made last night on drinks and a dinner." She gives a nod toward the deck. "So why are you here?"

"I'm just waiting for that guy who plays piano to show up. You both know him. Robert Todd who comes into the Pit Stop," I tell them. "Hey, who's minding the store with the both of you here?"

There goes another slap to the arm.

"Abe and he better not let any of his buddies get anythin' free or he'll be out on his ass," Annette says. "I don't care if he's my kid."

Now, it's Marsha's turn to speak and thankfully my arm is spared.

"That Todd guy you just mentioned was in the other day buyin' gas and those hoity toity cigarettes he likes. He was payin' me when he saw that front page story about you from the Bugle. Annette cut it out and tacked it on the wall behind the counter cause you're kind of a celebrity around here. Maybe you can autograph it for us. Anyway ol' Bobby bought that paper, too."

I am charmed Annette would do something like that but more interested in what the Music Man did.

"Did he say anything about it?"

"No, but I saw him readin' the paper in that Mercedes of his. He was parked there until a customer who wanted gas honked his horn for him to move his ass. Somebody was on the other side of the pumps and that Todd guy was just sittin' there hoggin' the space."

And after a thanks from me and another slap from Annette, the two women proceed to the deck. Sean did as I asked and kept the Music Man out of his story, but he might want to read it if he somehow is involved or perhaps it just caught his interest. I'm putting my money on the first option. Let me rephrase that. I am praying for the first option.

"So, how's the move goin'?" Dave asks, and for a second there I forget he is sitting at the table with me since I was focused on the idea of the Music Man reading that story in the Bugle.

"Jack's side of the house is all painted. It looks great. But we're kind of stuck though until that Lisa finds a place to live. Jack gave her a month. Heard of a decent enough place to rent around here? Maybe one of the cabins on the lake?"

He shakes his head.

"Sorry, but I'll let her know if I hear of anythin'," he says, checking the clock on the wall behind the bar. "I'm kinda surprised this Todd fellow isn't here by now. It's three-thirty. Usually he comes earlier and sticks around for a couple of hours. He tol' me he never wants to play when we have people eatin' here. He didn't want them to get the wrong idea why he's playin', that he's their entertainment."

"I'll give him another half hour or more if that's all right with you."

His mouth spreads in a smile.

"Aw, Isabel, I'm glad to spend the time with you. Anytime, really."

But the conversation goes no further after Dave is summoned by a waitress who says there is a problem with one of the customer's credit cards. He excuses himself. But I'm not alone for very long. Now, it's Gary Beaumont's turn to ask me why I'm sitting at Baxter's on a Sunday afternoon. He gestures toward my half glass of water.

"Dave cut you off already?" he jokes.

"No, wise guy." That's when I notice Gary is alone. Frankly, I have a hard time remembering if I ever saw one brother without the other. "Hey, where's Larry?"

"Home. I've got plans tonight and hangin' out with him ain't part of 'em. Anyway Larry's probably home playin' with that drone of his. Damn thing even takes videos. He just downloads them onto our computer. You should see the one of the bear tearing through our neighbor's yard. Besides, he's got that mutt Ricky to keep him company."

Gary tips his head to the other side of the room where a woman sits alone at the end of the bar. She's what the guys around here might call a hot babe. She's certainly dressed for the occasion with a top that has a scoop neckline on the low side and a short skirt. She worked on her hair, which is blondish and shoulder length. The woman keeps smiling with red lips at Gary and probably wondering why the heck he is still talking with me.

"I don't believe I've met your dining companion," I say.

I swear Gary blushes as he tells me her name is Virginia and that they met at the veterinarian office where he and Larry take Ricky. She is the vet's assistant. The woman grew up around here and recently moved back. She, Gary, and, of course, Larry went to the same high school.

"So, why are you sittin' all by yourself?" Gary asks. "You waitin' for somebody?"

"Yes, for your neighbor. He's supposed to be coming here to play the piano."

"Maybe he's on his way. I saw the gate to his place was open."

"He keeps it open when he leaves?"

"No idea, Isabel. I'm just not as nosy as you."

"I bet you aren't." I smile. "Enjoy your evening."

And then Gary, who I note is not wearing a tee-shirt advertising booze for once but a blue buttoned-down shirt and jeans, leaves me to join his date. His face is clean shaven. I believe he even had his mullet trimmed in the back. The woman smiles as he approaches. Ma is going to go nuts when I tell her about this.

Time ticks on. Dave is now in the kitchen tending to a problem there. Now, another familiar person enters Baxter's, but not one I like. Jim Hawthorne aka Thorny, dressed in a police uniform, walks past me with a bit of authority. I nod. He nods. I also detect a snotty sneer, but I don't respond in kind. That's all there's going to be between us as he heads to the bar, where he takes a stool far from where Gary Beaumont and his date are sitting, which makes for an interesting combination. I keep my attention on Thorny, who gabs with the woman behind the bar before she hands him a menu. I don't see any booze so he must be on Sunday duty.

The clock behind the bar says it's almost four thirty, and although I am aware it is ten minutes fast, bar time, it won't be long before Baxter's fills with Sunday diners. I'm wondering if the Music Man decided not to come after his piano tuner told him about my interest in meeting him. Maybe reaching out to Sean Mooney at the Bugle wasn't a brilliant strategy after all. And, no, I haven't heard anything more from Anna Robbins. Did I blow that one, too? But I'm not giving up. I never did it with a story. I won't do it with a case.

I fetch a few bucks from my wallet for the waitress who will have to clean this table. Dave walks over when he sees me stand.

"Leaving so soon?"

"Ha, I've been here over two hours." I laugh. "Thanks for keeping me company."

Dave nods.

"Are you still plannin' to find this man?"

"Yes, but it looks like I have to come up with a different way."

"You're not going by his house, are you? He should be back another time."

I am not so sure about that.

"I'll think about it," I tell Dave.

"It's not worth it, Isabel. I want you to be safe."

Dancin' Dave gives me a quick hug as if this might be the last time he sees me.

"Me, too," I tell him.

Safety Last

I decide to ignore Dave's advice and drive by the Music Man's house to see if I can still meet him today. What do I have to lose? Besides, it's on the long way home if I take a detour to Laurel Road where he lives. As I approach No. 17, the metal gate to the driveway is swung open just like Gary said. Has the man had a change of heart and is welcoming visitors? Maybe. Maybe not. The Piano Guy said Robert Todd would leave it open so he can tune his piano, but something tells me that's not it either. The warning sign is still there although I note a couple of fresh bullet holes strategically fired through the o's in the lettering. Somebody was a good shot and I bet I can guess who he was.

I pull to the side of the road to ponder my next move. Do I dare walk or drive? I believe I need some reliable advice. I get out my phone, which indicates I have barely any service in this location but enough to make the call home. I really should have done this when I was at Baxter's.

"Isabel, where are you?" My mother answers on the second ring, easy because she keeps the house phone beside her chair. "What was he like? Did you get what you need?"

"Uh-no. The Music Man was a no-show. Right now, I'm parked outside the entrance to his driveway. Get this. The gate is open. Maybe I should take that as an invitation or a sign. What do you think?"

"Hmm, what's your gut feeling?"

Gut feeling? Right now, it's that I must be nuts to be doing this line of work, especially for the amount of money I make, which frankly is less than what I get tending bar one night a week at the Rooster.

"I believe this guy is key to this case, so maybe I should take a chance. Besides, if he's home, he can see me coming with those cameras. I think I'll drive in case he tells me to leave. It might be a long walk out of there and at this point I have no clue what's at the other end of this driveway."

"Yes, do that."

"I'll call you when I'm done. By the way, you wouldn't believe who I just saw. Gary Beaumont. He was on a date at Baxter's."

My mother laughs.

"And Larry wasn't with him?"

"No, he wasn't. I'll tell you all about it when I get home."

I steer the car past the gate then along the gravel driveway that cuts through a rather thick forest, just the usual combination of hard and soft woods. After a quarter mile, I reach the clearing where the Music Man had his house built into the side of a hill. The only part visible is a large curved front made of wood and stone. The over-sized windows are likely its only source of natural light, that and a room with a roof atop the hill. I imagine this house is much larger than it appears from the outside. The Music Man has an in-ground pool, a nicely landscaped yard, and a three-car garage. A Mercedes is parked outside. There's no sign of a backhoe, but then again, he doesn't seem the type to own one. Perhaps, he doesn't have a gun either, at least I hope so.

My options are a front door and a glass slider on the other side of the pool, where presumably the Music Man can walk naked sight unseen, except for his nosy neighbors. It could possibly lead from his bedroom, so I break my rule again and go to the front door, which I discover is partly open. I stop outside. A man who uses cameras and a threatening sign wouldn't leave his door unlocked or open unless he were home. But what name should I use? Tim or Robert? Marsha says he told her his name is Robert although she calls him Bobby just to have fun. If Robert is the name he goes by, that's what I will use.

"Robert, hello." I knock politely, which makes the door open more. "Robert, are you in there? I'm Isabel Long, a private investigator."

Nobody comes to the door.

I don't hear a voice.

From my vantage point I can see this part of the house is a large open space with high ceilings, so my voice should carry easily to wherever he is.

I call out again.

Nothing.

Perhaps he's on the other side of the house.

I step inside and try again, this time louder. That's when I hear a moan, then another.

"Help," a man's voice calls faintly.

"I'm coming."

I hurry towards the voice on the right side of this house. But I don't have to go far. The man I recognize as Robert Todd lies on a carpet wedged between a couch and a coffee table. His face is contorted in pain. Shit, the man's been shot in the chest. His shirt is a bloody mess. So is the carpet beneath him, so I am guessing the bullet or bullets went through him.

I drop my bag, drag the table aside so I have space to kneel beside him.

His eyes open. He raises a long-fingered hand.

"Help me."

I've never had training for this kind of situation although in my mind the most obvious action to take right now would be to put pressure on the man's chest to somehow stop the bleeding and to get real help. I pull off my sweater, bunch it into a large square and with my left hand, press it against his chest, which causes him to groan. Using my right, I reach into my bag for my phone, get past the password, and dial 9-1-1.

Dispatch answers right away.

"9-1-1. What is your emergency?" the woman asks.

"My name's Isabel Long. Please send an ambulance and first responders to 17 Laurel Road in Caulfield. Robert Todd, the man who lives here, has been shot in the chest. I found him this way when I got here. Please hurry. He's really weak."

After answering a few questions and getting an assurance she will be sending help, I hang up and use both hands to apply pressure, the right on top of the left. Maybe it will help stop the bleeding or slow it down. I have no idea how badly he is hurt. Unfortunately, saving lives is not my area of expertise.

"Help is coming, Robert," I say in as calm a voice I can muster while I keep up the pressure. He groans. "Sorry. I don't want to hurt you. I'm just trying to stop the bleeding."

EMTs will be on their way although here in the hilltowns where we depend on volunteers to answer medical emergencies and fight fires, I don't know how quickly. The towns around here are too small and poor to have anyone full-time although the first responders, as we call them, are typically available 24/7. These people do it as a way to help their town, and if called upon, the ones around them through mutual aid. They tend to work locally or have their own businesses, so they answer calls whenever their beepers go off. I am not sure if Caulfield even has an ambulance and if not, how far one will travel from another town.

What can I say that will keep this man going? The most obvious question is to ask who did this. I seriously doubt this shooting was a self-inflicted accident or a suicide attempt since he's shot in the chest and I don't see a gun anywhere.

"How did this happen, Robert? Was it a robbery?"

His eyes open.

"Isabel?"

"Yes, I'm Isabel Long."

His lips move but his voice is barely audible. I bend my head closer.

"Under piano," he says with great effort. "Get it."

The grand piano is several feet away, where the light from the sliding glass door shines on its dark, polished wood. I don't want to stop applying pressure on the man's chest, but I can't ignore his plea.

"Okay. I will."

I lift my hands from his chest, get to my feet, and move quickly across the room. When I kneel and duck beneath the piano, I find a small manila envelope taped to its bottom. I stretch my clean right hand and yank the envelope free. No writing is on the outside and the flap is sealed shut.

"I have it," I say when I return.

"Hide it," he whispers. "It has everything you need."

I wish I could tear it open to see what's inside, but now's not the time, so I shove it into the bottom of my bag. Then I'm back with both hands pressed against Robert's chest.

Vehicles are coming up the driveway and in the near distance, there's the telltale sounds of an ambulance.

"Robert, the EMTs are here."

"Tell Anna I'm sorry," he whispers.

"Shh, shh, I will," I say.

"Tell her Gloria …" His lips move but he doesn't say more.

Two men with medical bags rush into the living room.

"We've got this now," one of them says. "You did good."

Actually, I feel like I didn't do good at all as I get out of their way, wiping the blood from my left hand onto my jeans since I don't know what else to use. Donning gloves, the EMTs remove my bloody sweater and get to work. I pick up my bag and stand out of the way beside the piano. As they help Robert Todd, they have questions I try my best to answer. No, I don't know how long ago he was shot. I wasn't here. I just found him. And he could barely talk. I tell them what I tried to do.

I don't ask if he's going to make it. The way the man looks, I seriously doubt it. Whoever shot Robert Todd wanted him to die. And the reason may be hidden inside my bag. I recall Chief Dutton telling me someone broke into this house when she was still only an officer. They didn't take anything but made a mess of his papers. Perhaps all they needed to do was look under the piano.

The town's ambulance has arrived. A cruiser is behind it. But I keep my attention on the EMTs attending to Robert. I recognize one of them, Barry Sweet, a semi-regular at the Rooster who brings his wife and likes to dance on Friday nights when it has a band. Right now, he and the other EMT are doing their best to save a life. I should leave them alone. I could leave by the glass door but decide on using the way I came since I don't want to touch anything more in this house now that it's a crime scene. Actually, the only things I have touched are the front door, that poor man I found on the floor, the coffee table when I slid it aside, and the envelope now stashed in my bag. I suppose my fingerprints could be beneath the piano.

I take one last look around the room. That's when I find a photo on a wall of what appears to be a mother and daughter portrait, from the shoulders up. I recognize the younger, smiling woman is Anna Robbins. I presume the older is the person who claims to be her mother, Gloria Robbins. Her full face has what I would call a determined expression. I remember Robert's words, "Tell her Gloria." Tell her what?

My attention is drawn to a familiar voice at the doorway. Jim Hawthorne is here. Not that long ago, he was ordering a meal at Baxter's. Now, Thorny stands in the middle of the room, with those ridiculous black leather gloves he wore when he was a dirty police chief as he studies what's going on here. It doesn't take long for him to notice me and the blood on my clothes. His mouth twists into that same sneer he gave me about an hour ago.

"Isabel, what are you doin' here?" he asks.

"I came to talk with Robert Todd for my case and found him like that. I called 9-1-1 and tried to help him," I say.

"Don't leave, Isabel."

"I'm only going outside, so the EMTs can do their job. You can find me out there."

"Just don't leave," he says louder as if I didn't hear him the first time.

The yard is filled with cars, trucks, and the Caulfield Police Department cruiser, which presumably brought Thorny here. My car is blocked, so there would be no easy escape for me. I choose a bench beside the pool, where I'll be out of anybody's way. Thorny talks with a couple of guys, who I am guessing are also part-time cops either from Caulfield or a nearby town. His gloved hands move as he talks. Where in the heck is Chief Dutton and the State Police? Surely, they are on their way.

An ambulance from Mayfield, the closest city, has arrived likely with paramedics on board who can give Robert Todd the advanced care he needs. They rush into the house.

I scan the area around the pool, looking for something amiss or perhaps even a gun. That's when I notice a man standing far enough in the woods he would be easily missed among the tree trunks and shadows. I smile when I recognize Larry Beaumont taking in the scene. He shakes his head when he sees that I've spotted him. I raise a finger to my lips and nod in response. Okay, Larry, I will let you be. I don't believe for one second he could have shot Robert Todd even though I know for certain the brothers own guns. He probably heard all of the commotion and decided to see what's what. He was smart not to bring that yappy little dog of his and blow his cover.

First responders roll the stretcher carrying Robert outside. Others have joined the original two. Thorny squeezes between them when they reach the ambulance. He hovers over the man, bending close to his face. His head jerks back before the stretcher is loaded into the back of the ambulance. The doors are shut.

Thorny marches toward me. His face is contorted. What now?

"He says you did it," he barks when he's a few feet away.

I stand.

"What? I only found him." My eyes lock onto his. "What did Robert Todd actually say?"

But Thorny doesn't answer.

"Stay right there," he orders me before he returns to the ambulance.

The man is lying. I don't believe for one second Robert Todd told him that. The poor man could barely talk. He wouldn't falsely accuse me or would he? What's in that damn envelope anyway? Hold on, Isabel. Stay calm. This is what Thorny wants. And there's no way I will give that envelope to him. I can imagine what he would do with it if he found out it would help me.

Thorny turns to check that I haven't moved as the ambulance rolls forward along the driveway. Barry, the EMT who was first on the scene, and Thorny are talking. Those gloved hands are moving here and there. Barry shakes his head and frowns. Something is going on between these two. But I'm not able to read lips this far away. Their voices don't carry.

Thorny marches toward me.

"Isabel, you might as well tell me what happened because I believe you're in big trouble."

"I want to hear what Robert Todd said."

"I already told you. That you did it."

"The exact words."

"He said, 'It was her.'"

That's all the poor man said? "It was her" isn't the same as "It was Isabel." But I am not going to say anything more even in my defense. I believe I might need a lawyer because Thorny is ready and willing to believe I would shoot a man. Never mind I don't own a gun or ever fired one in my entire life although he wouldn't know that. Would it make sense I would call for help and try to save him? Not in my book. I'm not a remorseful killer. Certainly, whoever shot Robert Todd isn't. That person left him to die.

Then again, I am the person responsible for Thorny losing his job as police chief. Actually, he didn't need me since he was a crooked cop and a lousy human being who couldn't face that as a much younger man he raped a woman, an incident that damaged her forever. Now being a part-time cop for the town of Caulfield is the best job in law enforcement he can have. Police Chief Dutton only hired him because she was desperate. I hope she changes her mind and the only job he will have from now on is being a rent-a-cop.

But I don't plan to open my big mouth and remind him.

"No comment," I say.

"What do you mean 'no comment'?"

"I'm going to wait for Chief Dutton," I tell him.

"Who knows when she'll be here?" He snorts. "She was visiting her folks in Vermont."

"What about the State Police? They know about this, right?"

"Yeah, yeah, they'll be here soon. Big accident on the interstate. I'm in charge until then. A couple of officers from Titus are here to help out. One's keeping guard at the end of the driveway."

"I'm not a cop, but it might be a good idea to secure the

house, so evidence isn't contaminated." I sit down again. "I'll be right here while you do that."

Thorny mutters "shit" and something more as he leaves me. He's bossing the other Titus cop to guard the home's front door, so nobody goes inside. I check the woods, but Larry is gone. He's seen enough or doesn't want to be seen and connected to this shooting. Smart guy. I need to call somebody to let them know what's happening. I don't want to worry Ma, but she must be wondering why she hasn't heard from me. Or maybe she thinks Robert Todd and I hit it off and he's been blabbing away. Jack? I love the man, but how could he help in this situation? I know just the person to call first. I remove my phone from my bag and scroll through the numbers. Luckily, Bob Montgomery answers.

"What is it, Isabel?" he asks.

"Bob, I need your help. I believe I've gotten myself into trouble."

So Many Questions

It seems like a real long time before an honest cop with some heft comes to the scene. Thorny shrugs and reminds me to stay put when I ask again for a status report on Chief Dawson's arrival. Does he expect I will escape into the woods or try to gun my Subaru out of here? I may have to if they don't let me use a bathroom soon. But I remain where I am, watching Thorny parade around the yard. Of course, that bastard is making it obvious he's keeping his eyes on me although I do manage to sneak a call to my mother when he's inside the house. All I tell her is that I found the Music Man had been shot, he's in rough shape, and now I have to stick around in case the cops have questions. That's enough information for now, I suppose.

I try Jack's cell once, but he doesn't answer. For all I know, he left the phone home or in his pickup. I won't bother texting him. I am still trying to teach him that. When I call the Rooster, it rings and rings until Carole picks up. She says Jack had to head home because those mutts got out and Lisa can't figure out how to catch them. "I'll tell him you called," she says.

The State Police are here. The two troopers, as these cops are called, wouldn't be coming from the same barracks where Bob Montgomery used to work because Caulfield is out of that geographic area. They meet first with Thorny, who presumably gives them the lowdown, at least his version, as he leads them into the house. Along the way, he points toward me. I can only imagine what that bastard has told those troopers. But I will find out soon enough since they have left the house and are coming my way. I stand when they do. The older trooper introduces himself as Detective Lt. Michael Green. His companion is Sgt. Kevin Daley. Like other troopers I've met, both are groomed, short-haired, and clean. No, they don't have to wear leather gloves to demonstrate their authority.

The detective surprises Thorny and delights me when he says, "I've got this, Jim. Why don't you keep an eye on things out here. The sergeant will join you." He gestures toward the bench. "Please have a seat, Isabel."

At his asking, I go over why I came here, what I found, and how I tried to keep Robert Todd going. I don't tell him about the envelope or bring up Thorny's accusations. This is not an official interrogation, and frankly, I need my boss's advice and a good criminal defense lawyer he can recommend if I have to face one.

Detective Lt. Green listens with a question or comment here and there.

"I came here once before, but the gate was locked and he had that sign at the end of the driveway. I saw surveillance cameras in the trees."

"Dummy surveillance cameras," he says.

I shake my head. The Music Man sure fooled me, but I'm guessing the person who shot him knew the cameras are fake. Chief Dawson said he put in an alarm system, but it wouldn't be activated unless he was gone. He may have been expecting a visitor since the gate was unlocked or maybe the person had a key. In either situation, the person was likely known to him.

"Dummy cameras? Too bad. They would have provided helpful information. Let me give you my card." I carefully dig for my wallet, leaving the bag wide open so Detective Lt. Green can see I don't have a gun. I hand him the card. "Here's my contact information. Maybe you know my boss, Bob Montgomery. He retired last year from the State Police. He recently bought the private investigation practice from Lin Pierce."

"Yes, I know Bob."

He nods but doesn't let on if that is a good or bad thing.

"I called him after Officer Hawthorne said I couldn't leave. Bob should be here soon."

"Is he a lawyer, too?"

"No, why? Do you believe I need one?"

"Officer Hawthorne thinks you might."

"And what do you think?"

"I believe we need more information," he says. "I will be talking with others who are here to verify what Officer Hawthorne claims."

Claims is one of those loaded words I avoided using when I was a reporter and then as an editor because it casts doubt that what the person said is true. I'm also smart enough to know it wouldn't be wise to speak badly about one cop in front of another even though it sounds like Thorny is making up shit about me.

"Fair enough. You probably will want to speak with the two EMTs who were the first to respond. They were near Officer Hawthorne before the stretcher was loaded into the ambulance."

With a nod, Detective Lt. Green leaves to rejoin Thorny. They are too far away to catch their conversation although I hear the word "arrest" when Thorny raises his voice. Crap.

My phone buzzes since I muted the ringtone. Jack's calling back.

"Isabel, what's going on? Carole said you called."

"Remember that man I told you I wanted to meet today? Well, after he didn't show up at Baxter's, I went to his house and found him shot. The ambulance just took him away."

"Is he gonna make it?"

Now, that's an important piece of information I don't have. If Robert Todd makes it, he would be able to tell the police what happened. If not, that's another story. But I keep that to myself.

"I dunno. But I have to wait around to talk with the police since I'm the one who found him. Bob is on his way."

"You're not in any trouble, are you, Isabel?"

"Why do you ask that?"

"I can hear it in your voice."

Ha, Jack is getting to know me well. But I don't want to worry him.

"I'm fine. I've just never been in a situation like this before.

211

I'll tell you all about it when I see you later tonight."

I'm surprised Bob isn't here yet. I could use an ally. He told me over the phone, "I'll be right there, Isabel. Don't say a word." I did ask if he knew a good criminal lawyer in case I need one. He answered, "Yeah, I do. She's the best around."

Maybe whoever is guarding the driveway's entrance wouldn't let him here despite the fact he was once a state cop. Now, he owns a small P.I. firm, so there's a difference.

I focus my attention on EMT Barry, giving him a wave as he loads his medical bag into his pickup. He nods and walks toward me.

"You all right, Isabel?" he asks.

He eyes the blood stains on my jeans.

"Sort of," is the best I can think to say. "What a mess in there. You go to many shootings?"

"A few. Hunting accidents. Suicides. Once a case of Russian roulette between two drunks. Nobody died but one guy lost part of his ear." He shakes his head. "No murders though. This is a first."

"You said murder. Is he going to make it?"

"I doubt it. Frank and I did the best we could, but he's in pretty rough shape. I reckon he was shot a while before you found him."

Bingo. Here is my opportunity.

"So you don't think I did it?"

"Nah, I know what Jim's sayin'. But the guy didn't say your name. He didn't say anything. He couldn't. The poor guy had lost consciousness. But that asshole kept on him, trying to get him to talk, until we told him to get out of our way. He needed to get to the hospital fast if there was any chance he'd make it. That's what I told that detective. Jim sure wants to pin it on you. What the hell's goin' on?"

"You might say we have a history."

"Oh, yeah, I forgot about that," he says. "Jack know you're here? Want me to call him?"

I smile.

"Yes, he does, but thanks for sticking up for me. I owe you a beer. Make it two."

He grins.

"I'll remember that."

The yard is crawling with cops. Happily for me, the State Police have taken over. Nobody pays any attention to me. This might be a good chance to see what is in the envelope that supposedly has everything I need. I pull the bag onto my lap and slip my hand inside. I try to act nonchalantly as I break the flap's seal, and after a casual glance around, I find a folded sheet of paper, a yellowed newspaper clipping, and the edge of a photograph.

But I don't get any further. Chief Nancy Dawson has arrived. As casually as I can muster, I slide the contents back inside the envelope.

There are no smiles from Chief Dawson. I start to stand, but she signals me to stay put before she sits beside me. She can't help seeing the bloody mess on my clothes.

"Looks like you've got yourself into some trouble, Isabel."

"I didn't shoot the man. I only found him. Where's the weapon?" I open my bag. "You see a gun in here or anywhere? They've been searching the house and yard for an hour now. And what would be my motive? I only wanted to interview Robert Todd for my case, not kill him. What good would that do?"

Chief Dawson's lips press hard.

"I hear you," she says quietly. "I'm just in a tough spot right now. They want to bring you in for questioning."

"I've already answered everyone's questions."

"This one would be different. If I were you, I'd contact a good lawyer."

"Wait. You're buying into this?"

"As you know, this is the second murder in our town," she says, alluding to the late Chet Waters. "I want to make sure we do things right this time."

"Robert Todd died?"

"He did. They didn't even bother getting a helicopter. Too much trauma."

"That's too bad." I sigh. "Just name the time and place for the interview and I will be there."

"Uh, they want to do it now."

"I'll need to call my mother, so she isn't worried. She's ninety-three and lives with me. Do you mind?"

"No, go ahead."

I shake my head as I go for my phone. This is bullshit. I'm the one supposed to be finding the bad guys, not be accused of being one. But I have no choice but to go along with it.

From the woods, somebody calls my name. Larry Beaumont is back standing among the trees. But this time he leaves them and makes his way through the parked vehicles toward us. He stops a few feet away.

"Larry, you can't be here," Chief Dawson says. "This is a crime scene."

"Yeah, I know." He holds out a cell. "You need to see what's on my phone. This is about what happened here." He glances toward me. "It'll help Isabel."

"What is it?" Chief Dawson asks.

Larry moves beside the chief. I am on his other side as he works the phone.

"I took this with my drone. I was just foolin' aroun' flyin' it over the woods and then over Todd's house. It ticks him off, but we do it anyway. Todd's not a friendly guy. Then I heard what sounded like gunshots, so I flew it over his house."

We watch the video as the drone flies above the treetops and over Robert Todd's house. On the screen, an older woman, definitely not me, leaves the house and gets into a Lexus before it drives away.

"What the hell," Chief Dawson says. "Is that a gun in her hand?"

Larry hands the phone to the chief so she can rewind the video.

"See? Isabel couldn't have done it," he says.

This is the second time Larry has come to my rescue. I feel like hugging him, but considering the circumstances, I don't.

"Wait a sec," I say as I reach for my phone.

I scroll through my photos to find the one sneaky Jack shot of the cars. Now, I am glad he did although I am sure I will never hear the end of it when he finds out it indeed helped my case.

"This Lexus looks a lot like the one in Larry's video. If you blow it up, you can even see the license plate." I do that for her. "I was in Morrisville on Saturday to try meeting Gloria Robbins for my case but she wouldn't see me. These cars were in her yard."

Chief Dawson studies the photo. She asks Larry to show her the video again. She looks at me.

"Your pal, Larry, just saved your ass, Isabel," she says.

I smile.

"I know. Thanks, Larry," I say.

Chief Dawson shakes her head.

"But what would be this woman's motive to kill?"

"I might have the answer," I say as I reach inside my bag. "Robert Todd asked me to find this envelope under his piano. He could barely speak, but he told me it had everything I needed for my case. I've got it here. Hold on a sec."

I remove the folded paper. At the top it says: **My confession.** Chief Dawson and I read it together.

I am not the one who took baby Elizabeth Pierce a long time ago in the town of Jefferson. But I know who did and I was an unwilling part of it. I am sorry I did, but I felt at the time I had no choice. I was being blackmailed. Will it make a difference? I will have to pay for it, but it no longer matters. I was a senior in college when I was driving a car that hit a woman who walked along the road. It was dark and I didn't see her until it was too late. I was also drunk. I should have stopped but I knew I would get arrested. The car threw her into the air. I later learned she died there. She was a student at the same college. She was coming back from the same bar I was at. I even knew her although not well. It was a terrible secret but one I shared with the passenger in my car. Her name is Gloria Todd Robbins. She is my sister. It was a secret that also cost another family. When I started taking music lessons with Jessica Pierce, I told my sister about the baby. Gloria got it in her head she wanted the child because of her eyes. She became obsessed. She didn't care how she got her. My sister shouldn't have had children. But she stole this one. She

215

had it all planned out, even coming with me several times when I had a music lesson, but she didn't let me know what she was up to until after she had taken the child. She threatened to tell the police about what I did if I told on her. I should have done that. She promised to give me whatever I wanted. I wanted to play music professionally. She made that happen. When she married William Robbins, she became a wealthy woman. She helped me out there also. I am not a good person. I couldn't face Jessica Pierce again after I found out. My sister named the girl Anna. She doesn't know her true story. Has she lived a good life with my sister? I've tried to make sure in my way. And now I've come clean. Forgive me, Anna, if you can.
Tim Robert Todd

Whoa.

Next, we read the newspaper clipping. The headline says: **Woman killed in hit and run.** It goes on to say the police are searching for the driver but there were no witnesses. Obviously, the driver was never found.

I remove the photograph, black and white, of a baby wearing a dress and lacy bonnet. I recognize the child. She is, of course, older than in the other photos I've seen of Baby Elizabeth. She sits on her own and smiles at whoever is taking her picture.

Chief Dawson shakes her head.

"I can't believe what's in here."

But I'm not about to let the police take this envelope out of my possession. While Chief Dawson shouts across the yard to get the detective's attention, I take pictures of the confession, clipping, and photo. Maybe this isn't legit, but I don't care. I don't want this evidence disappearing. And I have Larry as a witness.

"Am I free to go?" I ask Chief Dawson as I hand her the envelope with its contents.

"You will be, but hold on. Come with me, Larry. We need to show this to the detective," she says, grabbing his arm. "Don't worry, you're not in trouble."

Call at the Rooster

Jack is so relieved when I walk through the front door of the Rooster, he gives me a hug and a kiss in front of his customers, who laugh at this overt display of affection. Of course, they haven't heard what I just went through. Jack knows some from when I called him. My mother knows more. I stopped first at home to see her and to get out of my bloody clothes. Ma was a little shook until I told her the blood wasn't mine.

When I was finally allowed to leave the scene, I found Bob waiting alongside the road, a bit ticked off, mostly at Thorny, that he wasn't allowed to be with me, but I give him credit for sticking around. He told me about the TV station crews that showed up and the scant information, not even the victim's name or anything about him, Detective Lt. Michael Green gave them in a press conference at the end of the driveway. Everyone split to make their deadlines by time I finally could drive out of there in my car. Chief Dawson told me to expect follow-up questions. Funny, I didn't see any sign of Thorny as I was leaving. Hopefully, he gets canned.

"So, everything's all right now?" Jack asks.

"It's not over," I say. "Last I heard, the state cops were on their way to Morrisville to make an arrest. Boy, I sure could use a beer or something a bit stronger right now. This has been quite a day."

Of course, that gets everybody's attention, but I plan to be guarded about what I reveal since I live in a town of blabbermouths. Wait until the Old Farts hear about this one. The crowd at the Rooster is on the small side, all True Blue Regulars not ready to end their weekend, since I didn't arrive until after ten, which technically is last call on Sundays. But

217

Jack kept it open since he knew I was on my way. "You can help me clean up," he joked over the phone.

People have left their seats to listen. I don't give the victim's name out of respect. Besides, none of them would have heard of him unless they're classical music fans who go to concerts. I glance around the room and decide no. But I do tell them how Larry Beaumont saved my ass, as Chief Dawson aptly put it.

"What the hell were you doin' there anyways?" one of the True Blue Regulars asks.

"It was for a missing person case. A real old one. My former boss Lin Pierce hired me. The man was a person of interest."

"And he died? Too bad."

"For him, yeah."

Jack offers to make me any cocktail I want, even one of those fancy schmancy ones the newcomers and tourists request to his amusement or annoyance depending on how busy he is, but I take a beer on tap instead. I want to keep my brain in it and besides I haven't had a full meal since lunch, only something I grabbed out of the fridge and ate on the way here.

"I don't want you to get a big head, but remember that photo you took of those cars?" I tell Jack. "That was helpful evidence."

The man beams, no fooling.

"Really, Isabel? And you chewed me out for doin' that. Maybe I should be your sidekick."

"What and replace my mother? Uh, she wouldn't like that at all. I'll let you be her stand-in."

And so, we go back and forth like we do. The folks remaining at the Rooster have lost interest and are ready to head home finally. They were keener on hearing about a murder case than listening to our banter. Besides, all of them have jobs in the morning.

That's when my phone rings. I don't recognize the number, but something tells me I should answer it. I slide off my stool and head outside.

"Isabel Long? This is Anna Robbins. I would like to meet

with you."

"Are you all right?"

A pause.

"No. The police were here. They told me about my uncle. And what you did for him. Thank you." Her breath catches. "Now, they're looking for my mother, that she might be responsible for his death. I don't understand." Another catch in her voice. "She left this afternoon. I told the police I don't know where she went. I even let them search the house. I tried calling her about my uncle, but she didn't pick up. I left her a message that it was important she call me, but she hasn't. The police are still here in case she shows up. Please. Could you see me? I have questions about what you told me yesterday."

"Of course, I can meet with you. Tell me when."

We arrange that I will visit Anna at eight tomorrow morning, her request, not mine. I don't mind although it will take almost an hour to get there. I figure she is eager for information. I think about her so-called uncle's confession, but this isn't the right moment to share it.

I don't go back inside just yet. I make another call.

Lin Pierce answers right away.

"Isabel, did you hear there was a murder in Caulfield? They didn't give the man's name but a private investigator found him. Was that you by any chance? Was that Tim Todd?"

I weigh how much I can tell Lin.

"What I'm going to tell you is in confidence. The cops aren't giving out the victim's name just yet. I know it because I was there. That okay?"

"Yeah, yeah, I won't tell anybody. Not even my folks."

"Yes, it was Tim Todd although he calls himself Robert. I tried to help but he was too far gone." I give him a few sound bites. "And for a short time, I was a suspect. That cop Hawthorne wanted to frame me. But it was worth it. I got evidence the woman I met Saturday, Anna Robbins, is your sister. I'm seeing her again tomorrow. She just called."

"You found Elizabeth? Really? Oh my God. Is there anything I can do?"

"Just sit tight. I will contact you tomorrow."

News at Eleven

Ma tells me what she saw on the TV after I get home from the Rooster. She feels pretty smug that she knows a whole lot more than what was said by that well-dressed, well-coiffed reporter at the 11 p.m. newscast, especially now that I will be meeting Anna Robbins. Of course, there was the TV reporter's promise more will be coming, so stay tuned.

I run upstairs to my computer to check the Berkshire Bugle's website. Here's the headline on its top story: **Man shot to death in Caulfield.** Sean Mooney didn't write the story. He probably wasn't on the weekend rotation, which usually goes to the newest reporter on the staff. It is a glorified brief since this is a developing story and the state cops are being tight-lipped even about the victim's identity. It wouldn't take much to find out who lives at that address, but then again, the person who was killed isn't necessarily the owner or a person who lives there although it is in this case. The post is enough to get the news out to readers. It includes a photo taken of Detective Lt. Michael Green speaking at the end of the driveway. Here is the story.

CAULFIELD — State Police say they have a suspect in the shooting death of a man found at a Laurel Road home.

State Police have not released the name of the victim, pending notification of his next of kin. He was found by a visitor who called for help and tried to administer first aid.

"The woman is a private investigator who came to interview the man for a case," State Police Lt. Michael Green said at the scene. "She is not a suspect."

Green said the victim died of chest wounds as he was being transported to the hospital.

Police say the victim didn't identify his killer, but subsequent evidence has led them to the person who could

be responsible. No arrests have been reported.

This murder is believed to be the second in recent years for Caulfield, which has a population of about 900. The first was the death of Chester "Chet" Waters, who was killed in a housefire at his Rough Waters Garage and Junkyard that was initially believed to be accidental.

This story will be updated as new information is released.

I print a copy for my mother rather than bring the laptop downstairs since she finds scrolling on a screen beyond her skill level. She hands me the printout before she shoos the cat off her lap and uses the chair's arms to lift herself to her feet. The dog's head is up. Maggie knows my mother's bedtime routine by now although this is earlier than usual. Ma said worrying about me tired her out.

"I'm going to get ready for bed," she tells me as she shuts the reading lamp beside her chair. "Is Jack coming tonight?"

"He had to go home and check on those mutts. They've already gotten out once today and Lisa can't handle them." I glance at the windows as she leaves the room. "Oh, wait. I see headlights. That didn't take very long."

But something is off. The headlights coming down the driveway are too low to the ground to be on a pickup truck.

Dammit, the car is a Lexus.

Only one person I know owns one. Gloria Robbins. The woman has successfully evaded the police, but after all, she did have a head start. If I hadn't come upon the scene, who knows how long it would have been before Robert Todd's body was discovered? Or Gloria's likely involvement. Days even. Anna did say she tried to call her. And it's all over the news.

I'm guessing the woman has revenge on her mind. And given what information is available on the internet, it wouldn't take much of an effort to find out where I live. I lock the front door and run to the one in the kitchen to do the same. Next, I quietly call the dog Maggie and when she comes, I guide her down the hall to the bathroom. I knock.

"I'm busy, Isabel," my mother says. "Can't you wait? You

can use the bathroom upstairs."

"Ma, that woman is here. You need to take the dog and keep the bathroom door locked." Ma has worry all over her face when she opens the door and I push the dog inside. I put the toilet seat down for Ma to sit then turn off the light. "We'll be all right. I'm calling the police. Don't open this door unless you hear my voice or Jack's."

"Isabel, I don't like this."

"Neither do I."

I grab my phone from the kitchen counter.

I dial 9-1-1.

For the second time today, I hear, "9-1-1. What's your emergency?"

I give my name and address, then, "There's a woman outside my house I believe is wanted by the police for a murder in Caulfield. Her name is Gloria Robbins. She could be armed. Please send the police. Fast. My mother and I could be in danger."

The kitchen lights are on, but I leave them be. I stand far back from the windows as the woman gets out of the front seat of her car. She checks around her.

Then I remember Jack could be on his way.

I dial his cell but he doesn't pick up. So I watch and wait as Gloria Robbins walks toward the stone path leading to the front door. My heart beats hard.

"Hurry, somebody," I say to myself.

Gloria Robbins tries the door knob.

"I know you're in there. You and your mother," she yells.

There are no sirens yet, but headlights shine at the top of the driveway. Jack's here.

I flick the switch for the light above the front door on and off, on and off, on and off. Jack stops his truck midway down the driveway. Surely, he has spotted the Lexus, the one he photographed, and has put the pieces together. Jack shuts the pickup's engine and stays inside the cab. He flashes the headlights.

With woods on either side of the driveway, Gloria Robbins has no way she can drive her car from here.

She's trapped.

And that makes me worried.

What could I do to stop her? About all I have for a weapon is the baseball bat one of my sons left in the closet beside the front door. But that's no match for a gun. Maybe I can talk her into giving herself up.

"You bitch. You ruined my life," she yells.

No, that's not going to work either.

Gloria Robbins marches toward Jack's pickup truck. She fires a shot. Then another. Sirens in the distance grow louder. Gloria moves quickly toward the truck and yanks at the driver's door handle, but it doesn't budge. Please, Jack don't be a hero. Please be okay.

Flashing lights are at the top of the road. Cops are running down the driveway.

Behind me, I hear my mother speak, "Well, it's about time."

"Ma, you weren't supposed to leave the bathroom."

She joins me at the window.

"Shh, Isabel, I wasn't going to miss this."

A loud voice orders Gloria Robbins to drop her gun. She doesn't have a chance with the cops surrounding her. She shakes her head and does what she is told before the cops swoop in to take her. My view is blocked, but I've seen enough TV shows to know she's being searched, handcuffed, and led up the driveway to the back seat of a cruiser.

"I have to find out if Jack's okay."

"Go ahead," my mother says.

I rush from the front door toward Jack's pickup. I heave a sigh when I see him standing beside it and talking with a cop. Relief is written all over his face as his hand reaches for me.

"That was a close one." Jack points at the two bullet holes in the cracked driver's side window. "I ducked just in time. Too bad I gotta get that fixed. Makes me look like a tough guy, don't you think?"

I shake my head. Just like Jack to make a joke.

"No, just a lucky one. Real lucky."

Anna Robbins

It took a long time for the three of us to get to sleep last night. First, the state cops asked us so many questions, and after they left, the three of us were too wound up to go to bed just yet. Jack was still shook from that crazy woman firing her gun at his pickup. Ma and I were, too. I didn't get any phone calls from the media since it was the middle of the night although I expect them today when word gets out. I'm not sticking around for that. Instead, I got up early and left Jack snoring away in my bed to make the drive to meet Anna Robbins. I'm going alone since Ma thought it best given the sensitive nature of this visit. She will let all phone calls to our landline go to message. I did check the online news, which has been updated with Tim Robert Todd's name and the person who allegedly shot him, his sister. No motive was released. Nothing was mentioned about her visit to my house. A press conference was scheduled for 10 a.m., where more facts would be revealed.

Anna did call as I was leaving my house. She, of course, knew about her mother's arrest. I told her what I read on the news. "Do you still want to come?" she asked. More now than ever, I told myself.

Anna Robbins answers before the last chime. She's wearing a black dress, in deference I'm certain for the man she calls her uncle.

"How are you?" I ask.

She shakes her head.

"I still can't believe any of this."

I follow Anna to a room with a high ceiling, elaborate woodwork, and a stone fireplace at one end. There's a grand piano, the one I presume I heard being played on my last visit. Anna directs me to an upholstered chair near the fireplace and takes the one opposite.

"What would you like to ask me, Anna?"

She sighs.

"Where do I begin?" She reaches for a handkerchief in the pocket of her dress. "Sorry. It's just an emotional time. I loved my Uncle Robert. He was so good to me, so kind. He's the one who taught me to play the piano."

"Do you play professionally like him?"

"Yes, I did for many years in orchestras and doing soundtracks for movies. Uncle Robert opened doors for me." She sniffs. "I really didn't have to work. My parents are wealthy. Old money on my father's side. Very old. But I wanted to play music for others. I did so love playing with my uncle when he came here." Her lips form a sad smile. I could tell her that her mother, her real mother is a musician, too, but I decide to let her go on with her telling. "Why were you at his house?"

Anna listens as I share the story I've told now several times. Her mouth opens although she doesn't speak. She leans forward when I tell her about the envelope and what was found inside.

"A confession?"

"That's what it says at the top of the page. He said it would help my missing person case, that it had everything I need." I pause. "The police have his confession now, but I took a photo of it with my phone. Would you like to read it?"

She nods.

I find the image on my phone before I hand it to her. Her eyes, blue and brown, are on me and then the screen. I let her read as long as she wants. I try to put myself in her place, leading one life, to discover there should have been another.

"He wanted me to give you a message. He said, 'Tell Anna I'm sorry.'"

Tears form in her eyes.

"He wouldn't have written this unless it was true. I know my uncle." Her voice shrinks to nearly a whisper. "I had no idea although when I look back now … there were moments."

"Lin Pierce, the man who hired me, told me he met a

woman once who looked so much like his mother. She, too, had different-colored eyes. It was at Luella's, the restaurant in Mayfield. He went up to the woman, he even called her Elizabeth, but she told him he was mistaken. He said she was there with a man."

She raises a hand to her lips but shakes her head.

"Sorry, I don't remember that."

"Oh, he said the woman was wearing a silver necklace with a dangling black pearl."

Her eyes flicker.

"I have a necklace like that. It was a gift from my uncle. So, she could have been me." She bites her lip. "That man is my brother?"

"Yes, he is."

She thinks for a moment.

"My mother so sheltered me. I went to public school only one year. The rest of my education was at a girls' private school. I had few friends. A chauffeur would drive me every day and pick me up. I didn't go to college although I was smart enough. I only wanted to be a musician. I didn't need to, thanks to the lessons with my uncle and others."

I choose my words carefully.

"What were the people who raised you like?"

"My mother is quite headstrong. She wants to have her way. Always. She and my uncle would argue a lot, especially recently." Her head shakes side to side. "Still, I'm having a hard time believing what the police say my mother did. Killing my uncle. And then she came to your house? I'm so sorry."

"It's not your fault."

She nods.

"My parents married when I was about two. When I was old enough, she told me she got pregnant after she graduated from college, but it wasn't a serious relationship. She never wanted to talk about it. There is no father listed on my birth certificate in case you're wondering. How she got the certificate with her name, I have no idea, but back then, it probably could happen. If you have enough money, I suppose anything is possible." She sighs. "The man she married, William Robbins, was very

226

kind to me. I can't imagine he knew who I really was. He adopted me. I did think of him as my father. I called him that. Mother was always mother."

"You mentioned you were married."

"Once. Jerome was a musician, too. No children. A happy marriage. It ended when he died from cancer." She whispers the last part. "I've had nothing serious since. After my father died, my mother asked me to live with her. We traveled the world together. I handle running the house, overseeing our help. I stopped playing publicly. I didn't mind. I love this house and I suppose it's going to be mine someday."

"You seemed interested when I told you about my case."

"Something clicked inside. One time when I was organizing paperwork for my mother, I found an envelope with newspaper clippings about a baby being abducted from her front yard. It happened in the town of Jefferson, I believe. I read each one. When I asked my mother, she snatched the envelope from my hands and said it was nothing. Later, she burned it in the fireplace. I saw pieces of the newsprint the fire didn't burn completely. Funny, that was around the time my uncle's house got broken into although nothing was taken."

"Interesting."

"She was mad, real mad about that article about you and your case in the Bugle. I read it online after she burned the newspaper. After your visit, I told my mother what you had said. She, uh, got very angry. I heard her on the phone with my uncle accusing him of betraying her. I remember her saying, 'No, I will never admit it. You'd better not if you know what's good for you.' I didn't hear the rest because she slammed the door to her office. Yesterday, she left the house and didn't come back. The police woke me up to say they had arrested my mother."

"This has been a lot for you to take in," I say.

She nods.

"It has. I didn't sleep much last night," she says and after a long pause, "Please, tell me about my other family."

For the next several moments, Anna listens while I talk about her parents and brother, what they do, where they live, and how I know them.

"I don't want to put more pressure on you, but this story, about who you are, will come out very soon, I would imagine even today," I say. "It will draw a great deal of attention when it makes the news. If you don't mind, I will call your brother when we're done, so he can share this information with his parents. I don't want them to hear it from somebody else. It's too important." I pause. "I could arrange a meeting with them if you like."

She gives me a slight nod as the doorbell chimes. Then we are joined by an older man, clutching a chauffeur's cap in one hand.

"The police are here, Anna," he says in a voice I've heard before. I wonder what it took for his employer to have him impersonate the dead man, Pete Baker.

"Thank you, Steven. Please, let them in," Anna says. "Isabel, would you mind staying with me?"

The Reunion

As to be expected, the story goes national. It even makes the supermarket tabloids, which my mother scooped up when we were grocery shopping in the city. Here's one headline: **Baby lost and found after 49 years.** As a reporter, I would have killed for a story like this, not really. You know what I mean. As promised, I gave an exclusive interview to the helpful reporter Sean Mooney, which probably annoyed the editor and publisher of my old paper. Oh, too bad.

Bob Montgomery has been fielding requests for his P.I. firm's help, which is a big boost to his new business. And because my landline number was in that original story, I've changed the message to say they need to call my boss. Oh, by the way, in case anyone is wondering, Thorny is no longer a member of the Caulfield Police Department. Yeah, he got fired.

So far, Anna Robbins has not spoken with reporters. She hired a security outfit to keep out unwanted visitors to her home and prevent them from attending her uncle's funeral. Today, I'm introducing Anna to her lost family. She didn't have to do a DNA test to prove it as Gloria Robbins came clean during a jailhouse visit. "I wanted to give you a great life," Anna said she told her. Her reply was, "But it was not yours to give." She's still sorting her feelings about all of that.

The plan is for Anna to meet her family at Jessica Pierce's house today. Enough time has passed that it is unlikely reporters will be on the scene. Actually, this juicy story has been replaced by one about a serial killer in Arizona although I predict Anna would have the opportunity to do a sit-down interview with a national newspaper or on TV if she wished. But that's totally up to her.

Anna and I arrive at the same time in front of Jessica

Pierce's house. She joins me on the sidewalk and nods as I point toward places of interest like where her carriage was located and the woods where Gloria Robbins took her. I try to imagine what she must be feeling. But how could I really?

"I'm ready," she finally says.

By agreement, we let ourselves in through the front door after I make a quiet knock. I hear hushed voices in the living room, then silence. Jessica sits at one end of the couch. Ben, her ex-husband, is on the other. Lin stands near them. Anticipation is the word I will use to describe the expressions on their faces.

I make the introductions for Anna's sake. She smiles at each one as I do.

"Yes, I'm Anna. But you know me as Elizabeth. I am happy to finally meet you."

Fantastic Books
Great Authors

- Gripping Thrillers
- Cosy Mysteries
- Romantic Chick-Lit
- Fascinating Historicals
- Exciting Fantasy
- Young Adult
- Non-Fiction

Discover us online
www.darkstroke.com

Find us on instagram:
www.instagram.com/darkstrokebooks

Made in the USA
Middletown, DE
28 October 2023

41426283R00144